About the Author

Cláir Ní Aonghusa was born and reared in Dublin. She is a post-primary teacher and has been on a career break since 1992. During this time she has worked as a research officer in CDVEC Curriculum Development Unit. Her short stories have been widely published in newspapers and magazines and she has been short-listed for the Hennessy Cognac/*Sunday Tribune* Literary Awards. She lives in Dublin with her husband and two children.

Acknowledgements

The author wishes to express her thanks to Dublin Writers' Workshop for workshopping early drafts of sections of this novel, to Kate Cruise O'Brien for her enthusiasm and tireless professionalism, and to the Irish Writers' Centre for the use of their facilities during the final editing stages of this novel.

Four Houses &
a Marriage

Cláir Ní Aonghusa

POOLBEG

Published 1997
by Poolbeg Press Ltd
123 Baldoyle Industrial Estate
Dublin 13, Ireland

Reprinted October 1997

The Publishers gratefully acknowledge the support of
The Arts Council.

A catalogue record for this book is available from the British Library.

ISBN 1 85371 770 3

Cover photography by Attard
Cover design by Poolbeg Group Services Ltd
Set by Poolbeg Group Services Ltd in Goudy 10.5/14.5
Printed by The Guernsey Press Co Ltd,
Vale, Guernsey, Channel Islands.

For David

Chapter One

When Auntie Alice died I was staying in Imelda's holiday cottage on the edge of Connemara and had to race back to Dublin in a progression of bus, train and taxi to meet up with Eoin. He rushed out of the house when he saw my taxi. I froze as he approached but he grabbed my arm. "Imelda phoned," he said. "Your family left hours ago. It'll be a rush but we should make it."

"Thanks," I said. He threw me a bleak smile. Thus we found ourselves in his car hurtling along the road from Dublin to Cork. We arrived just in time, before the removal of the remains, and knelt to the sound of the rosary.

"I didn't know you were away," Aunt Moira whispered brokenly.

"Visiting a friend," I lied as she embraced Eoin. Over her shoulder his eyes met mine.

I looked at the mortal remains of my dear Auntie Alice. She lay on her bed looking much thinner than I'd ever seen her. It occurred to me that her death might have been less of a shock if I'd been more in touch with her during the last few turbulent months of my dying marriage.

"What age was she?" Eoin whispered.

"Seventy-six. Don't say it was time enough for her," I added fiercely.

"Wouldn't dare," he said. I heard the smile in his voice.

The rosary ended. The parish curate, a precise, cold, humourless man with a tremendous awareness of his own eminence, pressed my hand. "Father Guilfoyle," he said. It was the first time he had ever spoken to me. Aunt Alice loathed him. "Not a proper pastor," she would say darkly. He knew only the right people in the district.

"I've just come from a wedding," Father Guilfoyle said. "Quite a different atmosphere there." He sighed.

"The job must call for many changes of mood," Eoin said. I looked at him but his face was impassive, his tone urbane.

"Indeed it does, indeed it does," Father Guilfoyle said, favouring Eoin with a dry smile and blinking behind his thick-lensed glasses. He caught my arm and turned me about slightly. "Is that your father?" he asked, indicating my father. "Must have a word with him," he said and moved away.

"Auntie Alice would never have wanted him for her funeral," I said. "It's a pity Father Duffy's on holidays. With all his faults, she much preferred him."

"We'll just have to tolerate our smart friend, Father Guilfoyle." Eoin gazed down at her body. "Look at the bruises on her hands!" he murmured.

I stared at her hands. Tentatively I touched them. Cold. Petrified.

Eoin caught my arm. He had sensed my fear. It was strange how we'd put on the old habit of companionableness. The last time I'd seen him we had been at war with each other.

The crush in the room began to clear. For the first time I

looked around properly and saw my parents, sisters, brothers and one or two cousins in a huddle by the window. I smiled at some departing neighbours. We were all on automatic control.

"Come on downstairs," my mother said as the funeral directors came into the bedroom.

The stairs were too narrow to bring up the coffin so, after a quick slug of whiskey, the men coffined the body downstairs in the hall. We waited behind closed doors in the kitchen.

"Where were you?" my mother hissed. "We couldn't reach you at all. Only Imelda knew where you were."

"Not now, Mother," I said. "I was visiting a friend."

"Well, there's something strange about it all. When we finally contacted Eoin he had no idea what you were up to," she continued crossly.

"We weren't on speaking terms. It never occurred to me that this would happen."

"Couldn't you know it might happen at any time! I can't understand why you didn't at least tell us where you were."

Mercifully the door opened and we trailed out to say our final farewells. My lips brushed her cheek and felt such a coldness. She was really dead. I edged back beside Eoin. "Will you be here tomorrow morning?" I asked.

"Of course." He smiled warmly at me. "I do have a certain amount of family loyalty."

We looked at each other and looked away, each touched and hurt in some private place, as if we had rubbed an old sore.

My head began to feel giddy and I was relieved when they started to shoulder the coffin the short journey to the church.

The fresh air revived me, and I took my place in the little procession down the street. People watched from their doors and then joined up. I found myself beside Aunt Moira who seemed almost forgotten in the throng. She looked small and frail. She was very pale. I felt a rush of guilt. We linked arms and she smiled wanly. The crowd had swelled. For that I was grateful.

"But where were you?" my mother asked again that night as we munched sandwiches in the sitting-room.

I glanced up and saw my father glare at her. He motioned her to be quiet and frowned at me. I was out of favour.

I hadn't anticipated being with them when they realised that Eoin and I were at odds with each other. It seemed that no plan had ever been as luckless. I had been in Imelda's cottage barely three weeks when she telephoned news of Auntie Alice's death to me. It would have been churlish not to return. Anyway, I wanted to be there.

"You should confide in your family. We're there to help you," my mother said.

"Look, Sinéad told you what happened. We quarrelled and she took off," Eoin said.

My mother's eyes met his, wavered and fell away. She cleared her throat. "Yes, but she could have told us," she persisted.

"For goodness sake, I didn't know Auntie Alice was going to die," I said, exasperated, "and besides, I don't tell you about any of our quarrels."

"This one sounded serious," my father said heavily.

"Could we talk about it later," I pleaded, "when all this is over?"

"I suppose you have a point there," he conceded.

Somebody was pressing my hand. I turned expecting to see Eoin but saw Aunt Moira instead. She smiled tenderly at me and I tried to return the smile. "Go and get us some more tea, that's a good girl," she said briskly and I escaped to the kitchen.

There I found Eoin. "Interrogation unit left you off, did they?" he inquired thickly as he bit into a chicken sandwich.

"Only just," I muttered. "God, what persistence! I'm more interesting than the will."

"They smell a rat."

"As well they might," I said. He didn't say anything but turned away and, as he did, I caught sight of his face. His expression was set, his jaw jutted. I knew that expression.

"Sorry," I said. "I know we should try to keep things on an even keel. I just find everything very difficult."

"Right, we'll keep the peace," he said. I noticed he was buttering another sandwich. "Here, have this. I don't think I've seen you eat all day," he said and offered it to me. The kettle hummed as it neared boiling point.

I bit into the sandwich. Free-range chicken. It tasted delicious. Then I felt a niggle of guilt, repented my enjoyment.

"I should bring in the tea."

He smiled. "There's always a terrible run on tea at these affairs. Go in and fill up their cups and come back out here."

"You're an angel," Aunt Moira said when I appeared with the tray. "This is why one needs nieces."

When I got back to the kitchen it was deserted. Tiredness washed over me. I retrieved my sandwich. It was good to be alone, to enjoy a moment's respite.

I heard the back door close behind me. "A call of nature," my husband's brisk voice said as he washed his hands at the sink. "I'm glad to see you eating ," he continued. "You look ghastly. Whatever you've been up to doesn't seem to have done you much good."

"There's nothing wrong with me," I snapped. "I can take care of myself."

"Glad to hear it," he said. "By the way, we're staying with the Deasys tonight."

"We are not," I said sharply.

"No doubt about it. They've made up a bed for us and all your family agrees that it's much better than staying in a bed and breakfast. Your sisters and their spouses have been farmed out to O'Callaghans."

"That's ridiculous. I've no intention of staying anywhere with you."

"I dare you to go in and tell them that. Come on, you know that you'll do what's ordained. It's not important."

I stared at the floor. My head swam. "I don't want us to be in the same room," I said.

He snorted and gave a humourless laugh. "Don't worry," he sneered, "your virtue is safe. I haven't troubled you in months, have I? Sure, it'll add a frisson of excitement to our dreary lives. Cheer up."

The kitchen light seemed to bore into my head. "Must you be so flippant?" I asked.

"I'm just trying to lighten the atmosphere," he said.

"God, this is hard," I muttered. "I wish I were anywhere but here."

"Sure, I understand that. One day you flee the unsatisfactory life and, three weeks later, you're back in the thick of it. Very frustrating. Bad luck. Well, you can always try again." His normally pale face was slightly flushed beneath the eyes. He unscrewed a whiskey bottle and poured himself a large measure. In almost the same movement he gulped it down. All his movements were familiar and strange at the same time.

"The minute I got off the train," I said, " I knew it would be like this. It never changes. They always want me to account for myself."

" You didn't have to come back. Nobody forced you."

"Ah Eoin, she died."

"So? What difference did that make? You should have stayed away if you didn't want to fall into their clutches. The first rule of disappearing is to make a clean break. You can't keep turning up for funerals, marriages and christenings."

Reluctantly I smiled at him. "Anyway," he continued, "I'm glad we ran into each other." We smiled terrible, icy smiles at each other. "We have unfinished business. You said you wanted to be shut of me." He flashed me a grimace. "If you really mean it I'd like to see what we could work out."

I moved away from him towards the old Aga. "I can't deal with this tonight, not now. I haven't the heart."

He looked coldly at me. "Just thought I'd mention it when I got the chance. We probably won't be seeing much of each other from now on."

I sighed. My only escape that night would be sleep.

"Cheer up", he said. A fraction of friendliness crept back into his voice. "Have a drink." He poured me a whiskey. "Your father said to help ourselves and I intend to take him at his word." He poured out another measure for himself. We lifted our glasses and clinked them together. "Health and happiness," he said.

"*Sláinte's fadshaol agat*," I offered. We raised our glasses to our lips. I almost choked on the sweet sourness of the whiskey. Quickly I bit into the last of my sandwich. This stranger, my husband, made me another. As I watched him butter the bread my attention was snagged by his wedding ring, bulky on his slender finger.

"What were you two up to?" Aunt Moira asked as I sat down beside her.

"Don't know," I answered. She shot a look at me. "Just talking," I said.

Chapter Two

Later that night I watched Aunt Moira strip the covers from Aunt Alice's bed. She refused to let me help her. Her face was without expression as if she'd been relieved of her personality. I could make out the silhouettes of the old chestnut trees that grew at the top of the garden. From my seat by the window, if I craned my neck, I could see in through the lighted window of the kitchen. My mother washed up cups and plates and May, my sister, stood beside her drying them. May leaned across and said something. My mother laughed. I seldom saw her in good humour and it was odd to see her at ease with somebody.

"Help me fold up the sheets," Aunt Moira said, relenting from her solitariness. As we stood and stretched the sheets, matched the ends, advanced and retreated from each other, tugged and folded in easy rhythm it seemed that we were engaged in an elaborate, stately ritual like a court dance where we took each other's measure with carefully paced steps and movements. Our gazes bounced off each other. It seemed significant but had no significance at all. "Mrs Deasy will help me wash all the sheets when you've gone," she said. "Put them on the little table outside the bathroom door. You'll find a cloth there to cover them with."

"Do you want me to make up the bed?" I asked.

"No. I'll do that myself. I'm going to sleep here tonight." There must have been something shocked about my expression because she smiled and added, "Don't worry, it's not sacrilegious. I'm not going to snooze on any lumpy sofa bed tonight. I'll sleep well, surrounded by Alice's things. I'll be able to feel her presence here better than anywhere else. Don't you feel her spirit hovering about us? I do."

Since our return from the church I thought I sensed a presence moving through the house. It had been insubstantial like a breath, a sigh, a gentle gust of wind. It was pleasant to think that it might be Auntie Alice's aura lingering in the place she knew best, watching over us. "Yes," I admitted. "I put it down to that overactive imagination of mine that she used to criticise."

"She might have criticised it but she enjoyed it, particularly when you were a child. Remember that summer, when you were about four, and you insisted that you must have a tail? You were determined to be a cat. We had to stop you lapping your milk from a saucer."

I laughed. "No, I don't remember that, thank goodness."

"You were an amusing child," she said, shaking out a fresh sheet and spreading it over the mattress. "I don't know what happened when you grew up."

I went and put the folded sheets away. When I returned she was ramming pillows into starched linen pillowcases. There were no easy-care cotton and polyester sheets in the house. Aunt Moira sighed as she shook out the second sheet and began to tuck in the edges. "I'll clean out the room next week and go through all her things. I suppose I'll give the clothes to the nuns. They'll find some deserving person who needs them."

When she had tucked in the bedspread and pummelled the pillows into submission she darted a glance at me. "Alice left you some money," she said. "It's in the will."

"Money?" I heard myself say as though it were an alien concept.

"Quite a lot in fact," she said sharply as she gathered up the eiderdown to throw over the bedspread. I stood up and she let me help her push the bed against the wall.

"Are you serious?" I asked.

"Surprising, isn't it?" She laughed.

Suddenly my mother was at the door. I had heard her coming up the stairs but assumed she was going into the bedroom she and my father shared. "Yvonne's downstairs," she said to me.

"Yvonne? What's she doing here?" I asked.

"Offer her a drink. We'll be down soon," Aunt Moira said.

"She wants to talk to Sinéad. I didn't want to turn her away."

"What a time to turn up," I grumbled. Aunt Moira shot me a warning glance. Not a word to your mother, the glance said.

"You'd better see her," she said. "You were great with each other when you were children. Go on. You used to be very fond of her."

I went downstairs. Yvonne was standing in the hallway. She had hugged me warmly in the church but I wasn't pleased to see her.

"Hello, Sinéad." She smiled. "It's ages since we met. I just thought that tonight would be our only chance to see each other. After the funeral you'll all head off and then it might be ages before we meet again."

"It was good of you to call," I said. I felt flat and stale. She exuded an air of expectancy and anxiety that irritated me. I sensed a force of will behind that wavering smile. "Will you have a drink?"

"No. You don't want me here tonight but later you could slip up to our house for a while and we could catch up on all the gossip. What about it?"

I shook my head. "I'd better stay. You know the way it is. They'd only get annoyed if I went out. Wait till the next time I'm down." I heard my mother's step behind me on the stairs.

"Excuse me, Mrs Power," she said to my mother, "I'm sorry to interrupt you tonight of all nights, but I was hoping that Sinéad could come up and see me for a while, and she says she shouldn't. It'd be all right, wouldn't it? I wouldn't keep her long."

"Why shouldn't she? We'll all be in bed soon. There'll be no all night sessions here," my mother said crisply. My heart sank. She turned to me. "You and Eoin go up. You know you mightn't see Yvonne for months again." She passed by us and went into the sitting-room.

"There you are, you see! No problem," Yvonne said. She was elated, as if we were girls and she had succeeded in getting me out to a local festival. She danced out the door. "I'll be expecting you soon," she said.

There was nothing for it but to go. I heard my mother announce our impending departure to the assembled

12

company in the sitting-room. Upstairs Aunt Moira was bringing clothes and toiletries into her new bedroom. I heard her open the hot press door.

Eoin came out into the hall. He took the news of our expedition calmly. "It'll get us out of the house," he said. "I'm not usually invited along."

"Mam invited you," I explained. He knew my mother's imperious ways. We poked our heads into the sitting-room.

"Are you not gone yet?" my mother asked, and waved us away. I hesitated, uneasy at leaving the censorious company to pick over the bones of our marriage. I didn't want to struggle up the hill to Yvonne's house in the cold.

"You'd better go, if you're going," May said sharply.

"How many offspring has Yvonne to her credit now?" Eoin asked as we flinched and turned our faces away from the sharp, easterly wind.

"Three at the last count."

"They breed a lot here," he said.

"If it was up to us to populate the world it'd be in a bad way."

He moved closer to me. "Oh, I'm willing to give fatherhood a try," he said. "The idea isn't altogether unappealing."

I edged away. "Men and their egos," I scoffed. "Why don't you impregnate your lady friend? I'm sure she'd be keen."

"More willing than you've ever shown yourself to be." He sounded cross.

"Well, you can forget about that idea," I said. "That's a closed chapter."

"All right, my little iceberg," he said. "I won't force the issue."

Yvonne's bungalow was immaculate, crisp in the fading light, with a neat, cultivated garden and a paved path leading to the front door. When she opened the door she seemed taken aback to see Eoin but I was glad of his company. She wouldn't dare to ask probing questions with him about. She showed us into a small, gaudy little sitting-room I had never been in before. It was crammed with old, handed down furniture and cheap ornaments. There were no pictures on the walls. Eoin moved over to the fire and warmed his hands. He looked sullen and withdrawn. I saw Yvonne throw an apprehensive glance in his direction. She went to a drinks cabinet. Eoin raised a quizzical eyebrow when he saw the full glass of whiskey she offered him but said nothing. She probably didn't notice his mood. The men of the district weren't noted for their loquacity.

"I got great news today." She smiled at me. Eoin sat down on a creaky armchair. I realised that she was almost radiant. She could hardly wait for the follow up question.

"Oh," I said, "what was that?"

"I'm expecting," she announced.

I saw Eoin start. "What are you expecting?" he asked. She looked at him, puzzled.

"You know . . ." she began. I took pity on her.

"She's pregnant," I said.

"Ah," he said dangerously, "in the midst of death, life. How wonderful."

"Thank you," she said happily. "What about you two? Any news?"

An angry, twitching energy radiated from Eoin. "Auntie Alice's death is about our only news, isn't it, Sinéad?" he said.

14

"You know what I mean," she said. "Are you expecting or anything, Sinéad?"

"Well what do you think, Sinéad?" he asked me. "Do you think you might be a touch pregnant?"

I glared at him. He stared back impassively. Yvonne shot him another puzzled, confused look. "No, darling, not even a tiny bit," I said evenly. Yvonne looked defeated, even annoyed.

"Ah sure, God is good," Eoin said unpleasantly. He turned away and stared moodily into the fire.

"Sit down, Sinéad," she said. "I'll fetch the children for you."

"Don't snipe at her because you're annoyed with me," I said when she had gone.

"Her fecking curiosity got me," he said. "Our business is none of her business."

"You know what they're like around here. They're mad to know everything."

"I've no intention of humouring them, Sinéad," he said. "I'm not up to it."

"We won't stay long," I promised.

"Half an hour, forty minutes at most," he said.

Yvonne returned with three scrubbed, polished children dressed in their night clothes. "They wouldn't go to bed until they saw the visitors," she said, as she pushed them in before her. The children shifted uneasily. I felt sorry for them. It was hard to know who suffered most, the children who knew they were on show, or we who felt little inclination to admire them.

Eoin called the boy over to him. "What's your name?" he asked. "Tom," the boy said slowly.

"He's called after his father," Yvonne said.

Eoin called over the two little girls. "Who are these two splendid creatures?" he asked. They giggled shyly and whispered their names. "Rena and Caroline," Eoin exclaimed. "You'll take the eyes out of them here when you're grown up." He looked at Tom. "You won't be bad looking either, I can see." I never understood how children were always so completely at ease with Eoin. They responded to him instantly and never seemed afraid of him.

"They have to go to bed now," Yvonne said. "Say goodnight, children."

Eoin stood up. "They can't go until I've given them something to remember me by." He rooted in his trouser pockets, extracted three pound coins and held them up to the light. "You're lucky," he said. "Sometimes I have no money." The children stared at him expectantly, eyes rounded. I watched as he ordered them to hold out their hands and placed a coin on each little palm. He knelt down and they hugged him awkwardly. I felt Yvonne's eyes on me and suffered the children to plant a moist kiss on my cheek as they passed by. They waved to Eoin at the door and scampered out giggling.

"I'll be back in a minute," Yvonne said.

"Where's the husband?" Eoin asked. He seemed in better form.

"Probably down at the pub. I don't think she has an easy time with him."

"Remember now," he murmured as we heard Yvonne's step in the hall, "a hasty retreat. Tell her we're exhausted."

Whatever Yvonne had intended, the occasion must have disappointed her. We drank our whiskey quickly and made small talk. Eoin said very little. She looked despondent when we said goodbye.

"You could have been a little more sociable," I complained. "You hardly spoke at all."

"Tut, tut," he admonished. "That was a bit of a damp squib. I get us out of an awkward situation in record time and you show no gratitude. Ungrateful wretch."

"Where are we going?" I asked, as we strode down the village street past Aunt Moira's house.

"I'm going to that old, deserted graveyard you told me about once. I've never seen it and I don't feel like going to bed yet. I might never be in this village again so this could be my last opportunity to see the place. You can come, if you like, or you can go into that miserable family of yours. I don't care."

"You won't see much at night," I protested.

"Full moon, clear sky and," he fumbled in his coat pocket and extracted something, "a torch." He strode off down the hill towards the river road. I watched him go. Behind me I thought I heard a door open. I ran to catch up with him.

Chapter Three

"Funny, isn't it, the moon, the stars, the frost and you and me? An unexpected interlude in our turbulent lives." Eoin shone his torch on one of the tilting headstones. "Still, I quite like this place. It has a certain ambiance. We should have come here before."

We were at the edge of the graveyard, just inside the gates and the low wall. The eerie light of the moon threw a phosphorescent glow over the broken headstones and the ruins of the old church as it dashed across a shimmering sky. I shivered in the blue, silvery sea of light.

"It looks calm and untroubled," I said. He turned to look at me. His eye were dark and unfathomable. An agitation like an electric charge sizzled between us. If he touched me I would combust.

"Restful," he mused. "I suppose the dead are untroubled."

"What on earth made you decide to come here?" I asked. "You could have gone to a pub."

"It wouldn't do for us to show our faces in one of those dens of sin and drunkenness, not tonight with your aunt lying in the church. Can you imagine what a stir it would cause? We'd be the talk of the county. No, this is a good place to be. I came here on impulse really but perhaps it could have a special meaning for us. We could bury our dead relationship, an ideal spot when you think about it . . . an abandoned graveyard, a ruined church, a monument to dead loves and forgotten lives." He laughed. "Won't you come in to my parlour said the spider to the fly," he said.

His voice echoed around the deserted and chilly graveyard. After a long silence, while he shone the torch on tombstones and tried to make out their faint inscriptions and I followed him about, I said, "There's supposed to be a relation of mine buried here."

"Any idea where exactly?"

"Not a notion. All I know is that some grand-aunt of mine died in childbirth. She was buried here around the turn of the century."

"We should seek her out and commune with her spirit."

"I don't even know her full name. Helen something. Some of the headstones are missing. The others are piled up against a wall of the church. We'd never find her. "

"Ah, but don't you like the idea of a search?" he asked. "I'd quite enjoy having a good look around. It'd give us a sense of common purpose, don't you think?" His voice rang out clearly in the gloom.

"I don't see the point of that."

"I suppose you're right," he said. "It would be a bit of a fool's errand. You know, Sinéad," he said softly, "this isn't the way things should be between us." He was looking at me but, in the darkness, I couldn't see him clearly. Suddenly he shone the torch directly into my eyes. Blinded, I turned aside. When I could see again I moved away from him.

"Your face looks like stone in this light," he said. "Very

severious. Suitable enough, I suppose, for somebody with a heart of stone."

His sourness stung me. "You think that you're the creature of flesh and blood and feelings," I snapped.

He paced about the path for a while and then jumped back up on the grassy mound that contained most of the graves. "I remember nights like this years ago." His voice was flat, almost monotonous. "Do you? We were in love then. We were happy. Happiness doesn't last for long, does it? And yes, I'm human and I'm vulnerable. I want things. I need things. I'm not ashamed of that."

"Yes, yes, I know. We've said all this before." My voice sounded weak and false.

I heard him sigh. "It's all passion spent with you, is it? Everything is just words. Nothing touches you."

"You know what they say. I usedn't understand things but felt them. Now I understand things and feel nothing."

"Wrong," he said. "You understand nothing and feel nothing. We've had one fairly serious crisis in our marriage and, from that, you've simplified and generalised everything out of proportion."

"That business showed something. That we were finished."

He rounded on me. "Rubbish," he said. "It certainly showed up the weaknesses in our marriage but it didn't define it. That's a crazy misrepresentation of everything. Nothing's that simple."

"Sure, you know that wasn't all," I said dully. "Even before that we were fairly rocky."

"I don't see why we couldn't have improved it. All marriages have rough patches."

"I've no intention of enduring something out of a sense of duty," I said. "I've had enough of that all my life and don't see any point to it."

"That's wonderful," he sneered. "Reduce everything to a formula. Don't tolerate weakness or failure. I agree that the notion that everything must be endured and accepted is ridiculous but all you're doing is turning it on its head and coming up with the equally ridiculous idea that anything that isn't perfect can't be tolerated at all. Don't you see how ludicrous that is?"

"Don't lecture me," I spat at him. "Don't you dare talk to me as if I'm the one who's behaving unreasonably. You're still living with that woman some of the time, aren't you? All I hear from you is talk."

Christ, I thought, what do I know about men? I remembered a night when he had begged me to love him. His directness surprised me. I was stunned when he caught me to him and knelt at my feet pulling me over so that I fell with him. I escaped quickly. There was something repellent about the display, a rawness that was almost ugly. Such neediness was frightening. Soon afterwards he transferred his needs to another object of affection. The desires had to be satisfied, the outlet didn't much matter.

He laughed gently. The sound of that laughter enraged me. "I could throttle you," I said.

"You can have me back again tomorrow, if you want to try again. Just give the word and I'll be all yours."

"Don't," I muttered. "It's sickening. You don't know what it did to me when I walked into that pub and found you with her. You have no idea."

He strode towards me so purposefully that I backed away

and tripped on a stone. I went over on my ankle but he caught me before I fell. "Are you hurt? Is it sore?" he asked.

"A bit." I was conscious of his hands gripping me.

"Run it under a cold tap tonight if there's any swelling," he said. We stood quietly together. If I stood still for long enough, he might let the moment pass.

"Be reasonable, Sinéad," he said after some time. "You bolted without a word. You've hardly given me a chance."

"That's good," I said. "I ran off? You left first, remember? Ah, let it go. If I came home you'd drift back to her, I'd leave again and it'd be the same as before. I'm not able for all this chaos in my life. I want to simplify it."

"People are untidy and messy. Relationships are complicated. Maybe we should try mediation. At least we'd find out if there was anything to be salvaged."

"Make do, you mean? Not bloody likely." What was it I wanted? What would satisfy me?

"We could see if there's a way out of this. If you leave again then you'll be opting out altogether."

I shifted uneasily. "I can't think. This is a bad time," I said. Let it go, I really wanted to say but I felt he might fight that.

"It's never the right time," he said. "There's no perfect moment. Don't wait for a sign from the gods. Take a chance. It's all farce, all farce. It doesn't matter all that much. Being impetuous does as well as anything else."

"This isn't the time," I protested. "Aunt Alice . . ."

". . . is dead, and we're alive. Come on, Sinéad. Think about it. Give us a chance. All it needs is the will to give it a go."

Despite everything – perhaps I was slightly flattered by his persistence – I sensed a faint weakening of my resolve.

"I'm really sorry . . ." I began but he pushed me back against the raised earth and kissed me. He pressed against me and I let him kiss me, let my body go limp, aware of his quick breathing, conscious of him straining to press closer to me. It was almost hypnotic but a tiny, disembodied voice in me shouted, this means nothing. This means nothing at all. The kiss lasted for ages, tongue on my tongue, lips against lips, a whiskey breath on my skin, his hands on my body. I looked up at the stars.

He groaned and sighed deeply and then let go. I sat up quickly and pulled away, then looked down at his long face and that slightly crooked nose as he lay on the grass breathing deeply and slowly. His pale profile looked at the moon. I felt an almost detached curiosity as I watched him.

"That meant nothing to you, did it?" he asked. I started.

Suddenly he pushed himself into a standing position. He jumped on the wall, raised a fist and yelled, "I'm the king of the castle. Get down, you dirty rascal!"

He jumped down and sat beside me again. "Oh, well," he said.

"You never take anything seriously," I complained.

"Untrue," he said. "You're the one who doesn't appreciate the seriousness of things." He patted my knee in a brotherly fashion. This miffed my vanity slightly. I was almost tempted to reach out to him and to find out if sex could ever again feel urgent or exciting, but the thought died. I stood up. My whole body ached.

"Ladies first," he said as he helped me over the wall. He vaulted over it then. "There's life in the old dog still," he declared.

"You're not that old."

"Madam, no talk of age. It's too depressing."

I thought of Aunt Alice's body locked behind the doors of the new church over the hill, across the ocean of darkness, close to the road that led to the new graveyard, where her freshly dug grave awaited her. Was she lonely on her own? Age snapped away lives. That was all there was. Disappointment, age and death.

"Are you thinking about her?" he asked.

I nodded. "She'll be buried tomorrow morning. I can't think of anything more horrible, don't understand it. We're all struggling against this dark force that will swallow us up."

"We do a lot of living before that. I'm not prepared to give up on life because of death," he said.

We shuffled along the dark road. The moon went in suddenly and we were plunged into an even more intense darkness. He caught me as I stumbled and shone his torch in front of us, giving us a faint light to see by. After a while I could pick out the village lights in the distance. I pulled away from him.

"What are you going to do when this is over?" he asked.

"I haven't the faintest idea."

"Stay in our house, if you like. I won't bother you."

"Sure, and my parents would come knocking at the door to sort me out. I couldn't bear it."

"Tell them about us. They'll have to be told sometime. Bad and all as they are, they are your parents."

"I'll write them a letter. They can cut me out of the will and strike the memory of me from their hearts." I spoke despondently. Parents, brothers, sisters and husbands demanded time, explanations and justifications and I didn't intend to humour any of them. In that moment I thought of

Maggie, my old college friend. If Aunt Alice had really left me a fair sum of money I could take off on the strength of it. It was years since I'd been in London.

Aloud I said, "I've jumped through enough hoops for them all my life and never managed to please them."

"They might react better than you think."

"And pigs might fly. I've had a bellyful of duty and good advice. Anyway," I turned to him, "you don't even like them. I don't know why you're sticking up for them."

"They care about you in their own way."

"They care about moulding me."

We reached the first street light in the village. Eoin was silent. He kicked a stone. I heard it hit the pavement on the opposite side of the street. "I've had enough criticism from them to last me the rest of my life," I said.

"I still think you should talk to them."

"You want them to tell me to go back to you."

We strolled into the village. A delicate stillness hung in the air. Even the pubs were quiet. The tap tapping of our footsteps broke the silence and echoed in the empty street.

How could I break with this life? Only by going away. Maggie might let me stay with her for a while. The break would have to be sudden and surgical; no explanations, no letters.

Then I thought about Aunt Moira and ached at the idea that I might never see her again, but she too had to be excluded. It was altogether possible that she would confide in my mother and it wasn't beyond my father to go to England to fetch back his errant daughter, his perpetual child.

In Deasys there was silence. Mrs Deasy poked her head

round a door. She was in her dressing-gown. "This way," she said and led us along a corridor to a small room. She flashed us a gummy, bashful smile and shuffled away. Our bed was in a living-room converted into a bedroom for the night. The head of the put-me-up was jammed up against a mottled old mahogany sideboard. I smelt the damp of a little used room.

There was a sour look on Eoin's face. He undressed before me and watched me watching him. I picked up my nightdress and padded barefoot along a cold linoleum corridor to the bathroom to change. It was a cheerless little room, almost an outhouse. When I got into bed beside him we turned our backs to each other. The bed dipped in the middle and I caught the edge of the mattress to keep the space between us. My back and arms ached from the effort of trying to keep away from him. I couldn't tell whether he was awake or asleep. At times I could barely make out his breathing. Occasionally he let out a deep sigh. My own breathing seemed fast, almost laboured. We were restless, continually shifting and moving, unable to settle.

Eventually I was conscious of my fingers loosening their grip on the mattress and I dropped into sleep. I dreamt that he undressed me. He slavered in unsavoury excitement as he penetrated me. I woke in terror to find him holding me. "You were dreaming," he said and put me away from him. I clutched my pillow. "Go to sleep," he said. "Tomorrow's a long day."

I dreamt of Auntie Alice, met her on the road to the graveyard. She looked gaunt. Her face was unfamiliar. She didn't know me. She passed by. It was night-time but the graveyard gates were open. She walked towards an open grave. I ran after her but she had disappeared. The grave was filled when I got to it. Underneath the earth I heard muffled cries. I awoke in darkness. Somebody flicked on the light. Eoin was dressed.

"Time to get up," he said. He seemed subdued and distant. I felt hollow, as though someone had sucked out my entrails, and struggled out of the deep bed.

If Auntie Alice were alive I might have confided in her. She had been the most approachable person in my family. She probably wouldn't have condoned my behaviour and we might have rowed, but I felt sure that she wouldn't have condemned me. I would never know. She was dead. She was gone. And now we had to bury her.

Chapter Four

The church was an old, stone building with a faulty heating system. Outside, in the sun, the day was warming up but inside the stone released its store of iciness.

The coffin rested on a wheeled platform in front of the altar. My mind was overrun by memories of her. At some stage in my life a definitive image of her had crystallised and, from the moment of her death, that would be my mental picture of her, frozen like a portrait on a wall; a frail, slender, lame woman with iron grey hair drawn into a bun and fine, lightly lined ivory skin. I would have to consult photographs of her to allay or diffuse this image.

A pang, some deeper grief, pressed down on me. I felt that I was playing a part, that of the bereft niece, simulating all the appropriate emotions but not actually experiencing them. Would anybody sniff out this terrible coldness? Could they tell by looking at me?

In the pew in front of me Aunt Moira's small, sturdy frame sat hunched, utterly motionless, oblivious of everything, her pinched face frozen in an expression of bewilderment.

The Mass ended. When the priest returned from the

sacristy to say the prayers for the dead the congregation rose. He hurried down the altar steps, stopped in front of the coffin, made a great show of clearing his throat, opened his missal and began to read. Finally he blessed the coffin with holy water and the funeral directors wheeled it down the aisle. The wheels rolled on the cold tiles of the floor and creaked their way along. My mother, Aunt Moira, my father, May and Emer were the first in the front row to follow. We filed out after them. My brother, Joe, nudged me, kissed my cheek and we shook hands. In other circumstances a handshake between us would have been outrageous but in this situation it was appropriate. The rest of the congregation followed us but I couldn't bring myself to meet anybody's eye. Eoin touched my hand and I winced. My stomach churned. Too many whiskeys the previous night.

Outside the morning was foggy. I looked about me. Eoin had disappeared. Then I saw him standing with the men beside the coffin. He would shoulder it again this morning. The church bell tolled and the walk to the graveyard began.

As we moved out of the village the fog slipped away and the autumn fields were revealed in all their dying glory. We walked with a rhythmical slowness. My mother paced beside me, studiously avoiding my eye. At public events her behaviour was always very rigid, very proper. "You're walking much too quickly," she whispered.

"Sorry," I muttered and slowed down. She bottled up all her disapproval and resentment of me behind a tight, downturned mouth. Her mouth and lips were spare. She had no surplus flesh. "Dried up and wizened," I thought. I tried to put a stop to my mean thoughts. I felt like a trapped fifteen-year-old, frightened of everything.

"This way," my mother's cold voice said as she pushed me to the right. Aunt Moira's rigid little face stared up at me. May held her arm. Behind her walked Emer clutching on to her husband, Jimmy.

In the graveyard we passed one or two new graves strewn with domed plastic flowers already hardening into grotesque caricatures of themselves. No plastic flowers for Auntie Alice, I thought and remembered the bright wreath of flowers Eoin and I had bought for her. To my surprise I discovered tears on my cheeks. I touched and tasted them. Father Guilfoyle stood by the open grave, awaiting the arrival of the coffin. He strained towards us. He seemed impatient.

"He wants to get home to his dinner," I said.

"What a thing to say," Aunt Moira whispered. Father Guilfoyle was noted for his ruthless efficiency, his was the fastest Mass in the county.

The coffin bounced and tilted on its way down into the grave. Suddenly it was over. Father Guilfoyle snapped shut his prayer-book and the workmen laid sheets of wood over the hole. I was disappointed. I wanted to throw a handful of clay on the coffin. Father Guilfoyle shook hands with all the relatives, drew back his mouth in a strange, wolflike smile and walked away briskly.

People milled up to Aunt Moira and began the intonation of "Sorry for your trouble." Complete strangers shook my hand. People I knew slightly rushed up to us. A small crowd hung back, gimlet-eyed and glum.

Above the murmur of voices I heard my father talking to Eoin. "Not a bit windy, thank God," he said. "We were nearly blown away the day of my mother's funeral. A desperate day." He rubbed his hands together as though he might spit on them and finalise a dreadful bargain.

"I can't believe she's gone," I heard Aunt Moira say to a neighbour and the refrain "God is good" drifted towards me on the thin, cool air like an ephemeral blessing. I stood absolutely still, stiff with formality. Although I don't remember reacting the next thing I knew was that Aunt Moira's collapsing form was in my arms. I staggered, managed to keep my balance and steady the two of us.

"The poor woman. She's exhausted," I heard a voice say.

"Best get her home quickly," my father muttered. May ran back to the church to bring up a car.

"Let her have some air," I said fretfully but nobody heeded me.

"Move back everybody. The woman needs air," my father ordered, for once throwing a look of approval in my direction. Unwillingly the crowd shuffled back.

We were sitting on the path. I could feel Aunt Moira tremble as I held her but the dreadful greyness left her face. She sighed, seemed to revive and struggled to get up.

"Take it easy," I whispered.

"She's coming around," somebody said.

"I haven't done anything like that since I was a girl." She laughed. "I feel so silly." The crowd began to disperse. There would be no more graveyard drama. They might as well go.

"She took bad," they would say in satisfied tones when they returned home. "Ah sure it's terrible hard on her, the poor woman. She'll be all alone now."

"Take her up to the gate," my father's voice boomed down at me. He was in his element. Other people helped me lift her. She was quite unsteady on her feet. We plodded slowly towards the waiting car. May reached back and opened a back door. Eoin took Aunt Moira's arm and guided her in and she smiled wanly up at us. She looked as if she might expire at any moment. They drove off with her, my mother in the back, my father in the front like an outrider pointing the way.

"She could do with a good dinner," Eoin said. "She's worn out."

"I should be helping Mrs Deasy with the dinner," I said. "Better get back to the house."

"What's your hurry?" Brian, my eldest brother, asked. I hadn't noticed him. "The house is full of women to set tables, serve drinks and fuss over saucepans. You won't be missed. How're you, Sinéad?"

"As you see," I said. Since he and his family had moved to Wicklow we hardly ever saw him. I suspected that this was a clever manoeuvre on his part to distance himself from my parents.

"How's Isolda? How are the children?" I asked. Isolda was Brian's blondly glamorous and startlingly remote wife.

"All flourishing." He smiled. "I didn't see much point in dragging them along."

"Aunt Moira'd have appreciated it," I said.

"I suppose you're right. Didn't think of it like that. Not to worry. I'm staying for the dinner so I'll gain approval points there."

"Listen, I'm off. I've got to get back for a meeting this afternoon," Joe said. "I just managed to get time off for the funeral. We're incredibly busy these days." Hurriedly he shook hands with us all. "I hear things aren't going so well with you, Sinéad. Bit of trouble on the domestic front," he said.

"Don't you know that you're talking to the black sheep of the family," Brian gibed and nudged me.

"Take care," Joe said and kissed the air close to my cheek, threw me a searching look, hesitated as though he might change his mind and stay, thought better of it and moved off. "Cheerio, Eoin. Sorry to be in such a rush. Brian, I'll give you a ring."

"Promises, promises," Brian mocked. Joe backed away, waved, turned and ran.

"Our brother's a man in a hurry," Brian mused. "I hope he knows where he's going." I had forgotten what good fun Brian could be. We seldom met but, when we did come across each other, I enjoyed his company. We were a funny, disparate family group. The link that bound us was our parents and I suspected that when that link snapped we would be disconnected forever.

Brian linked my arm. "Tell me what you've been up to," he said. "Whenever your name is mentioned there's a terrible tightening of lips on our dear Mama's part. I'm intrigued."

His grin was infectious. I conceded a smile. "Wait for the next instalment, Brian. It gets worse."

"Shocking," he said, "Shocking. What's the world coming to?" He leaned close to me. "Give 'em hell," he murmured in my ear.

Later, as we sat around the table and drank a toast to Auntie Alice, I looked at the various members of my family. With the exception of Joe we had all made it to the funeral and dinner. Nevertheless, we were still a family ill at ease in one another's company with little or nothing to say to each other.

Across from me, at the other end of the table, Eoin chatted with Aunt Moira. He looked after my mother and her, refilled their glasses and leaned into the centre of the table to spoon vegetables on their plates. They were utterly charmed. I glared at him and he shot me a sweet smile. "Hypocrite," I mouthed but he faced me with an expression of deepest incomprehension.

Mrs Deasy collected the dessert dishes and that left the drinking of coffee and Cointreau. I longed to get away.

As Eoin packed the boot with our overnight bags Aunt Moira grabbed me by the arm and propelled me up the stairs. In Aunt Alice's room she pulled out drawers, sighed impatiently and shut them. Finally she rummaged in her handbag. "Here it is," she said and pressed an envelope into my hand. "Look at this when you get home. You and Eoin could book a good holiday on the strength of it." She shooed me before her down the stairs. "Don't keep him waiting," she said. I lost her in the round of hugs and farewells.

* * *

On our way through the city we passed the old school. "You don't want to stop, do you?" Eoin asked.

"Keep on driving," I said. My voice sounded hoarse. As we approached, the traffic lights in front of the main gates turned red and we had to stop.

Some girls in games uniform wandered towards the changing rooms. I saw Fintan and Simon stroll down the avenue of trees to the gate, deep in conversation. As the lights changed and the car moved off Fintan looked in our direction and I gave a little wave in case he had seen me.

"Sure you don't want to call in?" Eoin asked. "I'll turn the car around if you like."

"Go on," I urged. I glanced at my watch. The final bell was about to ring. I would miss all those young girls surging out past the school gates on to the road to catch buses and lifts home. I had been spared the flurry of bicycles and farewell shouts, and the thrust of their expectations.

Chapter Five

Eoin brought our bags from the car into the hall. "Have to go to work," he said.

"Now?" I looked at my watch. It was just after four o'clock.

"There's a meeting tomorrow morning. I'm expected to have a report ready for it. It'll take me hours to do. There's no food in the house. Well, anything you find'll be rotten."

"I've eaten enough to keep me on the march for a week," I said.

He edged towards the door, bouncing the car keys in his hands. "Well, see you later," he said. He looked uneasy. He looked exhausted.

"You'd better go," I said. I strained towards the kitchen.

He ran a hand through his hair. "There's quite a mess in there."

"Doesn't matter. I'm not living here now."

He let out a wheezy whistle through his teeth, turned on his heel and was gone.

The kitchen was a dump, the sink full of unwashed dishes, the bin overflowing and the floor littered with food droppings. I put on the kettle, extracted a cup from the unsteady pile in the sink, washed it and made myself a cup of coffee. A carton of milk in the fridge was rancid. I drank the coffee black.

In the hall I picked up an old newspaper from the floor. "New school opens," the headline shouted and showed a photograph of a minister opening the school on the front page. Schools and teaching, I thought. How quickly one forgot that world.

The previous September our staff had gathered on the first day of the year. I tapped my pen impatiently on my folder as I waited for the meeting to begin. Laughter erupted from different groups as people swapped holiday anecdotes.

"There you are!" Imelda yelled and hurled herself into my arms. "You old rogue you, I haven't seen you in weeks! You promised to call out to me."

She turned and shouted something at George and then settled in the seat beside me. "I'm pregnant!" she announced, her eyes sparkling. "Isn't that marvellous?"

"Tremendous." We all knew how she'd longed for a baby and how she suffered when she'd lost one. She was embarking on this adventure with her usual enthusiasm and confidence. Somebody pushed in on the other side of me.

"Woe is me. This is bloody awful," Constance muttered. She eased the chair in front of her away to make room for her long legs. "It's dreadful to be back."

I smiled. "Going to grumble all through the meeting?"

"Of course I am. I'd give anything to be in France. Got back just this morning, raced up from Rosslare."

"The hair is stunning," I murmured. The Vice Principal shook hands with Constance and then with me. She moved on to the next group. She was a small woman. Over the years the colour had drained from her face and hair and, as she aged, whatever compensating liveliness she once possessed vanished and her colourlessness became a negative force which reduced her to a ghostlike presence in the school. "Welcome back," she said to Imelda. "I believe congratulations are in order." There was no warmth in her voice. Imelda flashed a smile.

Constance nudged me. "The hair," she said, "is Titian red. I fancied a change from the blond."

"Any comments from the kids?"

"Of course. They think it's great." She looked around. "I don't see Sister Ruth. Where is she?"

"Surveying the property, no doubt. They had all the windows painted during the summer," Imelda said. "Here she is, girls. God, she looks dire!"

I looked up to see our Principal pass by. She walked slowly. Her eyes were watery and her nose red as though she had a cold. She sniffed and dabbed her nose with a tissue. All thirty-five members of staff appeared to be present. I watched Sister Ruth greet Fintan. She smiled a glassy smile and shook hands with him. "Welcome back," she said.

"God, I wish I were anywhere but here," Constance hissed.

"How's Eoin?" Imelda asked, tearing herself away from George, the staffroom toy-boy.

"Fine, fine," I said. "He'll be pleased to hear your news."

"Isn't it great to be back?" Marianne called out to me and smiled ironically. George and Jack were deep in conversation.

"What are you two yapping about?" Constance asked.

"George has an idea about how to get more computers for the school," Jack said.

Imelda groaned. "You're not at it already, are you? Give us a break. It's only the first day."

I counted all seven male members of staff. Simon caught my eye and saluted me like an army cadet. I was delighted to see everybody again, even Anita, my old adversary. It was soothing to feel caught up in the buzz of activity.

George leaned across Imelda to me and asked, "Any idea what's on the agenda?"

"Not a notion. Didn't see anything up on any of the notice boards."

"Jack swears there was an agenda but it vanished."

"Lo and behold," I heard Constance say. I looked up and noticed three nuns walk in. In turn they embraced Sister Ruth and kissed her on the cheek. The laughter and talk stilled as people watched and resumed when they lost interest.

George whistled. "Attention folks. We're being visited by the Commander in Chief."

"Who?" Imelda asked.

"The nun talking to Ruth is the Superior of the order," he explained. We watched as she talked and Ruth listened. Then suddenly the nuns sat down.

"How'd you come to be the expert on who's who? Is there some sort of anniversary? Is any nun dead a hundred years?" Constance asked. George shook his head.

"Bet we're due an inspection or a pep talk," Imelda said.

"They're going to start. Who's on for lunch at the pub?" Jack asked.

"Count us all in," said Constance.

Sister Ruth rang the bell for silence. Suddenly I felt despondent. Eoin hadn't been home three nights in succession. When he did appear he brought papers with him and worked in the kitchen until the early hours of the morning. I was tired of living in a dead house and hungry for activity, ready to be devoured by the demands of the teaching year.

Imelda nudged me. "Christ Almighty," she said, "cheer up, will you? She always lets us go on the dot of twelve. We'll be into the pub before the lunchtime crowds."

When we were all quiet Sister Ruth cleared her throat. "I think we can start now," she said. "In the name of the Father, and of the Son and of the Holy Spirit . . . " We bowed our heads while she prayed. "Hello everybody," she said. I thought she looked pale. She paused. Normally she was brisk to the point of brusqueness.

"I'd like to introduce you to Sister Antonio," she said. "She has something to say." The little nun vacated her place and walked to the top table. Ruth sat with the other nuns. The three of them sat in identical uniforms with heads bowed, hands joined and ankles crossed as though posing for a photograph. Sister Ruth dipped her head and stared at the floor.

"Good morning, everybody," Sister Antonio said.

"Good morning," we chorused. She smiled slightly.

"I'm here today with a message from the order," she began, "I've come to tell you something very important." She spoke deliberately as though preaching to a dull laity.

"The suspense is killing me," Constance whispered. "Hope it's a day off."

"As you know, these are hard times for religious orders

and, as you also know, this is a difficult time for education. Numbers are dropping in national schools and, quite soon, the secondary system will feel the effects of the drop in population and many schools will close." She paused like a teacher checking to see if a class was keeping up with her.

"Our order controls four schools in the country. Not a single novice nun has joined the order in the last five years. In the light of dwindling numbers we've had to consider our situation. We searched our hearts but found no easy solutions. I have to tell you that we will close all our schools in three years' time. There'll be no assessment tests in December. No enrolments will be accepted for next year or following years. Fortunately the redeployment scheme will ensure that you'll all have jobs . . . "

She was forced to stop because a discord of sounds drowned out her voice. The room was in turmoil. She paused and drank water from a glass in front of her.

"You can't be serious! You don't mean this," Marianne, our union representative, shouted.

Once again we fell silent under Sister Antonio's impassive gaze. She placed the empty glass on the table. "The decision is final," she said. "All the appropriate authorities have been informed."

Fintan stood up. He was shaking. "I don't believe what I'm hearing. Why would you close this school? We're doing well, as well as any other school in the area."

"Population patterns in this area indicate that local schools will suffer a sharp drop in numbers in the next three to four years."

"Why act now?" I asked.

"We don't want to prolong the process. We want to give the staff a better chance of being relocated quickly."

"Sister Antonio, how can you put it so clinically?" Imelda asked. "You're talking to people who've worked here ten, twenty, twenty five years. You're a religious order, not a multinational company."

"We had to make a rational, not an emotional decision."

Imelda looked at Sister Antonio as if she were some rare animal. "What I can't understand," she burst out, "is why you never prepared us for this. You walk in and land this bombshell and expect us to walk into classrooms tomorrow and teach as normal. How do I face my students knowing that there's no future here? Where do you suggest our little first years go?"

Sister Antonio picked up a piece of paper and glanced down at it. "There's the community school and there are other convent schools in this district. Certainly some will have difficulties, but they'll find some place."

"Jesus Christ, Sister, I can't let this pass," Imelda called out. "At the sixth year Mass at the end of last year Sister Ruth told us how the sisters appreciated our contribution to the work of the order. Why say it if she didn't mean any of it?" Her voice broke. "This all sickens me." When she sat down she buried her face in her hands.

Fintan began to walk up towards Sister Antonio but George intercepted him, held his arms and spoke to him in a low, persuasive voice. Reluctantly, Fintan sat down.

"Who decided this?" Anita wailed.

"The decision was made at a Council meeting of the order a few days ago. I came to tell you as quickly as I could. We didn't want to break the news in a letter."

Anita stood up. "What if we refuse to accept your decision? What if we decide to fight you?"

This caused consternation among the nuns. A frisson of indignation convulsed them. Despite herself Anita smiled. She repeated her question.

"You don't have that option. The order owns the school and we're within our rights to close it."

"We'll see what our union says about that," Marianne growled.

"This is terrible! I can't believe it," Constance said. All at once other voices were raised.

"You're not a bloody factory manager. You can't treat people like this."

"What about your Christian ethos? Aren't you worried anymore about passing it on?"

"What are we going to tell the children?"

"What are we going to tell the children?" Imelda echoed. "What can we tell them?"

Sister Antonio withstood the abuse, the questions and the hostility. She seemed possessed of an extraordinary calm. "There's no need to distress the students," she said. "We're asking you to treat this as confidential for the time being."

"Rubbish! We haven't taken any vows of obedience." Marianne's voice rippled with contempt. "We won't collude with you on this. The students have the right to be told."

"I know this is hard for you," Sister Antonio said. "It's obvious how distressed you all are. I feel for you. Believe me I do."

Nobody answered. I looked around. I saw heads bowed. Some people seemed on the verge of tears. A few compressed their lips as if to control themselves.

"This is amazing," Constance said. "It's easy to imagine you don't want to be in a place when you know you have to be there, but it's different altogether when it's suddenly whipped away from you."

I couldn't speak. Sister Antonio sat down. I noticed a slight, pink tinge on her cheeks. It wasn't even vaguely reassuring to observe this evidence of stress.

Suddenly I realised that Imelda was sobbing. George rubbed her back awkwardly, his face contorted. "What can we do?" she sobbed. "What can we do?"

"She'd want to look after herself and her baby," Constance whispered.

A tense silence fell. Sister Antonio sat rigidly upright. I've no idea how long that silence lasted. It seemed as if we sat there for at least an hour. Perhaps only minutes passed. With strange clarity I saw a blackbird fly into a bush outside one of the windows. I heard his piercing song. It sounded wilfully singular and wildly inappropriate. I struggled to keep my eyes open. The silence beat in on my consciousness . . . Surely somebody would call out and break it? Surely we couldn't endure it any longer?

"What will the order do when they've closed the schools?" Simon asked. His voice was controlled, almost toneless.

Sister Antonio looked up. "We're going to sell the land here and in two other schools and convert the remaining convent into a retirement home for the sisters."

"What work will the order do?" Marianne asked.

"We'll be involved mainly in parish and community work. The Bishop has given his approval."

"Why not hand the school over to us and set up a Board of Management? It's been done elsewhere."

As if speaking to a particularly slow child Sister Antonio said: "The estates you draw your supply of students from are long established. In a few years there'll be very few children coming from them. The school would experience a sudden fall in numbers."

"Why couldn't we look for students from other areas?"

A look of distaste flickered over her features. "The order doesn't approve of poaching students from other schools."

"Promoting the school could hardly be called poaching, could it?" Imelda burst in. There was a murmur of assent from the staff. Heads nodded vigorously.

"We don't believe in undermining other schools."

"That's doublespeak," Imelda said. "There's nothing wrong with a bit of healthy competition. You don't care about the school, the students or us."

"We have thought of the good of everybody."

"I'd like to ask you something, Sister, just out of interest, since talking to you is merely an academic exercise," Fintan said. The nun inclined her head slightly. "Don't you believe in what you're doing? Isn't what's going on here worthwhile? Don't you care about the students?"

"We can't change that situation. Of course we care. We care very deeply. This isn't easy."

"Don't you trust us to carry on your work? Is that it?" Fintan asked.

Sister Antonio stared at him. I was shocked by the venom I saw in her face. "Nothing will make any difference to the eventual outcome," she said finally.

"Nonsense," George broke in, "all we have to do is to

promote the school properly. We'd have students banging down the door. We have marvellous facilities here. Schools like this shouldn't close."

For the first time since Sister Antonio had taken charge of the meeting Sister Ruth raised her head. She looked at George with a marvellous expression of deep reproach. He met that look calmly and outstared her. She dropped her gaze again.

"You forget the overall situation," Antonio said. "There won't be enough students to go around. Schools are going to close."

"I can see smaller places having to close," he said, "but it'd be a crime to close a fine place like this."

She stared at him and, slowly and quite deliberately, shook her head from side to side.

"Is this final? Is that what you mean?" Imelda asked wildly. She threw her arms up in the air in an eloquent gesture of despair.

"If I say it a thousand times it won't change. The decision to close the school is final," Sister Antonio said. A collective sigh filled the room and then there was a lull. Most heads were bent. There was a slight rustle. Sister Antonio's mute companions stood up.

Sister Ruth staggered to her feet. "Thank you for coming," I heard her say. She clutched Sister Antonio in a farewell embrace. Antonio's eyes pierced hers as though testing her resolve. When I looked again the strangers had left. Sister Ruth stared out through the window for a long, long time.

"Why didn't she open her gob?" Constance whispered. "Does she have no say?"

"Don't, Constance," I muttered. "Don't make it worse."

After a while Sister Ruth spoke. "Shall we continue the meeting?" she asked. Nobody answered. She swallowed. "Do you wish the meeting to continue?"

For a long time there was no answer. "Why not, Sister?" Imelda said finally. She let out a snort of derision. "We'll have to keep up the good work!" she said.

Chapter Six

"Did that impress you as an act of gross moral turpitude?" Imelda inquired.

"Have we grounds for sacking them?" I asked.

"Somebody should hit that bloody Superior. She's much too superior for me."

"I thought Fintan was going to," Constance said. "I was expecting high drama. I thought he'd hit her or spit at her or kick her. I was even hoping he'd try to choke her. Why did George stop him? I was raging."

"Imagine the newspaper headlines," Imelda said "'Teacher assaults head of order' . . . or, even worse, . . . 'Male teacher attacks nun'."

"All grist to the mill," Constance said. "A pity he didn't land her a little punch. I was mad for blood."

Fintan came back from the bar. "Drinks are on their way."

"Never mind, Fintan," Constance said, "some dark night the two of us'll team up and mug Sister Antonio."

"You're on." He grinned. "We'll give her a good working over."

"Where's Marianne?" asked Imelda. "She took off after the meeting. Does she know where we are?"

"She went to ring the union," Fintan said. "See how things have changed. Years ago in a crisis people turned to God. Now they turn to their trade union."

"Haven't you heard, Fintan?" Constance said, "God's dead. He packed his bags and hightailed it out of education."

Anita arrived. "You've come at the right time," Constance said. "We were deep into God, philosophy and the meaning of life."

"I was particularly impressed by the silence of our wonderful principal," Anita said. "Not a word out of her when your woman was there, and nothing afterwards."

"Ah, come on, Anita, she's in a rotten position," Imelda said. "She's got to do as she's told."

"She should recognise her responsibilities." Just then the drinks arrived.

Marianne strode in. "Is that all that's here?" she asked. "I expected a better turn out."

"Perhaps the others went to Delaneys," Fintan said. "There was mention of it. Give them a while."

"What'd the union say, Marianne?" Constance asked.

"They haven't been told a thing. It's all news to them. They're trying to set up a meeting with the principal, the manager and the mother superior. They'll ring me back in an hour."

"What'd they think of its chances of staying open?"

"As far as they know we're not on the list of schools to close. I rang the Department of Education but they wouldn't tell me anything."

"I'll be waiting for that damn phone to ring all the time," Imelda said.

Just then the telephone rang and a silence fell. "It's the

nuns inviting us up to the convent for a cup of tea," Constance quipped. We all laughed.

"Marianne, there's a Mary Drabble on the phone for you," Fintan called.

"That's them," Marianne said.

"So quick!" Constance sighed.

When Marianne returned she sat down. "The nuns were in with the Department weeks ago to confirm the closure. It's been on the cards for months."

"The bastards wouldn't tell you."

"Bigwigs only talk to bigwigs," Constance said.

"They're trying to get in touch with the mother superior, but she's gone down the country to another school."

"Poor devils, "Imelda said. "The Angel of Death is on her way."

"Much too flattering a term," Constance said. "On physical appearance alone she fails to qualify as an angel!"

"Sister Ruth must have known all the time," Imelda said.

"She didn't," Marianne said. "I was speaking to Sadie in the office when I rang the union. She said Ruth hadn't a notion until this morning. I believe her."

"You're right," Constance said. "I was in the office this morning and she was on the phone accepting an application for next year."

"She got another phone call after that," Marianne said. "She nearly passed out during it. Sadie said she never saw anything like it. She had to put a chair under her."

"I'm not looking forward to the rest of this week," Simon said. "It's going to be a long haul."

"I'm afraid I might break down tomorrow. I really am. I

could be in trouble if a student smiles at me or something," Anita said.

"Say nothing for the time being till we see how things work out," Marianne said.

"Are there any precedents for this situation?" Simon asked.

"Only one example of a staff and parent body successfully thwarting a closure as far as I know," Marianne said. "Usually what the order wants is what happens. It's early days. I just have to have a drink," she gasped.

"Get this woman a drink, Fintan!" Simon called.

"Certainly, sir," Fintan saluted him, "will do."

"Poor nuns," Anita said suddenly.

"I wouldn't cry too much for them," Constance said.

"Keep that radical under control!" Simon said crisply. She stuck out her tongue at him.

Anita wouldn't be deflected. "No, this means that everything they dedicated themselves to is a complete washout. It's sad really."

"I don't agree," Simon said. "They're not defeated idealists, they're a pragmatic bunch."

"They're an organisation," Constance said, "big sister instead of big brother."

"How the mighty are fallen," Fintan said. "They were always the ones to set the standards, to dictate to others how they should behave."

Imelda laughed. "I wasn't one of their greatest fans but I thought they'd behave in an honourable fashion. I expected them to practise what they preached. I feel conned."

"They did a lot of good," Anita said.

Imelda considered. "Yeah, true. They educated

generations of people, poured their resources into the schools, trained their own people to teach and now they have to give it all up. It must seem a funny old world to them."

"All the religious weren't benign," Fintan said. "Those brothers beat the bejaysus out of me when I was at school. They were bad bastards. I hated every one of them."

The telephone rang. I jumped. "It's hardly the union," Constance reassured me but Marianne hurried to the phone.

When she returned she had a thoughtful expression on her face.

"Go on, tell us," Imelda urged.

"That was George," Marianne said. "He wants to know what the hell we're doing here when the rest of them are in Delaneys getting scuttered!"

We organised meetings with parents and gathered names for petitions. We became needy, came to depend on each other. Often we met up at night to review progress.

I was glad of the distraction. Sometimes I stayed in Imelda's. Whenever I went home it was time to sleep. Sometimes Eoin was there.

Months passed. Just before Christmas a union official called to the school to talk to the staff. He confirmed the closure. "It's their property. They can do what they damn well like with it." He shrugged. "We've no big stick to hit them with."

"That's it then?" Fintan asked.

He nodded. "'Fraid so, folks! Sorry."

"Touch of spring in the air," George commented one morning.

"About bloody time. It's almost May," Anita said.

"I'm on the panel," Constance said.

"You and six others," George said.

"I wish I knew where I'm going to end up," Constance said. "It's like a lottery."

"They won't place you farther than Athlone," Simon said. "Mind you it'll be a job to find schools for seven of us."

"Seven?" Anita said. "How can that be? The school's here for three years. They'll need staff."

"No, lovie," George said. "Remember how many transferred to other schools last term? From the look of it we won't have any fifth years next year and they're trickling away from the other years. We won't knock another two years out of it. We're gone."

"It just snowballed," Constance said. "They can't wait to get out of the place."

"Can't say I blame them," Anita answered. "It's horrible being somewhere that's dying."

"We're a godsend to the other schools in the area," Fintan said, "took the pressure off them."

"They'll never place so many of us in one year," Constance said. "I fancy an easy year or two."

"Don't bet on it," George said. "They don't want us hanging around getting paid for doing nothing. I'd be amazed to be here next year. I'm last on the staff so I'm the first to go. We have plenty of English teachers."

"I wonder where you'll end up," Constance speculated.

"Saint Ultan's needs an English teacher and that Belview Community School needs one too. I'd prefer to go there. It's supposed to be awful in Ultan's. The Principal's a loolah. He's off the wall."

"George, what'll we do without you?" Constance wailed. "We'll have no one to admire. We'll all go into mourning and wear black for a year."

"Those of us who are left," I said.

George said nothing and threw back his head to swallow the last of his coffee. A bell shattered the silence and signalled the end of morning break.

"No glad sound," Simon said behind me. As the others got up he sat down beside me. "You're free this class, aren't you?"

I smiled at him. Simon was small, plump, grey bearded and a good deal older than most of us. He was unmarried and claimed that all we "young ones" in our thirties were his substitute daughters.

"How's Imelda?" he asked. "How's the baby?"

"Anita was out last week. Mother and child are thriving. He's a big baby."

"Haven't you been out?" he asked.

"Not since the baby was born. Still haven't bought him a present."

"Don't let things slip. You go out and see her, miss," he said.

I smiled. Simon was addicted to dispensing good advice.

"I intend to go and see her," I said.

"The pathway to Hell," he said, and wagged an admonishing finger at me.

I pulled out a bundle of copybooks from my bag and sighed. "I really should correct these."

"Never mind about those. How's the teaching these days?"

"It's hard. They're terribly subdued. They sit in their

desks like sullen lumps. I find them very changed, very difficult."

"They're angry with us. They blame us for the closure."

"Maybe," I said, "if we'd tried harder the place wouldn't be closing down."

"Come on now, Sinéad," he said, "what else could we have done? There was no legal comeback. The union couldn't force their hand. The parents were helpless. The Department couldn't care less. In fact, they're only delighted. It makes life easier for them. We had meetings, petitions and a sit-in. I don't think Moses could have changed the outcome."

"I'll never forgive the nuns, never."

"Don't be like that," he said. "Bitterness is a dreadfully corrosive thing. You have to move on to the next stage in your life. Have you seen her ladyship yet?"

"No, tomorrow afternoon. What does she say?"

"Don't worry about it. She'll be all sweetness and light. She's anxious to do the right thing by everybody. She wants us to love her."

"I'm going to hand in my resignation," I said.

He sat back in his chair. "Jesus, Sinéad, you can't do that. Don't do anything hasty. Look on the closure as a death in the family. People do mad things after bereavements. They sell their houses, throw up their jobs and go off and live in Peru. It's a kind of craziness. Stick it out. Ask for a career break."

I laughed bitterly. "I'm hardly going to get a career break, am I? I'll probably be on the panel."

"Get your doctor to help you out. Get a certificate. Make

it say that the situation is stressing you, that you're not coping."

I laughed without humour, accepted a tissue from him and dabbed my eyes. "Sorry, Simon, my mother always said my bladder was very close to my eyes. I wouldn't have to tell any lies to get a doctor to say those things. My whole life is going down the tubes. Sometimes I think I'll go mad."

I couldn't tell him how I wasn't correcting work from students, how I couldn't concentrate on preparation, how my teaching was slipping, how I now dreaded going into classrooms, how I feared that the students would soon find me out and turn on me. I was terrified of becoming that most abject of creatures, the teacher who has lost control.

"Don't be so extreme," he said. "You're not thinking rationally."

"Ah, look around you, Simon. Can't you see what a pathetic lot we've become? We sit together in sad little groups at lunchtime. Friends who never had a cross word between them are having major rows. It's so easy to get under people's skins. It's like living on the edge of a volcano. You never know who's going to erupt next."

"It's hateful," he said. "God knows, the atmosphere here is oppressive and there's probably worse to come but that shouldn't distract you from your main preoccupation, your future." He took my arm. "Don't throw it away!" he said with urgency. "You're letting the nuns defeat you. Do whatever it takes to swing a career break. Promise me you'll do that."

"I'll think about it. Everything gets to me. The students are suffering too."

"They're not your concern now . . ." He put up his hand when I gasped in protest. "Nothing more can be done for them."

"I'm no good to them these days," I muttered.

"Look to yourself." He got up. "Mind what I say, young woman, look to yourself." He lingered a moment. "Things aren't so good at home, I gather."

I smiled. "That would be putting it mildly, Simon."

"You have to expect ups and downs in marriages. I don't have any experience myself but it seems to be the accepted wisdom."

"It's over, Simon. He's going to leave me."

"That's serious then, but not necessarily fatal. The brother's been married thirty years. Sarah, his wife, left him once for six months and refused to come back, but they worked it out. How long are you married?"

"Eight years."

"A drop in the ocean. It'll sort itself out."

"I doubt it. There's another woman. That's been going on now for the best part of a year. It started at the end of last summer. Sometimes we're under the same roof, but not as man and wife. He'll leave me or I'll leave him in the end."

"That's bad, all right. The timing isn't too good either. Still, these things happen and sometimes they work themselves out. We're all mad at some stage in our lives. Remember my advice."

"I'll cherish your words of wisdom, Simon."

"Mind you do, young woman."

He returned with two cups of coffee and handed me one.

"For me?" I asked, amazed. Simon usually charmed people into serving him food or drink. "I'm privileged," I said. He bowed. At that moment I felt a positive fondness for him.

"By the way," he said, "my consultation bill will be in the post." He grinned. "My fees are quite reasonable."

Chapter Seven

A key turned in the lock and woke me. I sat up in the bed. The room was dark. Where was I? It took a while to remember. Back in Dublin. Back from Auntie Alice's funeral. I heard doors slamming in the kitchen and then somebody moved into the sitting-room. It must be Eoin. Was I likely to be left in peace? Presently he called out my name.

"I'm here," I called from the top of the stairs and started to walk down slowly.

"There you are." He smiled.

"Fancy meeting you here," I said and staged a yawn.

"Tired, dearest chuck?" Coldness or tenderness? I couldn't tell.

"Report finished?" I asked. He didn't answer. He was poker faced and still. I brushed past him.

"Dinner?" he said.

"Dinner?" I echoed.

He smiled. "Dinner, such as it is. Yeah, woman, I have scoured the earth at this ungodly hour" . . . He consulted his watch . . . "What ungodly hour is it anyway? Ay, past the witching hour, into the madness of magical night, ripe with possibilities." He licked his lips. "Yeah, to the ends of the earth I have travelled in pursuit of sustenance for my weary companion in life. To the footed peninsula of the wild-eyed Italians seeking out luscious regional dishes with tingling sauces, pasta and rice accompaniments, to the Indian subcontinent sampling tongue tingling or mouth numbing culinary delights, to the land of the Red Indian tasting the pounded beef their conquerors call hamburger and lastly to that most populous place on earth, land of the wok and sizzling fires. There, my love, I chose a delicate blend of dishes, wondrous in their variety and exquisite in taste, complemented by boiled and fried rices. Then I flew across an ocean and swooped over the vineyards of the dispossessed and outcast Aborigines and brought back a true colonial wine, a ripe Chardonnay."

"Chinese takeaway, Australian wine," I said, exasperated. His good humour irritated me.

He grinned. "Recent earthquakes have reduced our restaurant to a rubble heaped ruin but the sky is clear. The moon will light our way."

I pushed past him into the kitchen and opened the fridge. He had disposed of its former malodorous contents. Three bottles of wine gleamed in its dim light.

He was close. I smelled a faint whiff of pungent underarm. I turned. "What is this?" I asked.

Still in Byronic mode he struck his brow. "Tush, sweet woman, don't limit every moment. Why this craze to prescribe and prohibit? See how the night unfolds. Purpose will reveal itself. You cannot know the end when you do not know the beginning."

He opened the double doors into the sitting-room and

indicated the coffee table set with cutlery, place mats and glasses. "Madam, your table awaits you."

"You've been busy," I said.

"As the proverbial bee."

So we sat on the sofa. He poured a dry sherry, handed a glass to me and smiled. He raised his. "To the future, whatever it may be." He smiled.

"To the future, whatever it may be," I rejoined.

"Ha!" He reached behind him and plugged in a side lamp, stood up and turned off the main light switch on his way out to the kitchen. He returned bearing saucers, bowed to me and ceremoniously placed them on the place mats. "Spare ribs," he said. "Could be the makings of a few fine women in there!"

"Ah!" I said. Eoin's sense of humour was what had attracted me to him initially. Of course it had taken him months to get me into bed. I was resistant to blandishments and flattery. We went to films, concerts, plays, visited galleries, museums, the zoo and every beach in the greater Dublin area. We even made a trip to Fota island in Cork, taking the early morning train, spending most of the day there and returning late at night. I allowed passionate kisses and other intimacies on an experimental basis. I was testing myself, monitoring my reactions. Eventually his persistence paid off or, and I'm not too sure about this, in or about that time I fell in love with him. There was no warning. During one of his passionate embraces – he had me up against the wall in his parents' kitchen – there was a sudden fiery response from me which took me and I imagine him by surprise. Then I was hungry for kisses, where before I had allowed them, and crazy for his touch, where before I had endured it.

"You're giving me some strange looks," he said.

I was rushed back to the present. "Do you blame me?" I picked up a spare rib to gnaw.

"The question of blame is complicated," he said. He was going to be serious. A coldness washed over me. I wanted to rush away from him but there was nowhere to go so late at night.

"We're not going to go through all that again, are we?"

"How do you do it?" he asked.

"What?"

"How does your mood flip like that? I always feel the change. You disconnect yourself and pull away. You do it like flicking off a switch."

"We should put this on a tape," I said. "Then we could listen to it instead of having to say it."

"That'd suit you," he said. "You don't want any involvement with anyone. I don't know why you married me."

"Because I didn't get that job and I wanted to get away from home." The truth sounded ugly and calculating. I had always guarded myself against it. "I was in love with you as well."

He carried the saucers out to the kitchen and returned bearing a tray of dishes. He had warmed food and heated plates. Solemn as a waiter he laid them out, put away the tray and faced me.

"Choose," he said.

Appetite, if there had been any, enthusiasm, if any had existed, and curiosity, if that had been there, had shrivelled with my words. I'd have given anything to have them recalled to rectify the fault. I spooned rice on to a plate and passed it to him. He handed it back. "Fill it for me," he said.

He poured wine and nibbled a prawn cracker. His eyes skidded away from mine.

"Eat," he said when my plate was full. He watched me. My mouth dried up. Each mouthful tasted like dried cotton balls. After a while he sat beside me, took up his plate and proceeded to eat.

"What job?" he asked. "You never told me about any job."

"Nothing. Something I didn't get years ago."

"Do tell," he said. "Your indiscretions are fascinating but I need the fuller picture, something more revealing."

"You don't want to know."

"I'll decide that." He pushed a prawn against my mouth. I bit it and looked at him. He had never looked back so coldly at me. Now his consideration, that habit of helpfulness, was mechanical. This is how it is, I thought, when all the pretence is stripped away and the protective covering of lies ripped through.

"Eat first. Then talk." He fed me because because I didn't want to eat. I constructed fine phrases and careful sentences over and over again.

He seated himself away from me and turned the chair so that his face was in shadow. He said "Begin" and I found that I couldn't move.

"Well, you know that my parents weren't prepared to keep me when I wanted to do a Masters. They were happy enough to let me do a Higher Diploma but that was as far as they were prepared to go. They thought it was time I paid back some of the money I owed them. I couldn't keep myself so I applied for a special work scholarship in France. French was my best subject," I said.

"Why don't I know about this?"

"Hardly anybody does. You didn't know me then."

"Continue." He reached for his glass of wine. I saw his eyes. Steel trap, I thought.

"I'd all the necessary qualifications, first class honours degree, that scholarship I won in second year, and I was sure that I'd be called to interview. I was never called. In fact I didn't receive an acknowledgment of my application. All the time I waited for a communication. In the end I overheard somebody say that such and such a person had got it. His marks weren't anything as good as mine so I couldn't understand it. Then I thought my application had been lost and rang them up. It had arrived but I hadn't been short-listed for interview. Well, I was demented, utterly confused."

"Your future was going down the tubes," Eoin said. I couldn't make out his face. The room had darkened.

"Yes." I said. "The next morning I went to see my tutor. Our relationship had never been easy. Once or twice he bought me drinks in the bar but you couldn't say we got on well. He gave me good marks but he was never enthusiastic about me, didn't encourage me. He seemed displeased to see me. There was a coldness, how do I explain, a nastiness in his manner that I'd never noticed before. It crossed my mind that I should leave but then I was desperate to talk to somebody about what had happened. He fiddled with his pen, scribbled while I spoke, and I had to force myself to keep talking. 'Why are you telling me this?' he said when I'd finished.

I was bewildered. 'Because you were one of my referees,' I said.

'Oh that,' he said. His words are etched in my mind. 'I didn't recommend you,' he said.

I remember saying 'Was it my work?'

And he laughed. It was a particularly unpleasant laugh. 'Not your work' he said.

'Not my work?' I said.

He bundled his papers together and put them in a brief-case. 'I told them that I didn't consider you a good bet, that in my opinion you wouldn't complete the course.'

I was stunned. 'Why? Why did you tell them that?'

He looked as if the question offended him. 'Well, there was that business of your crack-up,' he said.

And of course it was true. I came close to a nervous breakdown in the second year. Home was just so awful that I seriously considered giving up college. My tutor at the time, a woman, persuaded me to stay and finish the exams. She was very nice really. Funny thing. I did extremely well in those exams, got one of those small money scholarships. Obviously this cut no ice with my final year tutor. He gave me a really contemptuous look. I blanked for a while.

When I came to he was smiling at me, said, 'It's not the end of the world', said he had to go and we left the office. He left me in the corridor. I think I must have wandered about for hours. When I came around people were having their tea in the restaurant. It was evening time."

"What did he say when you went back?" Eoin asked.

"I never went back. I took up teaching instead."

"He was unbalanced or it was something else."

"He thought I was unstable."

"No he didn't. There was something else behind that.

Either the other student had a hold over him in some way or he was a sadistic bastard. Did he fancy you?"

I laughed. "He was years older than me. He never made a pass at me."

"Did he ever invite you out?"

"Once. To a concert. He had a spare ticket. It was very embarrassing, I made a hames of turning it down."

"Well either that or he was twisted in some way."

"I don't know. I couldn't bear to think about it for years. It hurt my mind. I blanked it out. It doesn't matter now. It's all in the past. I think what he said was probably true."

"You never challenged it?" Eoin sounded astonished.

"Never occurred to me. It sort of wiped me out. I wasn't like a person for a while afterwards."

"Very meek, turn the other cheek sort of stuff. How did that make you marry me?"

I looked across at him. "You're relentless," I complained.

"This is important."

"You, I met you. You made me laugh. I buried that self then. I wanted to try a new life."

"One that never satisfied you." He sounded angry.

"Why do you say that?"

"I see it now. I was your fallback. Plan A failed so you moved on to plan B but plan B failed too."

"You make it sound so calculated."

"Not consciously. You were running away from things, not choosing a life."

"You're being very simplistic," I argued.

"That's the way I see it," he said.

It was impossible to guess how angry he was. I knew we had reached the close-down situation I had tried to engineer for so long. Now that I had achieved it my grief was immeasurable. The darkness in the room swallowed me up and spun me about.

He stood over me. I could hardly see him. "I think that's as much as we can bear," he said. When I looked again the room was empty.

Chapter Eight

The following morning I woke up on the sofa. Somebody had drawn the curtains and thrown a blanket over me. The remains of the previous night's meal cluttered the coffee table. A half consumed bottle of wine stood on the mantelpiece, two empty wine glasses beside it. Through a gap in the curtains I saw daylight.

I struggled to my feet and made my way to the kitchen. It was desolate as before. A stale smell hung in the air. I tried the back door but it was locked. Then I toured the house but Eoin was nowhere to be found.

The fridge yielded nothing save the two unopened bottles of white wine. You cannot know the end unless you know the beginning, I thought. The beginning is the end.

"Into the bright blue sea the sun
drops out and all our day is done."

What would I do when Eoin came home? What would I do if he didn't? What did I care? What could I do about it? As I rooted in my bag Aunt Moira's envelope fell out. I retrieved it and opened it. A slip of paper and a cheque fell out. "Spend it on a holiday for you and Eoin," Aunt Moira had scrawled on a page. "There's more to come." I looked at the cheque and looked again. Noughts winked up at me. Three of them. Thousands. There must be a mistake, I thought. Back to the letter. "Alice inherited some money and was very careful with it," I read. "I want you to have it now when you need it. I'm past wanting things now. It's Alice's money really." I reread the letter, took the cheque to the window light to scrutinise it and laughed. "Bless you, Aunt Alice," I said and kissed the cheque.

Time was heavy, minutes dragged. I filled waste bags and put them in the back yard, cleared the sink, ran hot water and began a wash up. When I finished it was early afternoon and I still hadn't eaten. Hunger drove me out.

At the gate I met Eoin. He nodded and walked past me and I stared after him. I followed him into the house. He went upstairs without a backward glance. "Eoin," I called. He paused, hunched his shoulders and continued. "Eoin," I said but I had nothing to say.

He came downstairs late that night, eyes bloodshot and hair dishevelled. He didn't speak but slouched on the sofa to watch the television. Once or twice his glance flickered in my direction but seldom for long. After a short while he went back upstairs.

The next morning I ventured into what had been our bedroom and found him tossing in the bed. I put a hand to his forehead. It was hot and moist. His dull eyes looked up at me. "You're sick," I said. He didn't respond. His eyelids drooped. I called the doctor.

Two days later he stumbled downstairs and filled a glass with water from the kitchen tap. "My head feels full of rocks," he complained.

"You have a dose of flu. The doctor gave you a sick cert for a week."

"The doctor was here?"

"You didn't pay him much attention."

He turned a dull gaze on me. "I thought you'd be long gone. What are you doing here?"

"You're sick."

"Wouldn't have thought you'd let that bother you," he said and drifted upstairs.

That night he came down and I cooked him a meal. He ate without interest. "What day of the week is it?" he asked.

"Friday."

He looked up at me. "We were in Ballycourt last Monday."

"Yes."

He shook his head. "It seems like years ago." It was true. Days seemed like months and time was playing games.

"What are we going to do?" he asked suddenly. The Eoin I knew had died and this morose stranger had taken his place. His face was gaunt and sickly.

"I'm going to go away," I said.

He nodded. "Thought you might." He pushed the half eaten meal away from him. "Thanks," he said as an afterthought.

"You're welcome." The response was automatic.

"Will you be all right for money?"

"Yes." He looked up. "I have some saved and Aunt Alice left me quite a bit."

He sighed. "I can give you some if you want."

"No need."

"Suit yourself." Speaking seemed to cause him great effort. "When will you go?" he said after a long while.

"Next week."

"I'll see you off." I shook my head. "No, I might as well. It's appropriate." His smile mocked us both.

"You look a little better," I said.

"Feel really fucked up. Weak as a kitten."

"Eoin, I'm sorry . . ." I began.

He waved his hands as if to fend off my words. *"Cuir na mairbh leis na mairbh,"* he said.

On the plane I found I couldn't help thinking about him, our restrained final day in the city, the last few drinks in the dingy little pub around the corner from our house, his terse silence when he dropped me off at the airport terminal. I remembered how he looked when he said goodbye – tall and dark, his hands rammed into the pockets of his long coat, his eyes glittering in his pale face as he stared angrily at me. Then he jumped into the car and drove away without a word or a backward glance.

As the engines of the plane screeched into life and it began to taxi along the runway I saw a rabbit scurry across the tarmac to a green verge. The plane turned to accelerate into the sky.

Then it was in the air banking over fields, roads, industrial complexes and housing estates and moving out over the sea. I stared down at the foaming water and watched the gulls. I was on my own and leaving Ireland.

Eoin, I thought, someday I'll think of you. A week before I had been angry with him and sorry for myself. Now I was sorry for him and angry with myself.

I remembered my last interview with Sister Ruth in her tidy

office which was full of shelves lined with computerised records and neat files. She had advised, urged, begged and finally ordered me to take a career break.

"You'll thank me for this one day," she said, when she handed back my unopened letter of resignation. "You need a break, but you shouldn't throw up teaching until you know where your life's going. Don't do anything rash."

When I stood up to go she surprised me by coming out from behind her desk to shake hands with me.

"Don't think too badly of me, Sinéad. Learn to forgive us."

"I don't know if I can."

"Condemn the sin, not the sinner," she urged.

I looked at her. "You admit there was a sin," I said.

She sighed. "Impossible to know. It wasn't my decision, but it wouldn't have been my choice." She lifted a black file from her desk. It had a large label on its front with "Closure" marked on it in bold type. "See this," she said. "This is my Calvary. It nails me to the cross every day." She smiled wryly. "I pledged my obedience to the order thirty years ago. They told me to open the school. Now they tell me to close it. I live in a big house with empty rooms. When I joined as a novice the house was bursting with activity."

"Nothing lasts forever."

"No, things don't last. I pray to God every day to give me the grace to accept this."

I moved away from her. The unusual intimacy made me uneasy. "I should go," I said. "I have a class."

She made as if to embrace me but I dodged her and bolted out into the corridor.

I reached the staffroom and it was deserted as it often was

then. When we were united in our attempt to keep the school open we lived in one anothers' pockets but when all efforts failed we began to avoid one another.

Misery is contagious. Anita became quiet. Marianne sought out others and offloaded her unvarying litany of complaints on anybody who would listen. The women lost interest in George and he wilted from neglect. He knew where he would be the following year. The community school had claimed him.

I didn't want to teach if I couldn't stay where I was. I didn't like the idea of being shunted from place to place like a nomadic journey-woman.

"Pig-headed you are," Imelda hissed at me when we met up for lunch. Her mother was minding the baby for the day. "Stubborn as a mule. I'll never understand you. Do what Ruth says. Take advice."

I hunched over an inflight magazine, flicked through pages of advertisements and tried to imagine my new life. How much had London changed in six years? Perhaps going there would trigger a magical resolution of my problems. Some employer would spot me, recognise in me something that everybody else had missed and take a chance on me. In my heart of hearts I guessed that this was unlikely.

"Anything I can get for you?" a voice asked. I blinked myself awake from my stupor to see a young man with dark, greased hair staring across at me. His jaws worked. He was chewing gum. "Do you want tea, coffee or a drink of some kind? The trolley's here."

I stared past him. A hostess flashed me a professional smile. "No thanks," I said and turned away.

"You might as well. It's all on the house or, should I say, on the plane." Something insidious and insistent in his voice rippled along my nerves and jangled their ends. I stared down at the sunless sea and the surging foam thrown up by the passage of a ship on the water. When I looked again the hostess had gone and he was pouring tonic into gin.

"I'll get you something if you change your mind," he said. "If you suffer with your ears you should swallow."

"I said no."

"No need to be like that about it. You could be a bit more gracious."

I wished I had a book or a companion, anything to ward off these unwanted attentions. "Leave me alone," I said levelly. When I looked again he was no longer there.

My stomach rumbled and I was overcome by a nauseous weakness. Just then he returned.

"Duty free's on its way," he said. I closed my eyes. "Do you live in London?" he continued, "I've got a meeting tomorrow." His hand touched mine. "Forgot to introduce myself. I'm Joseph Sheehy from Blackrock." I ignored his outstretched hand. What arrogance, I thought.

"Perhaps you'd leave me alone," I said.

"Don't be like that." He offered me a sweet.

I sat up sharply and favoured him with a long, hard, unblinking stare. He stared back.

"If you don't leave me in peace I'll report you."

He said nothing but sat where he was with a sneering smile on his face. I longed to smash a fist into that face, dig a knife into his ribs or into his stomach. "Go and annoy somebody else," I said and pushed past him to go to the toilet.

On my way back I spotted an air hostess. I pointed at my tormentor. "That man's annoying me," I said. "Could I sit somewhere else?"

"There's a seat at the back," she said. "Take that. No one will mind."

On the shuttle train to the terminal building at Stanstead I saw him engage a young girl in conversation. She didn't look more than eighteen. He laid a hand on her arm. She seemed dazed by his attentions but I left her to her fate. That was life. Dog eat dog.

I remembered Aunt Alice's death and burial and burrowed into memory for details of her life. She had married and gone to live in London but her husband had died of tuberculosis. She lived in London for many years but then, in the manner of the time, returned home to live with her mother and sister.

People of her generation didn't tear around expecting to attain love, happiness or self-fulfillment. They accepted whatever life offered.

The journey to the city centre dragged. The rapid rhythm of the train's progress jiggled me in and out of an uneasy doze.

That evening I found myself outside Liverpool Street station and stood in the rain on the steps. Bodies brushed against me as I consulted an underground map. I was washing off the tang of Ireland. I traced out my route. Maggie would be expecting me.

Chapter Nine

As a student I had worked summers in London as a chambermaid and barmaid. I had happy memories of warm days, hot nights, a bedsit of my own and wonderful freedom. But London had changed. It wasn't the place I had known. When I arrived autumn had established itself and was thinking of becoming winter. Dried, crumbling leaves crackled like starched book pages on park bonfires and the wind whipped the survivors through grey and dispirited streets.

At Twickenham station, as instructed, I rang Maggie and she came to meet me. "You found us," she said.

"It took ages to find the right platform in the underground in Richmond," I said.

"In future change at Waterloo and use British Rail to get here. The train comes straight through."

"You're a good bit out."

She grinned. "There's only a small mortgage on this place and we don't want to live in the city. It's so shabby and dirty now and the homeless roam the streets." She dropped my case in the hall. "Want a guided tour?" she asked.

I followed her down some steps to a kitchen. "Double

doors to the handkerchief garden," she said and led me outside. "It's lovely in the summer. Jean planted shrubs last year. It was a kip when we moved in, overgrown, fences falling down. We spent last spring digging it up."

She led me through the kitchen into a back room. "This is the work room. Out of bounds to you, I'm afraid, but you're free to wander the rest of the house." I followed her into the front room. A fire glowed. "Gas," she said. "We spend a lot of our time here or in the kitchen. Do you like the kitchen?"

"It's very clean," I said remembering my own.

"The decor I meant."

"Oh yes." I strolled down again and looked this time. A huge wooden table divided the room. To one side were shelves laden with cookery books, a white cast iron fireplace, a large framed abstract print, potted plants on the hearth and a cupboard on which rested an expresso coffee making machine. To the other a Belfast sink, resolutely plain kitchen units and a large window which caught the light.

"Pine units?" I asked.

"Maple."

"Can you have wooden worktops?"

"They're sealed."

"And terracotta tiles on the floor. Very nice. 'Homes and Gardens' will be around any day to feature it."

She opened a unit door and showed me a washing machine. "We got deeper units made to fit it and the dishwasher in. Neat eh?"

"Oh very."

"Come upstairs." She was eager to show me the rest of the house. "Pokey little bathroom," she said. "We haven't done much with it yet. We're working on the sandwich principle. We did the roof, damp-proofed, rewired, replumbed and decorated downstairs. It gets threadbare from now on. There are blinds on the windows and we've stained the floors but it's quite spartan. My room." She indicated a door and threw it open. I peered in.

"Grey on the walls? I would never have dared," I said.

"Goes brilliantly with the red, don't you think?" She pointed out the bedspread on her double bed.

"Sumptuous." I said. I touched the material. "Silky."

"Cost the earth," she said, "but worth it to wake up under it every morning. I bought two quilt cover and pillow-case sets before I even thought of curtains. I'm going to have everything I want in this room. I won't make do with what I can afford. At the moment I'm in love with some curtains but they're hideously expensive. My next job should pay for them." She laughed. "Then I'll get a wardrobe."

She tapped a door on our way to another staircase. "Jean's room," she said. She ran up the stairs. "We've put you on top of the world. You'll have a bed, table and chair and a row of hangers but that's it. I did warn you that we're not the Ritz." I followed her into the room. It looked down on the street below.

"You and Jean bought this?"

"Yeah. One buys the other out if the arrangement changes." She ran down steps to the bathroom and led me over to the window. "Look at the English suburban garden. It's not a myth. The English love their gardens."

I looked down on back gardens, neat rows of garden sheds and greenhouses, manicured lawns, extensive patios and landscaped flower beds. "Sickening," I said.

"See why we did the garden," she said. "It would have been last on our list but we felt under pressure to whip it into order. Now we can hold our heads up in the street." She pointed under the window. "There's a radiator here but it can be chilly in the depths of winter so I've left a heater."

I stared at the bare boards and the narrow bed by the window.

"Home sweet home." She laughed.

We descended to the fire. "Let's break open a bottle of wine while we're waiting for Jean," she said. "She'll be home soon. Now, you have to tell me all. Why have you left Eoin and come to live in this wicked place?"

"It's too complicated. I wouldn't know where to begin."

She didn't miss a beat. "How long are you going to stay?"

"Until I get fixed up. I'll pay rent a month in advance," I said.

"We'll work all that out. You'll have no trouble finding a job," she said. "There's a real shortage of teachers here."

I smiled. "I wouldn't like to work in schools here. Too tough from what I hear."

"Oh." She shrugged. "What'll you do then?"

"I took a word processing course last year."

She was unimpressed. "That wouldn't count for much. You'll need to smarten up if you're called to interview. You can't turn up in jeans or floral skirt." She surveyed my well worn jeans.

Suddenly I felt very tired. Maggie seemed a stranger – a streamlined, sharper version of the Maggie I remembered. "I'll see what happens," I said.

"You haven't come at a good time. Have you seen the unemployment figures?"

"I know all about that. It's worse at home. Don't worry, you won't have to keep me."

She looked exasperated. "It's not that. I don't think you realise what you're up against. Jobs are scarce and you need to look well if anything turns up. Appearance is important."

The door opened and a woman in or about our age looked in. "Jean," Maggie squealed. "Meet Sinéad!" I had heard of Jean but never met her. She was overwhelmingly glamorous; slender and dark with widely spaced olive eyes and abundant, black, wiry hair. It was hard to believe she was Irish. I'm tall but she made me feel small.

"I've heard so much about you from Maggie." She smiled. She kicked off her shoes. "Wine," she said. "I could die for it."

They toasted me. "Here's looking at you, kid," Maggie said.

I spent some days trying to compose a curriculum vitae. The more I struggled with the reinvention of myself the less I believed it.

At first I waited until the others had left the house before I went down to the kitchen. I would eat breakfast and stack the dishes in the dishwasher. Autumn sun poured into the kitchen all day. It was too cold to sit outside but I could sip tea and look out at a green world.

Maggie and Jean led comfortable lives. Maggie was a stage designer and Jean worked for a publishing company. Looking back on it now I know I expected them to help me find a job. I resented them when they showed no inclination whatsoever to do this.

Jean's working hours were flexible and occasionally she

worked from home. Sometimes I would find her in the kitchen when I came down for breakfast. She spoke politely when we talked but we talked very little. Her brother lived at home on a farm with her parents. "A big Meath farmer." She laughed. "They wanted me to hitch up with a local fellow with lots of land. I think that's why I left home." She talked of her work and her troubles with the taxman. What she was really like remained a mystery and I wondered at the arrangement she and Maggie had arrived at. It suited me in that I saw reasonably little of either of them.

The initial warmth of their welcome cooled into something like indifference. I felt some affinity with Maggie, but when I talked with Jean, I felt as if I was swapping anecdotes with a stranger I had met on a bus or in a pub. I drifted between them like a slow ping pong ball. Occasionally I came up against one or other of them and received a sharp thwack and then wandered off aimlessly again.

I visited an employment agency but the woman there could barely bring herself to talk to me. She indicated a notice board and waved me away. I was strongly discouraged by this but tried another agency soon after.

"Maybe you should sign on," Jean said. "It could be slow."

When the hope of finding a job faded, my visits to the job centre tapered off. It became difficult to get out of bed in the mornings. I waited until I was sure they had left the house before I got dressed.

I started to take long walks down by the Thames to fill in the endless days. Then the walks became tedious and I stayed indoors.

In the beginning Maggie and Jean used to ask me about

job prospects and offered all kinds of unsolicited advice but, after a month, they became silent on the subject. I found I could not broach the issue with either of them. If we ever found ourselves eating together I felt that a fourth chair was haunted by the spirit of the unfound job.

"Don't give up," Maggie said. "Keep at it."

I spent more and more time in my bedroom, doing nothing in particular or nothing at all. I opened books I had bought in London but usually closed them after a few lines. I seldom reached the end of a page.

I sensed a change in the atmosphere. There were pauses in conversations when I entered the kitchen or living-room. "She's doing her best," I overheard Jean say to Maggie. Were they talking about me? I felt eyes scrutinise and dismiss me. "How are you these days?" Maggie asked once. I couldn't speak unless spoken to and drifted from day to day in a haze of tiredness and sleep.

"You never go out these days," Jean said. I lurked on the edge of their lives like a brooding slug.

I became more and more stupid. I moved from bed to chair to window or crept down to bathroom or kitchen. These manoeuvres should have been simple but they became complicated. Eating, drinking and washing were tedious chores.

Sometimes I made a decision. I might decide to wash my hair. This then became the imperative. The hair had to be washed. I had to wash it. It had to be done. Yes, I would agree with myself, this was necessary. The process of washing the hair involved the will to wash it but I had no desire to perform this task.

Nevertheless, the problem remained. The hair became

greasy and limp, the scalp itchy. I imagined that I had nits in my hair. I scratched my scalp until I drew blood. Other people washed their hair. Why couldn't I?

When I reached the bathroom, shampoo in hand, it took an age to persuade myself to actually run the water. I would offer myself all kinds of excuses. It would do the following day. It was too late in the day to wash the hair. It would never dry in time. In time for what? I would never go to bed with damp hair. Since I hardly ever slept how was that stopping me? It took a stunning act of resolution to initiate the procedure and complete the sequence of actions. Once I showered and washed myself and, utterly spent, went to lie down on my bed. Later, it must have been considerably later because the sky had darkened, I overheard Maggie complain about the uncleaned shower and the wet towel she had found on the bathroom floor.

Thus I filled the days forcing myself out of my room and into the kitchen or into the bathroom, dragging myself out to the shops to buy food, making myself load clothes into the washing machine, when the laundry situation became critical, and forcing myself down to the bank to withdraw money for rent or food.

I became careless and bold and took to wandering the streets at night. I hoped that some maniac would waylay me, drag me into a dark alley and kill me. I could see my gory body with its bloodied locks stare up at me from the grey pavement. I seldom met anybody. Once I came across a tramp lying on a park bench. He was in a deep, drunken stupor. I wandered further afield and lost track of time. One morning I returned to the house to find a stone-faced Maggie waiting for me in the doorway. "You left the door wide open," she said. "Anybody could have walked in." I smiled as I passed her. Do it, I thought. Throw me out. I stared at her from the stairs and she looked at me strangely. Then she walked down to the kitchen.

It was as if I were trapped in a capsule that was hurtling, at tremendous speed and with tremendous force, towards an unknown destination. I was terrified that it would crash but I had no control over it. Nothing could halt its progress.

In a way I longed for the day when I would get my comeuppance because I could see how I deserved it. Like a person outside of myself I watched the creature who was me walk, eat, drink, urinate and defecate.

To talk to others was the severest test. I felt uneasy all the time. When I spoke I wondered if my words made sense or if I mouthed gibberish. When what I said appeared convincing I felt like a hustler who had carried off some incredible confidence trick. Other times, when I imagined that my words lacked conviction, I faltered. I intercepted uneasy looks on Jean's or Maggie's face. At times it seemed that the phrase "I see" was a euphemism for their bafflement with me. I would laugh or leave the room in a sudden state of agitation.

I tried to practise ordinary, incongruous phrases that would pass for normal but knew that if I got them in the wrong order, or used them out of context, they would give me away.

I watched their reactions, fearful that one of them might at any moment lift the telephone, call the authorities and arrange to have me taken away. Perhaps all my life I had been heading towards this point, this critical moment.

It wouldn't matter if they locked me into an asylum and institutionalised me for the rest of my life.

It would become clear to everybody why I was the way I was. It would be obvious that I couldn't be blamed for something I couldn't help.

"She's mad. She was never right," they would say to each other. Had I always been mad, skimming on the edge of sanity, or had I become mad?

I waited for Maggie to give me notice. The idea filled me with giddy terror. Nevertheless it must happen. It was logical. It made complete sense. I left fires unattended, abandoned meals, ignored them, forgot to lock up when I left the house and locked my door against them. How could they bear me?

Whenever I spoke to Maggie my words misfired. A terrific barrier had sprung up between us. She must loathe me. I was unfit to live, a despicable creature. I thought of suicide. It was pathetic. I would never do it. I would funk it. I lacked a sense of purpose or the will to effect anything.

Chapter Ten

In light, in shadow, in twilight you rage. This rage reaches out, seeks everything and touches nothing. It returns to you, weakened, listless and spent, like grief, desolate and hopeless, which surges through you. The rage is dead.

You hunch yourself up, cocooned in a bed, and flinch at the sounds that seep through the walls of the room. A sound is heard, then identified. Doors shut, doors slam. You hear voices, laughter, footsteps, the static of a radio, the blare of a television, the clatter of cutlery, the swirl and vibrations of washing machine or dishwasher, the splash of water in the shower, the swoosh of the toilet flushing, the roar of a vacuum cleaner, shouting, loud laughter, loud voices, whispering and giggling, the ring of a telephone, the absence of sound, stillness, quietness, the creaking of bodies turning in beds, the peace of night. The darkness sucks in all sounds and holds them, deadens the air.

At night, when the street noises subside, you awake from this drifting in and out of wakeful sleepiness; which is like a dream, like a nightmare, which envelops you as though you are trapped down a well, where your voice resonates, reverberates, clangs and echoes off cold, stone walls, where this echo weakens as it rebounds from stone to stone, and your cry, unheard, unlistened to, unlistened for, returns to you.

You drag yourself from the half world of perpetual wakefulness, perpetual dreaminess. You wander about this room, stand by a window, stare down at the street lamps, stare at the blue-green grass, at the stiffening, whitening grass, stare at the yellow pools of light on the pavement and stand; dry eyed, pale, dispirited and desolate. Your eyes feel tight. They strain, peer at the landscape, watch it for only a while, only for some time, when you find you have been standing there, suspended, inanimate, as if your soul has deserted your body and left you a shell, containing only the hollowness, the void.

You creep out in the dark, in that blackness, driven by thirst, find your way by touch, push back doors, avoid furniture, finger cupboards, extract a glass, turn the tap, fill the glass with water, drain its contents, greedily suck and gulp down that wetness, the liquid that trickles through your blenched, dusty mouth and throat, like a reviving stream, filling your mouth with moisture and allowing you to swallow.

You crouch down and huddle into yourself if you hear a sound, half breathe, hardly breathe at all until that other passes by, returns to its room and closes the door, yawning, sighing or moaning to itself. Then, furtively, uneasily, you slouch back to your room, your refuge, tiptoe up the creaking stairs, hardly dare to draw breath until you are safely behind the door with the lock drawn.

Through all this impotence, while you dangle and bob

about in this fading, this erosion, you sometimes hear the echo of your own silenced voice, its message lost to you, especially to you.

You buckle and collapse until the collapse becomes a terrifying plunge into darkness, a pit, the deep sleep or death that has eluded you for so long, the longed-for, yearned-for, dreaded, prized insensibility.

Nothing looked different but something had changed. I padded across the floor boards to the window and saw a pale sun flickering through the bare branches of the trees. I laid a hand on the cold radiator, shivered and drew on my dressing-gown.

In the kitchen I made a pot of tea, toasted a stale slice of white bread, covered it with butter and marmalade, sat at the table and switched on the radio. My continuous headache had lifted and taken off like a bird. I savoured the tea and toast.

Back in the bedroom I looked at the graceless image in the wall mirror. My hair was dank and limp, the skin on my face pale and blotchy and my nightdress grubby and frayed. I scowled at this unattractive, skinny stranger for some time and she scowled back.

I resolved to take a bath. I would scrub off the staleness and shed the skin of dejection.

Later I stared at the clean reflection of a stranger. I was exhausted. The air in the bedroom was flat, heavy and stale. When I opened the window slightly the rush of chilly freshness stunned me. I left the window ajar to give the air its chance.

Maggie was in the kitchen, standing by the French doors

and staring out into the back garden. "Good morning," I said. She looked coolly at me and then smiled.

"Thought you'd be at work."

"Not on a Saturday." She poured a jug of water into the coffee machine. "Fancy a cup?" I nodded. I was eager to explore the sensations of taste. She measured coffee and switched on the machine. I noticed a calendar and saw it was showing October. "Black or do you take milk?" I heard Maggie ask.

For a moment I couldn't remember. "Black," I decided.

I noticed bright auburn and blond streaks in Maggie's brown hair. She caught me staring. "I've had them for ages," she said, "not that you'd have noticed." She darted a look at me. "You know you look better. You even sound better," she said.

"Sound better?"

"Your voice, it's more alive. For a while there you sounded like an old record played at slow speed. Still, it's good to see you back in action," she continued, "you had us quite worried."

Stupid tears spurted from my eyes. I couldn't stop them. She came around the table and put her arms about me. "There, there," she crooned. "You'll be fine. You're allowed to cry."

"Sorry." I pulled away.

"Have dinner with us tonight," she said. "You've hardly eaten in the last few weeks."

"I don't feel hungry."

"We won't force you to eat. You can just sit there and talk to us. That'd be a novelty."

"I'll listen. I haven't got a brain any more." I looked at

the calendar and looked away again. October? "Have you got today's newspaper by any chance?" I asked.

She handed me a paper. "Yesterday's," she said and I scanned it for a date. "It's nearly November." A month of my life had been swallowed up. I put the paper away.

"Come out with me," she urged. "You've been cooped up for far too long." The invitation carried with it an imperative that couldn't be ignored.

"I'm very dull company."

"Dull is infinitely better than the way you were. God, I'm glad you're better. We didn't know what to do with you."

"I'm such a nuisance."

She pulled a face. "Not great, but we'll let that pass. You don't need our absolution." She checked her watch. "Half an hour's time, all right?"

In my room I consulted the mirror like a demented queen. Again I saw the slack mouth, tired skin and lustreless hair. I rehearsed a smile but only the lips moved.

Maggie knocked at the door. "Let's go," she shouted in.

I shivered in the cold. "Hop into the car," she said. "You're not dressed properly for this weather." As the car flashed past trees, parks, recessed houses and across the bridge over the Thames on its journey into Richmond I felt fragile.

"What's the time?" I asked.

"It's two."

Two o'clock in the afternoon, I thought. Saturday, I thought.

She parked the car. "Here we are." She hopped out, came over to my side, linked arms with me and dragged me with her some distance. Then she pushed me into a newsagent's.

Suddenly she was chatting to a young man. I hoped she wouldn't forget me. My gaze swam over photographs of scantily clad women, banner headlines, exclamation marks and minute print that dazzled my eyes. People came into the shop and picked up papers or magazines with frightening decisiveness.

"Do you want something?" Maggie asked. I jumped at her closeness.

"I've no money. Forgot money," I said.

"I'll treat you. What do you want?" She grinned at my choice. "Doubt if you're after the *Financial Times*." She replaced it. "I'll choose for you and take the *Telegraph* for myself." She took the papers to the counter and paid for them.

On our way back to the car she forced me into another shop, a bookshop this time. "Come on," she urged, "if I see you pick up a book I'll know you're on the road to recovery." I tried to dodge away but she pulled me back. I doubted I'd ever read a book again.

"Maggie," I said, "we'll try this in a few days."

She wouldn't hear me, wouldn't listen. "I insist. Go on. Please me."

I felt most peculiar. "Show me something," I murmured. The noise in the shop dipped to an almost inaudible level and, as suddenly, rose to a ridiculous pitch. I passed too close to a protruding lower shelf and stumbled. We stopped and I heard Maggie's voice. I think she was telling me things. It was difficult to hear her, hard to concentrate on what she was saying . . . "That should interest you" . . . "not really all that good" . . . "I must say I enjoyed this" . . . "got excellent reviews but . . ." Phrases crashed into my ears or got sucked into the air.

"I see," I said. Through waves of light and air I sensed her impatience. "You'll have to make allowances for me," I said. Rushing noises pierced my ears and hissing sounds engulfed me.

"You've gone very pale. Are you all right?" she asked.

"Fine," I mouthed but suddenly I felt almost feverish and found myself tilting, felt the drag of gravity. In a moment of clarity I saw a chair by the cashier's desk. As I lurched towards it I felt the power ebb from my legs, felt them tremble and contract, became aware of a flailing arm movement as I struggled to maintain my balance. As I reached the chair I relaxed my concentration and crashed to the ground.

Next I was turned over like a piece of meat to face upwards. I saw the ceiling of the bookshop, the blinding lights above and blurry faces looking down at me from a great height. A face came closer. Maggie peered at me. I think I smiled.

"Shouldn't someone call an ambulance?" I heard a tight English voice say.

"She's fine," Maggie said. "I shouldn't have taken her out. She wasn't up to it."

"Are you all right, dear?" the owner of the English accent asked. Another face came into focus as it peered down. A woman smiled.

"Yes thanks," I answered politely.

"You gave us such a fright, dear. You had quite a

spectacular spill, scattered ever so many books. Do you think you can sit up?"

"I'll try." Arms pulled me into a sitting position. My head was sore. I rubbed it. Somebody pressed a glass of cold water to my lips. Where had that come from? I drank thirstily. "Thank you," I murmured.

"You gave your head a nasty knock as you fell," the woman said. Her fingers sifted through my hair. I was so glad I'd washed it. "Yes, here's a little lump. You should get it seen to."

"I'll be as right as rain," I said.

A hand was thrust in front of my eyes. "How many fingers do you see?" a male voice asked.

"Three." I said. Don't be silly, I thought.

"Now how many?"

I looked again. "Thumb and index finger."

"Good. Now follow my finger." It wagged first one way and then the other. I followed its progress with my eyes. Then the hand was taken away. I looked into the owner's eyes and met the gaze of a clean, dark man. He looked fresh and young and energetic.

"What are you, a doctor?" I asked.

"No. You lost consciousness for a moment. Get yourself checked out."

"Let's get you back to the car." Maggie helped me to my feet. Other customers looked us up and down. If their eyes met mine their glances fell away. Such restraint, I thought. Better say nothing.

"Bed for you, my lady," Maggie said as we drove off. "I was mad to haul you out. What was I thinking of? You can hardly keep your eyes open. I'm going to heat up some nice chicken broth for you when we get in."

"You sound like my mother," is the last thing I remember saying.

When we reached the house she made me stretch out on the sofa and plumped up cushions for behind my head. I felt pleasantly light-headed. "Right. I'll heat that broth up now," she said. I sat up to warn her that I was falling asleep but fell back against the cushions.

Chapter Eleven

Maggie shook me awake. "Breakfast," she said, left a tray on a low table and rushed out again.

I sat up, pulled the table closer and bit into crisp, brown toast spread with blackcurrant jam. I remembered the thrill of making toast in Ballycourt, the glowing log fire in the sitting-room, the plate on the hearth, pronging the bread on the brass toasting fork, thrusting it towards the heat, judging it, turning it and slapping runny butter on it.

There was a knock on the door and Jean's slender form slid into the room. She smiled. "I've come to rejoice in your recovery. You were out to the world when I got in last night," she said. She cast a look at me like a hesitant hospital visitor who isn't sure how to behave.

She had snipped that luxuriant hair to below chin level and it bristled about her face like a mad, black halo. "You have wonderful hair," I murmured.

She grimaced. "Always wanted it to be straight when I was a kid. The other children gave me a hard time about it. Accused me of having a touch of the tar brush."

"And did you?"

"Not unless there was some family secret I was kept in the dark about."

"It's exotic. I like it." With wonderful impassivity she studied her features in the mirror above the mantelpiece. She had grown used to herself. "The farmer's daughter from Timbuktu," she said. She looked about, sat on the edge of the sofa and stole a triangle of toast.

"Thief," I said. "Greedy gut."

"Breakfast." She smiled. "Don't expect me to be sweet and considerate. I'm not at all good at that. Maggie told me to come and talk to you."

"Don't stay if you don't want to," I said. My voice carried the sharpness I felt. "Anyway I have to change. I slept in my clothes last night."

"Stay put," she said. "Maggie's doing a special resurrection lunch for you. She thinks you're Lady Lazarus. It's best to keep out of the firing line when she takes over the kitchen."

"Bet you're sorry I came to stay."

She shook her head. "Maggie's told me about your folks and the business with your husband. I had an awful upbringing as well. My folks are tyrants too but it's something they can't help. It's the way they were brought up themselves. It does things to you. I've Maggie to thank for dragging me away from them. She made me do what I'd always wanted to do. If she hadn't I'd probably be bored to death and married to some self satisfied lump of a farmer."

She got up. "I'm off to fetch the newspapers. The morning looks lovely but there's a vicious nip in the air." She hesitated. "Heck," she said, "Maggie tells me you can use a computer. Would you be interested in a typing job?"

"A job?"

"There's something going, not much mind you. About a week or two's work if you work quickly."

"Oh."

"Somebody I know needs a thesis typed up. He has appalling longhand which won't be easy to decipher but he pays well. You could do it on my machine in the workroom."

I wanted to run up to my bedroom, huddle up and snuggle down under the bedclothes but, just as I would eat a Sunday lunch I hadn't any appetite for, I would accept this job. "I could do with the money," I said.

"Good. I'll phone him tomorrow," she said. "I warn you he's weird. He was in my first year in college. He's a sort of philosophy genius, lives in the head."

"Fine," I said. "Thanks." Jean left behind bursts, like detonating pellets, of her distinctive perfume. Would I have forgotten how to work a computer as easily as I had forgotten how to be myself?

"Lunch in five minutes," Maggie called. I slipped upstairs and changed into fresh clothes. Then I wandered over to the bedroom window to view the world, took a deep breath, stretched out my arms and exhaled.

After the chicken casserole and almond tart, we sprawled in the living-room, drank wine and glanced through Sunday newspapers.

The telephone rang and Maggie groaned. "I'll get it," she said. She returned a few minutes later and a secretive smile played about her lips.

"Anybody in particular?" Jean asked.

"Just Eoin."

Silence followed this remark, no rustling of newspapers, sipping of wine, tapping of glass or comment. "You mean my husband, Eoin?" I asked after a good while. I stared at the blurred newspaper print.

"The same. He's rung here a few times."

"You never said."

"I did once but you didn't seem to hear."

"I don't remember. What did he want?"

"He was asking after you."

"What the hell was he doing that for? Does he know what happened me?"

Maggie looked uncomfortable. "He guessed something was up. There didn't seem to be much point in lying to him. I told him not to come over."

"Very good of you," I snapped. "Why the hell did you tell him anything?"

"He's your husband."

"Technically yes, but really he disqualified himself in the husband stakes."

"That was only a flash in the pan," Maggie said.

"How would you know?"

"Some people don't know when they're well off," Maggie snarled. She glared at me.

"Oops, we're getting a bit nervy here. We should cool it." Jean stood in front of me and filled my glass. She went to pour wine into Maggie's glass but Maggie waved her away.

I think I said "Excuse me" as I left the room. I felt almost sick as I made for the bathroom. There I stared at the white wall tiles and at the gold rim that ran about the room at chest level. The bathroom had been decorated. The cold surfaces were curiously comforting. Perspiration broke out on my warm skin, rivulets of moisture between nose and chin, a dampness of forehead. I couldn't escape the pressure of my thoughts and wondered what they were saying in the living-room. I was angry with Maggie. How long had Eoin been in touch with her? Was the old life shadowing the new, others' stratagems working to manipulate me?

Maggie and Jean had reserved a place for Eoin in my life when I had edged him out. What extraordinary impertinence, I thought. How did they dare? I splashed cold water on my face and worked to calm myself.

There was a tap on the door. "All right, Sinéad?" Jean asked. "You're in there a good while."

"Fine," I announced. "The stomach isn't used to rich food, that's all."

I fixed my hair in the mirror. It was time to get a job. A job anchored a person to a place. Failing a job I would sign on for the dole. I flushed the toilet, ran the tap for a while and returned to the others. Their eyes followed me.

"Well, how's Eoin?" I asked Maggie. "Is he well?"

She threw me a black look. "Fine. He's very concerned about you."

"Touching isn't it?" I smiled. "Next time he rings tell him I'm going to be fine."

"Tell him yourself."

"No, you tell him to stop bothering me."

"Do you mean that?" Maggie asked. Jean winked at me. Was she encouraging me or laughing at me? "Jean, pour me some wine!" There was an acerbic note in Maggie's voice.

"Yes," I said. "There's going to be a new me. Wait till the new year. You won't recognise me. There isn't much of this year left, is there?"

"Just Christmas," Jean said.

"Yes, Christmas. What are you doing for Christmas? Where are you going?" Maggie asked suddenly. I scowled. Bloody, old Christmas, always demanding attention and clogging up the works.

"I've no idea."

They looked at each other. "We'll be in the west of Ireland," Jean said. "Neither of us has to go home. We're out of the loop this year." She glanced at Maggie. "We've booked a self-catering cottage. You can come if you pay your way."

I swallowed fruity wine. I didn't like the idea of being on my own in London in dark December. "Well, I've no other offers so I'd love to come," I said.

"Great." Jean stretched and yawned. "Make us coffee then. Wake us up."

"And calm us down," Maggie said. "Filter pot's in the cupboard under the sink."

"Yessum, mistresses," I grinned. Once the task of making coffee had been routine. Now it was a challenge that demanded concentration and effort.

As I left the room I thought I heard sounds of stifled laughter. I stood absolutely still. Easy, I told myself, steady on. Don't be paranoid. I had to go back into the room. "Black or white?" I asked.

"Black," they chorused. I stared at them but their faces were serious and calm. I made the coffee. Triumphantly I poured it into blue mugs and carried the tray into the living-room.

"We'll be able to put you to good use," Jean said. She smirked.

"What did your last servant die of?" I asked.

Chapter Twelve

I consumed cup after cup of coffee to keep me alert but I was easily distracted from the thesis. Hours passed every morning before I could force myself to face the task. A bird on the patio was enough to absorb me. A shower of rain was fascinating.

The author was a peculiar creature, incapable of making eye contact, clumsy, thin as a stick insect, with a long twisted nose, hardly any chin to speak of and a voice so low and indistinct that it was difficult to interpret his instructions. Sometimes I felt that I wasn't dealing with a member of the human race but with an extra-terrestrial from some far-flung planet. Compared to this strange being I felt sane.

"I can't wait for this to be over," I said to Jean. "I hate having to deal with him. I'd like to give it up!"

"He'll hold you to the deal. He's an extraordinarily stubborn man."

"He's a ridiculous creature, gives me the creeps."

She laughed. "Ah, he's harmless. He doesn't even kill flies. Anyway, you wouldn't like to miss out on all that frustration, would you? Angst is good for the soul!"

"You said a week or so. It'll take at least three weeks," I complained. "His index is a mess. Some genius!"

"He is," she said. "He's incapable of living an ordinary life. Existence is a series of ideas for him."

I watched a man in an overcoat shuffle about the garden of the house next door. He went into a greenhouse, moved a box of plants, arranged gardening tools, cleared a spot on a narrow bench and sat down. The earth was crisp with frost. "A lunatic," I said.

"Genius or idiot, you make up your own mind," she said. "Stop moaning." She got up from the kitchen table. "It'll be over soon."

Everything I said became a complaint. I couldn't muster up an enthusiastic phrase or sentence. If I said something as simple as "I'll do that" it sounded like a reproach or a whine.

I performed my share of the cooking and cleaning chores, took my turn at the shopping and paid bills. Initially Jean and Maggie seemed to appreciate this turnabout but they didn't want rotas posted up. "Don't you dare make out lists or timetables," Maggie warned, "or I'll throttle you!"

They became indifferent to me. It was aggravating to be a thing of such slight interest.

"Shopping, bills, cleaning and all in the one week. Receipts. Accounts. What will we do with her, Maggie?" Jean asked.

"Throw her in the river." They taunted and teased me and got on with their lives.

Often they were away from the house for days. One morning Jean came down for breakfast with a man. "This is Ted," she said or perhaps she said, "Meet Mike." She turned to the man. "This is Sinéad," she said, "she's staying with us for a while."

"We've met," he said.

"We have?" Had he seen me slouching about the place? I didn't remember him.

That's how she and Maggie introduced me to their men. Sometimes I met one in the hallway or emerging from the bathroom or passed a man I recognised in the street.

One memorable morning I rushed into the bathroom to go to the toilet. I pulled down my knickers, sat on the bowl and looked up to find a man in the bath watching me. "Hi," he said.

"Oh hi." I blushed. Fucking idiot hadn't bothered to lock the bathroom door.

"Don't let me put you out," he said.

"I think we shock you," Maggie said one morning. "I think you look down your straight nose at us and imagine that you're better than us."

"Not at all," I protested but I lied. Was I a puritan?

"We'll be a long time dead," Maggie said, "and soon we'll be old."

"Don't you have a special person?" I asked.

She grinned. "Nah, but I have tried serial monogomy in my time."

"Each to her own."

She looked at me. "I see little Ms Rabbit here. You're afraid of men. It's obvious. You'd run a mile if one looked at you. You wouldn't know what to do."

"I married one."

"Yes, that was extraordinary. Don't know how you managed it. Well, now's your chance to check out a whole new world." She laughed but there was no friendliness in that laugh. For the first time in all the time I had known her I looked at her with real dislike. Our eyes locked. Here, where I expected to be safe, was a hostile environment. After a while I dropped my gaze.

"Aren't you afraid of, well of . . . infections?" I asked.

She laughed scornfully. "Haven't you ever heard of safe sex?"

One morning she asked, "Have you ever slept with anybody apart from Eoin?"

"Once," I muttered. "We were both drunk and it wasn't much good."

"Once!" She smiled. "Aren't you curious about what it would be like with other men?"

"Not really." I rapped the kitchen table. "Men mean as much to me as this table."

"I suppose we all have our tendencies," she said.

"I suppose so."

I wanted to say: Maggie, where are you? Where's the person I knew? I didn't dare. I knew that she no longer existed.

The days, although cold, were dry. I layered myself like a Russian doll and rolled out into the world. In the street outside young couples were renovating recently purchased houses. The long term inhabitants of the slightly dilapidated houses kept out of sight behind tatty net curtains. Each day at the end of the road I passed a skip outside a house which was being renovated. Workmen whistled at me but I felt safe as a nun.

On one of my walks along a back-street I discovered a pub. It had been sufficiently neglected to look like a pub renovated to look old. The dirty windows, darkened counters and worn floors pleased me. When I ordered a pint the barman smirked and said, "Southsider".

"Wha . . . ?" I was baffled. He grinned and flashed a gappy, nicotine smile.

"Stillorgan, I'll bet, or is it Booterstown?" He spoke in a coarse Dublin accent.

"You're close," I said.

On my way out I spotted a notice. "Staff wanted. Apply within." Before I could change my mind I turned on my worn heel and walked back. I saw games machines in corners and the edge of a pool table jutted into view from a farther room, details I'd missed the first time. Nicotine smile raised an eyebrow.

"You're looking for someone," I said.

"Always looking for someone. Not too fussy either." He grinned. "Boss," he shouted.

The job got me out of the house two nights a week. Nicotine smile was called Steve. Older customers congregated in the snug while layabout youths lurked at the games machines and pool tables. The work was undemanding. The repetitive, rhythmical chores soothed my mind.

I glided out from behind the bar and moved among customers, collecting glasses and taking orders. I was an actress playing a person who was somebody else entirely. I could invent her, sometimes smiling, sometimes thoughtful, always dreamy. "Pint of bitter, luv," became a tenderness, the odd drink names, word play.

"Old-fashioned we are here, luv," the owner, a little man who chewed his false teeth, said. Nervy, impatient customers were told to "Hold it, mate".

On Saturdays, after the clearing of the bar, washing of glasses, cleaning down of surfaces, pooling of tips and distribution of envelopes, I changed into my own clothes in the ladies' toilet. It was difficult to believe that slumbering London dozed outside the doorstep.

Jean and her latest lover, Russell, disturbed me in the kitchen one afternoon. "You have a job, my lady," she announced.

I almost said "I know".

Russell filled the kettle, plugged it in and drummed his fingers on the worktop. He was good-looking in a carefully constructed way, wore tailored suits and sported a tiny gold earring in one ear. He chewed gum constantly. He looked like a North American Indian. I admired those strong, regular but slightly protruding teeth. When he spoke I was disappointed by his ordinary English accent. I wanted exotic foreignness and expected broken or accented English. He didn't like it when I asked him about his background.

"Well, aren't you going to ask about the job?" Jean pushed me playfully against the wall.

"OK, what sort of job is it?"

"Something really downmarket. Lousy pay. Hours not too bad though." Another ploy to get me out and about. "Chambermaid."

"Been there. Done it."

Russell placed coffee in front of me. I wanted to ask him to go into the other room. His impassive, restless presence made me uneasy. It was as though he was constantly assessing, evaluating and dismissing everything. In his presence Jean exuded a breathless jerkiness. She was unrecognisable as the person I knew.

"Look enthusiastic, Sinéad," she said. "I met an old friend today. He's manager of the Carolan. I've known him ages. He said he'd fix you up."

"I worked there years ago."

She grinned. "Student days. Yeah, I know. Me too. It'll keep you going till Christmas."

"It's bloody hard work."

"Come on," she snapped. "You have to start somewhere."

Russell's cold, flickering eyes shot out coded messages to her. "There's a recession," she said. "You won't find much this time of year."

"There's always a recession," I complained. "We're no sooner out of one than we're into another. Where are the boom times?"

Russell stood behind her, his hands worked on her hips, moved up towards the breasts. I squirmed. His eyes met mine and I remembered a man I had seen masturbating in an underground station who had stared insouciantly at me. Jean caught his hands, held them a moment. "The boom times were when we were children, only we didn't know it," she said.

"I'll do it." I wanted to leave the kitchen but they blocked the doorway. "Excuse me," I said. Russell smirked as I brushed past. "I'll go along tomorrow."

They followed me into the living-room. "You'll fossilise if you don't do something," she said.

"You're right." I moved back into the kitchen. From the living-room I heard them talking. They went upstairs. I heard laughter. I was the outcast, the skivvy, the one who had lost it. I ran past her bedroom to my room. I lay on the bed and turned my face to the wall.

Two days later I loaded up my trolley on the fourth floor of the hotel. Chambermaiding had a quality of solitariness to it that reminded me of teaching. I negotiated my trolley through fire doors, stripped and made up beds, cleaned out filthy bathrooms, wiped tiled floors, picked up the occasional tip and fended off randy male guests, over-stimulated by beds and girlie magazines. As I cleaned and dusted I listened to the radio. The hotel looked out at a streetscape on one side and a railway track on the other. I counted hours by bedrooms.

In years to come would I still be working in this place? Would I even come to welcome the monotony of the job? Could I end up in a grubby little bedsit heating lonely meals for one on a two-ring cooker?

When I became less preoccupied with my own thoughts, I noticed a familiar face at the housekeeper's morning briefing and saw it again in the canteen. The young, gum-chewing girls and the older women didn't tug at my memory the way this woman did. I looked at her dyed blond curls, her sallow, fine skin and her queenly walk and wondered if she just reminded me of somebody else.

One day she sat beside me in the canteen. She offered me her hand. "I Consuela," she said.

"I'm Sinéad." I forked tepid lasagna into my mouth.

"You new here?" she asked.

"This is my second week. Mind you, I worked here years ago as a student."

She chewed her bread roll. Suddenly she swallowed it

with a gulp and jabbed a finger at me. "That's it," she said, "I remember. You were Irish student who worked here one summer." She jabbed those dangerous fingers into her breasts. "Me too. I work here then," she said excitedly.

Finally I remembered her. "You must be a housekeeper now," I said.

"No," she said. She fingered her apron. "They only make their own kind housekeepers. I am still the chambermaid with the trolley."

I remembered she had a mother. "How's your mother?" I asked.

She shook her head. "Gone. Dead. Three years."

"I'm sorry. She was a fine old lady."

She looked hard at me, almost suspiciously. "How do you know my mother?" she demanded.

"I met her. You took me back to your place once. Don't you remember? You cooked a wonderful paella."

"Ay, ay, I don't remember that." She frowned. "But something like that, yes. How funny you remember." She squeezed my hand.

"You'd a brother, didn't you?" I said.

Her face darkened. "Yes." The word conveyed immeasurable bitterness and scorn. "Great big bully. He the reason my mother and I had to leave Spain. I could have live in Spain except for him. Bad man." I struggled to remember this story, something about an aggressive, violent brother.

"I keep on the rooms after my mother die," she said. "It's not so cheap now but the owner not worry about making lots of money." She pointed at my ring finger. "You married?"

"Yes. Did you ever marry?"

109

"No. Nobody marry me." After her mother's death she had lived with a man for a while but he had left her. "That was the end," she sighed. "There is nothing for me now, no one to cook for, nobody to talk to."

I sympathised with her, murmured platitudes.

"What happen your husband? He die?" she asked.

"No, I left him."

"Ah," she nodded. "Bad man. The world full of them."

"Not bad," I said. "The marriage didn't work out."

"Children, do you have children?" she asked.

"No. We didn't want children."

"So you had to find a job. Poor thing." She patted my arm.

"I had a job," I said. "I was a teacher but I gave it up."

"Crazy woman," she said. "You give up man and good job to come here. You want to work here. I no understand." As we left the canteen she shook a fist at me. "Crazy woman. Loca," she said. She pointed at her head.

The next time we met she was gloomy. "This life so hard, so sad. Nobody happy. Nothing last. People are greedy and selfish. The people in the city are bad. It's a bad place for the children." She tapped her chest. "You go back to Ireland where people have a soul. Go to your husband. Pray for help. You go home. I cannot."

"I don't pray anymore, Consuela," I answered. "I don't believe in anything."

"You too," she said. She touched my hand. "This is terrible." The next time she saw me she turned aside. Her eyes refused to meet mine.

Chapter Thirteen

"Letters arrived for you this morning," Maggie said one day as I came in from work.

I rushed to the hall table to find two envelopes addressed to me. Eoin had redirected them. I recognised the handwriting on one. My mother had written to me.

I opened her letter. "Since I don't know where you are I don't know if this will ever reach you," it began. As expected it contained reproaches and complaints but one sentence drew my attention. "Your father isn't at all well," it said.

I glanced at the other envelope. The name and address had been written by an unsteady hand. I tore it open and Auntie Moira's scrawl met my eye. I scanned the pages and picked out, "Your dad hasn't been too well lately" in the first paragraph and, towards the end of the letter, "I visited your Aunt Alice's grave yesterday. The earth hasn't settled yet. I must order a headstone."

I glanced at the postmarks. They had been posted on the same day.

"Any news?" Maggie called from the living-room.

"Aunt Moira and Mammy wrote. Daddy's been ill. They don't say what happened."

"Yeah, I heard he was ill."

"You never said!"

"I only heard it from my aunt last night. She rang. She was talking to Mrs Synge who lives on your road. You were working, remember?"

"Did she say what was wrong?"

"He was in hospital with severe pneumonia. He's home now, I think."

"He was fine when I saw him last."

"It happened suddenly. He was being treated for a chest infection and had a breathing emergency. They had to call an ambulance and rush him into hospital."

I sat down. For years I had resented my father but now I felt a thud of dread in my chest.

"The old mortality scare," Maggie said. "He'll recover but it'll take time. He's not young."

"I should get in touch."

"Why aren't you on the phone now?"

"I'll ring tonight."

"Ring now."

"I'll ring later. The rates are cheaper."

"It's up to you." She looked away.

"I have to work up to this, Maggie. It won't be easy," I said.

She had brought work home. She clutched a typescript to her chest. "Mind you make that telephone call," she said as I went upstairs.

Aunt Moira's letter was full of references to funerals. "Mrs Delaney died last week. I'll miss her. She was always very good to call in. Jack O'Brien passed away yesterday. The funeral is today. Winter is taking its toll. The cold weather tells a lot. I'm well enough, thank God, but I spend a lot of time in bed. I haven't the heart to get up in the mornings. Mrs Deasy lights a fire for me every evening so that I'll get up and watch the television."

I remembered the sweet breeze of a hot summer's day in Ballycourt. I walked to the top of the garden and leaned against the wooden stile that marked the start of the shortcut to the graveyard.

The days were dry and hot, the nights so warm that I tossed off everything except the cool sheets. Most nights I woke sticky with perspiration and got up to sit by the old sash window, stare out at the pale darkness of the night, smell the garden and savour the stillness.

The days pulsed with energy and heat. The world had become a furnace and stole my resolve. The farmers wanted rain. I wanted nothing of the sort.

That day, as I stood at the top of the garden, listened to a bird's song and watched a butterfly flicker about the cabbage leaves, I was restless but couldn't summon up the energy for a stroll.

Behind me I heard a light tap tapping on the hard earth and a swish of cloth. Aunt Alice's light-heavy footsteps beat out a rhythm. Now and again I heard her pause to check flowers or vegetables or pull out weeds. She resumed her slow walk and I listened for the crack of her stick against stone.

"I thought you two were going into the big smoke this afternoon," I said.

"Mrs Murphy's car is broken down so we can't go. If Father Duffy's going to Cork tomorrow we'll be able to go with him. No harm," she added. "We'd have been roasted with the heat today. It's awful going around those shops."

"It's a pity I don't have our car with me," I said.

"Don't worry about that. Eoin needed it and you're better off without a car. All this exercise is doing you a power of good."

She stood beside me and followed my gaze. "Come on," she said, "let's stroll down to my next home." She laughed at my reaction. "Better get used to it. That's where I'll end up. It may as well be said." She was preoccupied with mortality and her own impending death.

"It'll be a while before they put you there," I said. I hated these references to death and the graveyard.

"I'm seventy-three now. It's time for me to go." She paused and rested on her stick. Despite her limp, she had always been a great walker. Years before we used to tramp through lanes, farms, crooked little back roads and visit strange little houses perched on steep hills. She knew the whole district. Then arthritis set in and the walks stopped.

"You link with me and I'll make it down to the graveyard," she said.

"Turn back," I urged. "It's all uphill on the way home."

She smiled briefly. "It's a disgrace that an old woman like me has to drag a young girl like you for a walk. You're just lazy. What's the world coming to?"

"Well, take it easy, you know how you overdo it."

"It's only a little walk." She sat down on one of the low walls and tried to coax a tendril of grey-blue hair back into her bun but it escaped.

She got up and we walked arm in arm, dreamily and slowly. "How are you feeling?" she asked.

"Fine. I'm due a check-up when I get back."

"Never mind. You can always try again. Don't lose hope. One miscarriage doesn't mean anything. Losing babies is nothing new." I said nothing. "I hope you're not brooding. There could have been something wrong with it and nature took its course."

"I didn't realise I was pregnant. The miscarriage happened so quickly that I didn't take it all in. It's sort of unreal." I didn't tell her that I was relieved to lose the baby. She wouldn't have understood that.

"Well, the country air has done wonders for you. I expect Eoin's travelling the highroads and byroads of England."

"Oh, I don't envy him all that travelling around." I smiled at her. "Here's the proper place for a rest."

"Maybe you should have gone with him."

I suppressed a feeling of irritation. Best to say nothing. I was glad he was away.

"Don't think you can fool me, young lady. You think I'm just an interfering old busybody, but I know more than you'd expect. Husbands and wives should be together when times are tough. I'm not saying I'm not glad to see you. You're always welcome here."

Aunt Alice was a bit of an enigma to me. Years after her husband's death she came home to teach in the local village school. I had seen photographs of my dead uncle in her bedroom. He'd been an attractive man. Aunt Alice's face was remarkably unlined. Her bones told of her former beauty. Life must have disappointed her but she never complained.

The retired teacher and postmistress lived plain, simple lives. They had shared the family house for more than forty years. Their great passion had been their garden. It was a wonderful garden and they still supplied the church with flowers for the altar.

Years before, their pensions received an unexpected boost from a legacy left them by a long forgotten uncle who had absconded to America in the 1930s and never returned.

Despite this, they had hardly a good word to say about him. "He should have sent money when my poor mother needed it to rear a family," Aunt Moira said. "We don't need it now." Nevertheless the money made their lives comfortable. They could afford to be generous to people.

After an hour or so spent berating the unfortunate man they would pause and one of them would say, "Still, we shouldn't speak ill of him. God will be his judge."

The other would nod and say, "True. Even if he neglected his family, he didn't forget us in the end."

Their lives were full of formality and ritual. Birthdays had to be remembered, gifts acknowledged and clothes admired. News had to be told. A glass of sherry was drunk before dinner and a glass of whiskey before going to bed. "I never touched a drop until I was in my forties," Aunt Moira was keen to emphasise. On Sundays they visited the graveyard and renewed the flowers on their parents' grave. They did their best for their recalcitrant niece and looked forward to her visits.

Aunt Alice and I slipped into the graveyard by the sidegate. Long grass and weeds obscured some of the older graves.

"What are we paying the priests for if they don't maintain the graveyard? It isn't right the way they neglect the place. It shows disrespect for the dead. You come and weed my grave and plant some roses over me. I want real things to grow here."

Always this talk of death. It oppressed me. Cheerfully she pointed out some graves . . . "Madge, poor Madge. Were you old enough to remember her? Ah, you'd have been too small. Kitty Conlon, a nice woman, her husband gave her a terrible time . . . the greatest scoundrel you ever met. He nearly drank his family out of their home . . . Timmy Higgins . . . a nice quiet man, never did anybody any harm . . . Now, there's a right blackguard . . ." We worked our way through the gravestones. She pointed out some of my relatives. Some I knew of and some I knew nothing about.

She pointed with her stick beyond a freshly dug grave. "See over there. That's where our plot is. We fixed it up last winter when I didn't feel so well."

"You never said anything about being unwell in your letters."

"Oh, I was quite bad. We even had the doctor in. It took three doses of antibiotics to put me right. At one stage I wasn't sure I'd see the spring."

"If I'd known I'd have come to see you."

"I hope I don't have to be ill for you to pay me a visit. You can come and see me when I'm well too."

I looked at the fresh grave. "Who died?"

"One of the O'Reillys. He died the Sunday before you came. Ah, it was time enough for him."

"How old was he?"

"Seventy."

I smiled. "Aunt Alice, you're three years older than him."

"That's right. It'd be no harm if I was gone too."

"Do you want to die?"

"Well, I don't want to go on forever."

Aunt Alice had achieved her death and I hadn't visited her during her last illness. I never saw her in the final months of her life.

Chapter Fourteen

M aggie reached across me. "Hand me the receiver," she
said. "I'll dial and set it up, and you speak. When she
gives out say nothing. Silence is a great weapon."

She took the receiver, dialled the number – I could hear
the click, click as the connection was made – and handed it
over when it began to ring at the other end.

"Hello," I heard my mother's telephone voice say.

"Hello, Mam."

She made some strangled sound. "Sinéad?"

"Yes." The word dropped from me like a leaded weight.

Then, unusually, she was quiet. The power of that silence
pulsed through the telephone and surged into my sluggish
blood. "How's Dad? How are you all?"

"You got my letter?"

"Yes."

Again she paused. I waited for the jaws of her anger to
snap at me. "Your father's getting up for part of the day now.
He could have died, you know. Everybody visited him in the
hospital except you." Out of the corner of my eye I saw
Maggie wave her hands, flapping the lurid red of her
fingernails at me. Don't say anything, the hands said. Keep

quiet, they said. "Are you there? Can you hear me, Sinéad?" my mother's voice said from a great distance.

"Yes, I'm here. Is he going to be all right?"

"We don't know." Her words throbbed resentment. "When are you coming home?"

"I might see you at Christmas."

"What are you up to, Sinéad? Why don't you come back?"

"I've a job. I'm all right."

"Have you left Eoin for good?"

"Yes, it's all over."

"That's terrible. Your Aunt Moira will be very upset when she hears this. Give me your number in case we need to get in touch. I have a pencil here."

"I'll write," I said.

"Sinéad, give me your telephone number. What if anything happens?"

"I'll write. Goodbye. Give Dad my love." I replaced the receiver and turned to Maggie.

"Atta girl," she said. "Stood up to her. Good for you."

That night I couldn't sleep. I felt as though a large, heavy stone was jammed in my chest.

I saw the five of us as children in the sitting-room at home, May reading, Emer sewing, Brian and Joe playing a quiet game of scrabble in a corner and I staring at the leaping flames of a coal fire. My mother came in. "Is the homework finished?"

"Yes," we chorused.

"Well make yourselves useful about the house. Boys, put that game away and tidy up your bedroom. It's a mess. May, set the table. Sinéad, you can hoover the hall. Emer, some of your Dad's socks need darning."

"Why can't we have a television like everybody else?" Joe asked. "We're the only house without one."

"Your father doesn't want one. We don't want cabbages staring at it all day."

"It's not fair," Joe said. "You're too mean to get one."

Whack! Her hand swatted his face and left a redness. "Don't ever speak to me in that tone of voice. Get out of my sight, you brat!"

"I hate stew, hate it, hate it, hate it," Brian said.

"Don't talk like that, you insolent young pup you," my father said. "Your mother went to the trouble of making the dinner and you eat it."

"I won't. It's disgusting. I hate stew. It's runny and tasteless. It's revolting."

"Eat your dinner before I whip you, you foul-mouthed, ungrateful wretch."

"No I won't." Brian folded his arms and dared my father to hit him. "I'm full."

"You'll eat that dinner."

"I won't."

At teatime my mother plonked the cold stew in front of Brian. He left it there.

Next morning was a schoolday and she offered it to him for breakfast. "I haven't given you a lunch today," she said, "since you seem to have no appetite."

"It's cold," he said.

"You wouldn't eat it when it was hot."

When we came home from school Brian was starving.

My mother put the congealed stew in front of him. He ate it silently, tears running down his cheek and salting the food.

"In future eat what you get," she said.

It was spring, Mother's birthday. "We'll pick her daffodils," May said. Emer tagged along with us. We ran through local gardens and the field at the end of the road, rifling daffodils as we went. It took three of us to carry them back home.

"I hate flowers in the house," Mother said. "Throw them out. Were you too mean to buy me a present?"

One day a girl presented herself on the doorstep. My mother opened the door. "Yes?" she said.

"I've come to play with Sinéad," she said. "We're in the same class."

Mother called me to the door. "Do you know this girl?" she asked.

"It's Marie," I said. "She sits beside me in school."

"Did you invite her round?"

My heart sank. "No. She said she'd come around to play."

Mother turned to Marie. "Sinéad's doing her homework," she said. "She's not allowed out." She closed the door on Marie's face. Then she turned to face me.

"Don't lie to me, you little vixen," she said. "I know you invited her around." Thwack went her hand against my face. "Go to your room," she said.

Emer ran home one day. "Can I go to a party?" she asked. "I'm invited."

"Sit down and do your homework."

"But may I?"

"No. We'd only have to invite them back."

"No you wouldn't," Joe said. "We never have birthday parties."

"We never go anywhere," Emer cried.

"Any more lip from you and you'll feel the back of my hand on your ear."

May was the first of the girls to be let out to a disco. She was sixteen. "Can't I wear jeans?" she asked.

"You'll wear a nice frock," mother said. Behind her back May raised her eyes heavenwards.

"Be home by eleven," Mother said.

Emer and I huddled at the top of the stairs waiting for her return. We had almost fallen asleep when we heard the doorbell. Mother rushed to the door and, when May came in, caught her a blow across the side of the head. May doubled up.

"You little trollop you," mother said. "You dirty little whore. You can't be trusted to be let out. Get up to your room."

May stumbled up the stairs, sobbing bitterly. We followed her into the room she shared with me. She was lying on the floor facing upwards, her hands clutching her head. "I hate her, hate her, hate her," she muttered through gritted teeth.

"What happened?" Emer asked.

"A boy walked me home."

"Is that all?"

"He kissed me at the gate. She must have been watching." May dried her face. "I can't bear it here. That bitch'll never make me cry again. I wish I were dead."

Mother didn't speak to her for a month afterwards.

I was at home sick in bed while all the others were at school. I woke from a deep stupor to hear raised voices downstairs. I had almost recovered from my flu and crept down to see what was going on.

Being sick meant staying in bed and being ignored for the most part. My mother's usual irritability mellowed into a sharp gentleness. She gave me medicine and brought up meals but otherwise left me alone. Being sick was quite pleasant in many ways. It freed me from chores and I missed family meals.

The kitchen door was slightly ajar and I could hear my mother talking to my Aunt Sheila. "I can't bear it," I heard her say. "No matter what I do all I get is abuse. There's a limit."

Peering cautiously around the open door I saw Aunt Sheila look at her. She took a long, slow drag on her cigarette. "What can you expect?" she asked. "You married him. He doesn't beat you up. He doesn't starve you. What more can you expect?"

"I can't stand it. I've been stuck in this house for the last twelve years. I can't stand it, I'm telling you!"

"Lizzy!" My aunt's voice cut sharply through my mother's words.

"What can I do?"

"You have to stay. You have five children. You'd starve without him."

"If he dies I'll starve anyway. He told me he's made the house over to his sister. Wouldn't do her much good, stuck in a silent order. Anyway what do I care for those children? I never wanted them."

"That's no way to talk. I'm telling you he won't throw

you out. Those days are long gone. You're fretting over nothing. Don't mind what people say in the heat of an argument. He's far too respectable with his Vincent de Paul and his Knights of Columbanus. He has to keep up appearances. Be thankful he doesn't drink."

My mother sat at the table and put her head in her hands. Aunt Sheila lit another cigarette.

"I suppose he just wanted someone to look after the house and give him children," Mother said.

"That's about the sum total of it. When his mother died he was heading on to forty and he needed someone to take her place. We warned you. You can't say we didn't warn you. Always beware the only son. You couldn't expect to please him. Count your blessings. He's seen with you. He goes to Mass with you. Behave with dignity and no one can say a word to you."

"Dignity." My mother said the word with quiet contempt. "I don't see much dignity. I live in this miserable house and I mind his children."

"I'm tired of telling you. They're your children too."

"No. They're his. I mind them for him. He criticises everything I do. He owns us all."

"He has you where he wants you all right and there's no getting away from him."

"I wanted to go home to Ballycourt but Alice said I should stay. Oh, what's the use?" my mother said. "What's the use?"

"No use in the wide world. There's no point in upsetting yourself. He said it to torment you. You know what he's like. What can't be cured must be endured."

"I suppose so." My mother sounded defeated.

"Listen we'll have a nice little glass of whiskey. It'll do you good."

"He'll see we've been at the bottle."

"Don't worry about that. He won't notice a thing. I'll top it up. When do you use it, except for visitors? Mr Pledge Pin won't know the difference and the guests can't complain."

My mother laughed humourlessly. "Oh, go on," she said. "Get some."

"Merciful God!" Aunt Sheila hissed when she saw me cowering at the bottom of the stairs. She grabbed my arm. "Out of here," she whispered, pushing me up the stairs. "Up fast or I'll tan your bottom for you. If you say a word I'll skin you alive."

"What is it, Sheila?" I heard my mother call out. I stared imploringly at my aunt.

"It's just Sinéad at the top of the stairs. She wants a glass of water. I'll get it for her," she said. "Back to bed with you," she shouted. I scrambled up. My heart pounded. Was Dad going to throw us all out?

Aunt Sheila materialised at the door of the bedroom I shared with May. I looked at her rouged cheeks and varnished nails. She worked as a buyer in one of the large city department stores. We didn't see her all that often. Soon afterwards she stopped coming to the house and we never saw her again.

"How much did you hear?" she asked.

"Not much." I shifted uneasily.

She stubbed out her cigarette on the floor. One of us would have to take the blame for that, I knew.

"Tell me what you heard."

"Somebody's going to throw us out of the house and Mammy's miserable."

Strangely enough she seemed to relax at this.

"You picked it up wrong," she said cheerfully and tucked me back into bed. "Your mother isn't well, that's all. You'll have to be a good girl." I nodded fervently. "Your Auntie Moira is coming to help your mother. She's worn out. It's no wonder when she has the likes of you to look after."

She gave my wrist an admonishing tap. "Now, settle down. That's a good girl."

Suddenly she thrust her face close to mine. "If you ever mention what you heard to anyone I'll kill you," she hissed. I shrank back from her vivid face.

"I won't say anything," I whispered. Then she was gone.

Soon after that Auntie Moira came to stay and took over the running of the house. For a while there was harmony and we were happy.

My father treated us all to lunch in a hotel. "Very good of you, Maurice," Aunt Moira said.

"Not at all, Moira," he said. "It does us good to get out once in a while."

My mother took to going out during the day. She went to afternoon matinees and came back to tell us about the films she had seen. Under Aunt Moira's indulgent eye we blossomed. Even my father was civil. Then one morning Aunt Moira was gone. No explanation was given. Father reverted to his gloomy, volatile ways but mother was less harsh with us for a while.

Unhappiness breeds unhappiness. My father attended Mass, Benediction and devotions, displaying outer holiness. Austerity suited him. My cold, determined mother was a prisoner of his will and we were their victims. Mother wore a disappointed expression on her face and by and large we failed to please her.

Chapter Fifteen

Shortly before Christmas Jean decided to throw a party. "It's an idea," Maggie said. "We've never had a party but downstairs is presentable and the bathroom's been done. Yes we should. It could be a kind of housewarming." They sat at the kitchen table to draw up a guest list.

"I see you sneaking off," Jean called after me. "Don't think you're going to sit up in your room while we suffer. You're invited too."

"Leave me out," I said. "I'm no social butterfly but I'll help to get things ready."

"Don't be ridiculous," Maggie said. "Of course you're coming. You can borrow one of my outfits." I felt like the poor relation. "You'd look half decent if you bothered to do yourself up," she said.

The reflection in the mirror told me that my hair needed attention. It hung about my face in limp tendrils.

"Go to Gerrards," Maggie advised. "He's good, but he won't fleece you." Gerrard cost me the equivalent of my weekly food bill.

"*Très chic*." Jean smiled. She danced about me and surveyed me from all angles. She smiled all the time those days. "You might persuade some one to give you a proper job when you look like that."

"I like it," Maggie said. "I didn't think you had great hair but the cut shows it up well." I squirmed under this scrutiny which seemed to go on forever.

"Let's see," Maggie said, "all the chairs must go upstairs or people'll get rooted to one spot. Make them stand."

Jean said, "Leave the sofa. If anybody's dying on their feet it'll be there for them."

On the day of the party I raced home from work with bottles of wine and found Maggie and Jean deep in preparation. Jean took the bottles. "Excellent," she said. "This is good stuff." It was strange to be doing all the right things for a change.

We filled flans and pavlovas, prepared dressings for salads and stacked quiches and pizzas for reheating. Hours later we had finished. It was seven o'clock. "We've cracked it," Maggie said. "Bags the first shower." There followed a frenzy of showering, blow drying of hair, dressing and application of make up.

"Your skin is quite good," Maggie commented, as she applied foundation to my face.

"Not too much," I begged.

"You're going to look great," she said as she applied eye make-up. I surveyed the finished product in the mirror. "Go on, say something. I don't like this silence. Do you like it?" she said.

"I look so glossy. I think I'd be quite scared of me."

"Good bones."

"My mother's side of the family," I said, thinking of Aunt Alice.

"It's not excessive. Wait until you see how everybody else will be made up. There'll be a few Irish people so you'll feel at home."

I preened in front of the bathroom mirror. Who was that creature? Did I recognise her? Could I ever know her?

When the first guests arrived I hid in my room, overcome by a terrible stage fright.

"Come on out!" Maggie hissed in at me. "We need you."

I headed into the kitchen to pour out drinks. This would be my task for the night, I decided. Russell leered at me as I passed by with a tray of drinks. He didn't recognise me. In the kitchen I found Maggie and Jean in deep consultation, their heads almost touching as they talked.

"He said he'd come," Jean said fiercely.

"You couldn't ever rely on him," Maggie rejoined. "He'll probably turn up late, if he turns up at all."

"Bastard."

I offered the tray of drinks around and gulped a glass of wine. I needed alcohol to steady my nerves.

A thin, almost anorexic woman grabbed me by the arm. "You're Sinéad, the Irish friend," she said. "I work with Jean. I gather you've left your husband but there's no divorce in your wretched country."

"Yes, I'm Sinéad," I said and extricated my arm. I smiled at the woman. "Divorce is on its way," I said.

Back in the kitchen I found Maggie. "Go and talk to your guests. I'll set up the food," I said.

"Jean's in a pickle. Her author hasn't turned up."

"What author?"

"The new guy, Damien Varis. Everybody wants to have him and he promised he'd come."

"Poor fellow. Maybe he had better things to do with his time."

Maggie looked at me as if I were a fool. "Don't be daft. Jean's done a lot for him. He ought to turn up."

At that moment Jean dashed in. "He's here," she breathed and ran out again. Moments later she reappeared with a thin, rather nervous looking young man. He carried cans of beer under his arm. These he thrust at Maggie. "Folks, this is Damien," Jean said.

"How're yez doing?" he said.

"You're Irish!" I said.

"Ay, I'm from Belfast," he said in a deep, melodious voice.

"Have a drink," I said. "How can you be Irish with a surname like that?"

"Irish mother, Polish father. Cultural cross-pollination."

"What side of the religious divide did you land on?"

"Neither really. The mother's a lapsed Catholic, the father a non-practising Jew. Could I have beer?" he asked, looking doubtfully at the glass of wine Maggie had passed him. "I don't drink wine."

"Give the man a beer," Maggie said. I passed him a long glass.

"You two seem to have hit it off," Jean said. "Beer's in the fridge. Sinéad, bring Damien out to meet everybody. No hiding in the kitchen." They drifted out of the room.

"You're not what I expected," I said.

"You said it. I'm not what I expected either."

"You had a book published?"

"Aye. This is me second. I'm over for the launch."

I laughed. "I expected some sort of egomaniac," I said.

"Give me time. I'm only new to the game." He ran a hand nervously through his blond curls.

"You're the celebrity here. You should be enjoying this."

"I'm fed up to the eyeballs with it. All these bloody people leeching out of me and sucking me blood." He drank his beer thirstily.

"I bet you'd prefer to be down in a pub."

"Nah, I'm too grand for pubs now." He grinned. "Who are ye anyway? Ye're from Dublin."

"I'm Sinéad, a friend of Maggie's."

"I don't know if I heard anything about ye."

"I'm staying with Maggie and Jean for a while." I sipped my third glass of wine.

"You should drink the white stuff. The tannin in the red will give you an awful head in the morning."

"I'm going to have an awful head anyway. I have to keep on drinking or I'll run out of the place."

"Me too. I had a few pints before I could work up to coming here."

"You'd better go out and meet the fans. They'll be getting impatient."

"Jeysus, I suppose so. Ye'd better come and keep me company. I want to have a glamorous woman by my side." He looked down at my wedding ring. "Ye're spoken for, I see."

"We've split up. I haven't seen him in a long while."

"Well then ye can help me get through this. I'm sick of fucking parties and dinners. I'm going to lock meself in a room for a year when I get home."

Jean grabbed me as Maggie kidnapped Damien and

whisked him away. "He's terribly shy. How did you get around him?"

"We just hit it off. I like him. He's nice."

I looked over at Damien. He was trapped on the sofa with two middle-aged women. They were doing most of the talking. I helped myself to more wine.

"I'll start moving them into the kitchen for food," Jean said.

"I wouldn't have recognised you, Sinéad," a cool, female voice said at my elbow. "You've changed altogether."

I turned around. A fuzzy redhead stared back at me.

"I'm afraid you have the advantage of me."

She extended a hand. "Teresa Mannion. Don't you remember?" She smiled, showing good teeth.

"I don't think we liked each other much at college."

She chuckled. "You're much more direct than you used to be."

"It's the drink talking."

"What else does the drink say?"

"It says I'd forgotten you existed, but I remember you now."

"Come over this way and I'll introduce you to my husband."

"Have you got one of those too?" I asked as she guided me through the throng.

"You have had a lot to drink. You ditched yours, I believe."

"I'm not too sure who ditched whom."

She introduced me to a small, older man. He looked severe but then he smiled and suddenly he had great charm.

He lifted up my hand and kissed it. "*Enchanté,*" he said. I giggled.

"Delighted to meet you."

"My husband is Italian," Teresa said.

"Do you live in Italy?"

"Some of the time." She sounded bored all of a sudden, her voice frosted with formality. I cut away from them.

"Time for food. Ye need to eat," Damien said in my ear. He guided me towards the kitchen. "Ye'd better stick to the bottled water from now on. Ye're flying."

"This party isn't too bad," I said. He handed me a plate. "I'll never eat all this," I protested.

"Eat!" he commanded. "I'll feed it to ye if you don't." He gestured at other people. "Look, everybody's having food."

"OK, OK. No need to be so bossy."

He steered me over to the sofa. A man got up and walked away. "I'm going to look after ye for the rest of the night. I've done me authorial duty."

A long time later I realised my head was on his shoulder. The plate had disappeared. I thought about sitting up.

"What sort of books do you write?"

"Thrillers."

"You're joking." I tried to lift my head, but he pushed it back down.

"Nah. I don't write deadly serious stuff, ye know. They're just better than average for the genre. They sell quite well."

"That's all that matters. Can you make a living from it?"

"Yeah. I was able to give up the job."

"I gave up my job too."

"What did ye do?"

"I was a teacher."

"I always rather fancied teachers. I expect them to be quite resourceful."

"You wouldn't say that if you saw me in my last few months. I got out just before I fell apart."

"It's supposed to be a burn-out job," he said. His lips brushed my ear. A pleasant quivering sensation ran down my back.

I laughed. "Well, I was pretty burnt out at the end."

"Ye seem to be burning brightly to me."

"You say the nicest things." Suddenly I imagined he might kiss me but he just stroked my hair.

"When do you go back to Belfast?"

"I don't live in Belfast anymore. I've moved up to Dublin."

"Surely you've moved down?"

He smiled. "Up, down. Who cares?"

All of a sudden he seemed very desirable but I felt that I should get up and go away. I stayed. A number of party guests were leaving. I thought I might fall asleep on his shoulder.

I felt a strong urge to touch this man. It was such an unusual feeling for me that it made me nervous. I knew nothing about him really. Up to this, recklessness had never been a feature of my character.

"What are ye doing here in London?" he asked.

I laughed. "Not much. Just drifting."

"Are ye going to stay here?"

"I don't know. Probably. I'll stay until my money runs out."

"What'll ye do then? Go back to Dublin?"

"I've no idea."

His finger traced the outline of my cheek. "Have ye resolved everything with your husband?"

"Everything is resolved . . . and unresolved."

Suddenly I realised that we were alone in the room. Everybody had gone. Somebody had stacked plates on a table. The room was littered with empty wine glasses. I sat up in surprise.

"What time is it?" I asked.

"Four in the morning."

"I don't believe it. I didn't notice the time passing."

"I suppose ye want me to go?" he murmured into my ear.

I didn't want him to go but I was afraid to have him stay. "I'll make coffee," I said, disentangling myself from his arm and standing up.

He followed me into the deserted kitchen. "There's still some on," he said.

I filled two mugs, he milked them and we sat down. He reached out and took my hand. I let it lie in his.

"This is very strange for me," I said.

"I can see that," he said. "Still, we get on. Don't we?"

"Yes." I felt my pulses throbbing. Soon he would get up and go away and I would let him. I saw him to the door.

He caught me to him and I let him. He went to kiss me but I ducked. Then I kissed him on the cheek. It was easier than I had anticipated. I actually felt something.

"Do ye think ye could be interested in me?" he asked.

"Could happen."

He kissed my cheek and pulled me closer. It was pleasant

and awkward at the same time. I drew away. "I'd better go," he said. "This could go on all night and I wouldn't get anywhere with ye. Will we meet again? I'll be in London for a couple of days."

"Yes. I'd like to meet."

He smiled and looked into my eyes. "Good. That's settled. Now give me a proper kiss and I'll go. If I stay I might forget my manners."

Chapter Sixteen

The following day we met up in a city pub. It surprised me that he wasn't particularly good-looking. He seemed nervous and drank his first pint quickly. We were very quiet. I thought he looked tired.

"These bloody English pubs shut in the afternoon," he said. "Anywhere that serves booze is closed. We could go to a film."

"Let's go to a film."

He sat hunched over his drink and then looked up. I turned towards him. He caught me and pulled me against him. There was no time to resist his kiss. "That's for the one I didn't get last night," he said. "Tomorrow's my last day in London. Let's spend it together."

"I'm working."

"Ring in sick. I have to be at the publishers at ten but I should be free at lunchtime."

I shook my head. "I need the money."

"It doesn't matter about the money. I'll give ye the money."

"I'm on a short day. I'll be finished before three. Then we can meet."

"Meet me earlier." He kissed me. I shook my head but kissed him back. His mouth gave way and I felt almost sucked into him. It was unnerving.

We didn't go to see a film. We walked along the Thames near the Houses of Parliament. It was peaceful by the river.

Then he took me on a sightseeing tour and we visited the Tate gallery. He wanted to buy me a print but I wouldn't let him.

"I'll have to read one of your books," I said.

"They're not very literary, Madam teacher."

"I think I can live with that."

"Come back to me hotel room and I'll autograph two copies for ye. I'll write disgracefully intimate things on them. Ye'll be ashamed to show them to yer friends."

I shook my head. "I like it here. I don't want to move."

"Ye're going to have to stop resisting me sometime so why not now?" He seemed to tremble. His eyes devoured me. I shouldn't be doing this, I thought. I buried my face in his shoulder.

"This is happening too fast."

He sighed. "I know. Ye want to make sure I'm not just looking for a quick fuck. All right. Come on, the pubs'll be open soon. Drink will take away the capacity."

"Tomorrow," I said when we parted that night.

"Be there. Don't be late." At the barrier to the train platform he kissed the tip of my nose.

What'll this lead to? I asked myself on the train. What's going to happen?

The next day I shot out of work and raced up to Kensington High Street. I was in luck and caught a bus immediately. The bus-stop where I disembarked left only a short walk to his hotel.

The traffic lights were eternally green. When, finally, they turned red I dashed out. To my left I heard a screech of brakes. Suddenly I was lifted up off the ground by some terrific impact. I came down on a car bonnet. I could feel my head jerk back. Very slowly, it seemed, I bounced off the bonnet. I could see the halted traffic. I looked into the eyes of startled pedestrians. I saw a policeman watch my descent towards the ground. As I fell I willed my body to relax. God forgive me, I thought when I felt my body thump on the road.

I lay there. The car had stopped. Amazingly I felt all right and slowly got to my feet. What good luck, I thought, and smiled to show the world I was fine.

Somebody blocked my way. It was the policeman I had seen from the air. I tried to dodge away from him but his hand dragged at my sleeve. He spoke into his walkie talkie. Again I tried to pull away. His grip tightened on my arm.

"No harm done," I said.

"I've called an ambulance."

"There's no need."

"You can't tell. You gave your head a nasty thump. Sit over here on these steps."

I did feel a little dizzy then and let him guide me to the steps. Quite a crowd gathered. I stared at them and they stared at me.

The policeman indicated a swarthy, young man to me. "This is the driver of the car," said the policeman. The man stared at me sullenly. "The two of you will have to give me statements."

A feeling of mounting frustration agitated me. I looked at my watch. A quarter past three. "Look, I'm late. I'm meeting somebody. I have to go."

"You can't go until you've given me your details. The ambulance is on its way. We can do this now or you can do it down at the station later on."

I shrugged up at the driver of the car but he looked away. Then I gabbled off my statement. We exchanged details and, almost immediately, the policeman guided me towards an ambulance. When I saw it I realised that I had heard the sound of its siren but hadn't noticed its arrival.

"Really, I don't need to go to hospital," I protested.

"We've better things to do with our time, do we? Bit of an inconvenience this having to go to hospital. Sorry if we've mucked up your social calendar." The policeman smiled and helped me up the step. He sat down beside me. "I'm coming with you," he said.

Behind me somebody was dabbing at my head. I whirled around. "Easy, duck!" An ambulance man smiled at me and held up a cloth for me to inspect. It was full of blood and tiny fragments of glass.

"Oh," I said weakly.

"See!" The policeman grinned.

"She's got a hard head," the ambulance man joked.

"A tough Irish head." My policeman smiled. "What part of Ireland are you from then?"

"Dublin."

"I went on holidays to a place called Bantry once," the ambulance man said. "Went for a fortnight, stayed there for a year. Beautiful place. I didn't want to come home. Know it?"

It was surprising to find myself in such congenial company. "No, I've never been there."

"You go there. It's smashing!"

"She doesn't want to go to hospital," the policeman told him. "We've messed up her afternoon."

"Turn around, lovie, until I get this stuff out. It's not too bad."

"Did I break his windscreen?"

"Shattered it," the policeman said. "He didn't even ask you how you were, the bastard!"

I fretted. Damien would have given up on me by now. "I need to make a phone call."

"After your x-rays you can make all the phone calls you like," the ambulance man said.

"Do I have to have x-rays?"

"Yeah. They'll check anywhere you hit."

"She hit her legs," the policeman volunteered.

"They'll do your legs too."

"Will it take long?"

They laughed. "You're in an awful hurry, lovie."

I looked down at the plastic bag in my hand. My new bottle of shampoo had leaked over oranges I had bought.

"Throw it away," the ambulance man said.

I let them sit me in a wheelchair at the hospital and didn't protest too much at the wait. An orderly helped me off with my jeans for the x-ray. Afterwards they left me on a bed and closed curtains around me. The policeman looked in. "I'm off," he said and waved. I smiled at him but I was beginning to feel drowsy. I stared at the curtains. Then, as though an anaesthetic was wearing off, I began to feel sore.

"You're a very lucky girl," a voice said from above. I

142

opened my eyes. A white-coated Indian doctor looked down at me. His teeth flashed. "You haven't broken a thing. You're in the clear, free to go. Mind you don't go running out under cars again. You mightn't be so fortunate next time."

"May I go?"

He grinned. "You may. You'll feel some discomfort over the next few days."

"I'll be grand. Thanks." Long after he had disappeared from sight I could see his dark features and those white teeth. I remembered his smile.

I'll ring Damien now, I thought and looked down at my watch. Half past six! His flight was at half past seven. How could so much time have passed? Got to get my jeans and get up, I thought, and dragged myself into a sitting position. My body was stiff.

A tall black nurse looked in at me. She scowled. "Need some help?" she asked and watched me impassively.

"I'm fine," I said and leapt down off the bed. Hot needles of pain shot up through my legs. I thought of the little mermaid. I staggered and fell. It seemed that I could never get up again. I felt the cold floor under me.

Somebody hauled me into a sitting position. The nurse and I faced each other. Brown irises and yellowed whites stared into my eyes. Through the language of eyes I asked her for help. The pain was vicious, cruel, digging into my bones. "I don't think I can put on my jeans," I said.

"Can you stand?"

"Don't know." I defied the pain and got to my knees. I thought I might faint. As I clung to her I smelt a wonderful musky scent from her body, felt a different texture to her skin. I had never been close to a black person before.

"Lean on me," she said. "I'll take your weight." When she got me into a standing position she dragged me over to the bed. "No dancing on the town for you tonight," she said.

"What a shame. I had so many things planned." I tried to smile.

"Let's get those jeans on. Lie out. Here, I'll help." She fetched my jeans from the chair and, by dint of pushing, shoving and dragging the material, we forced the jeans back on. I stood up and tried to master this pain. She put a shoe on each foot while I clung to the bed. "Jesus," I said. "This is terrible."

"You've got some dreadful bruises and you're suffering from delayed shock," she said. I was conscious of her body supporting me.

"How will I get home? How will I get to work?"

"Didn't they give you a note for work?" she asked. I shook my head. "Doctors never think of practical problems," she said. We staggered into the reception area. "You sit down here," she said, edging me into a chair.

I'll never get up again, I thought.

She returned and handed me a note. "That'll get you off work for a few days. They always expect miracle recoveries here. Get another note from your doctor if you need it. And here, I got you some pain-killers." She smiled and put them into my bag. When she smiled her face was transformed. She looked beautiful.

"Thanks a million. Can I make a telephone call?"

"You want me to phone somebody for you?"

"Would you? Could you ring my friends?"

When she had gone I concentrated on staying upright in the seat. I felt unstable as though I might slide to the floor at any moment. Somebody was in the seat beside me. I hadn't the energy to turn my head to see who it was.

There was no relief from the pain. An attempt to stand brought on an attack of such ferocity that I immediately went limp.

"Your friend says to get a taxi to the underground station. She will meet you there. I rang for a taxi."

"You're an angel," I said. I fumbled at my bag and tried to extract my purse. "I never would have managed without you. Let me pay for the phone call."

She clamped her hand on mine and shook her head. "Forget about the money," she said.

She smiled her bright smile and helped me out to the taxi. As it sped away I realised that I didn't even know her name.

Maggie met me at the station. She looked pale and seemed indifferent to my plight. "More dramatics?" she said. There was a harsh note in her voice. As she bundled me into the car every muscle in my body screamed out. I moaned.

"Sore?" I heard her say as from a great distance.

"Yes, I'm very bruised."

"I rang your mother." I think she felt me look at her. "I know, I know. I did it instinctively, didn't think. Relax, she's not coming over or anything. I told her you were OK."

In the house I staggered once or twice on the stairs. When we reached my bedroom I fell on to the bed. "I'll help you off with your jeans," she said and dragged them off. I heard a gasp and then silence.

"God, I've never seen anything like those bruises," she said. "I didn't realise you were so bad." I couldn't speak so I nodded. Every movement or response demanded tremendous effort and concentration. I felt my body buckle as I tried to sit up. Maggie supported me and dragged off my top and bra. She handed me my nightdress.

"Maggie, in the morning could you ring the hotel and tell them what's happened?" I asked. No point in asking her to ring Damien. He was long gone.

"No problem." Was it my imagination or did she sound flustered? "I'll ring them before my flight."

"Flight? A plane? Where're you going? I didn't know you were going anywhere." Panic agitated me. How would I manage without her?

She hunched over me and spoke quietly. "Listen," she said. "I don't know how to tell you this. Jean's brother was wounded in a shotgun accident yesterday. He's dead, died in hospital this morning. I have to go over for the removal and funeral. I don't know what to do with you."

Her words exploded in my mind. "Her brother. Jean's brother?" I heard myself echo.

"He was only twenty, Sinéad, the only boy."

"Where's Jean?"

"Long gone. She got away on a standby flight."

"This is horrible." A wall of unconsciousness threatened to bury me. I pushed against it. "I can't believe it."

"Look, Sinéad, we have to think. You'll have to stay here. You're in no condition to travel. I'll make an arrangement with somebody. What exactly I don't know but I'll think of something."

"No, I'll come with you."

"Would you keep a sense of proportion! You can't sit up, never mind cope with a journey. You'd just be in the way."

"I know, I know," I groaned. "Damn. But I should be there, Maggie."

"Not at all. You won't be fit to travel for days."

"Of all the bloody times to get knocked down."

She gave me a tight, forced smile, more a grimace than anything else. "That can't be helped."

I was wide awake now. I struggled to sit up. "Maybe I'll be better in the morning," I whispered as I fell back.

"I doubt it. You look wretched. Did they give you any painkillers?"

I pointed at my bag. "Open it. They gave me pills."

Chapter Seventeen

The next day my eyes opened on a pale and murky morning. I reached out for the note on my bedside table.

"Spanish omelette in the fridge. Plenty of milk, butter and bread. I'll ring you soon. See you in Ireland,
    Maggie."

It was cold. The heating had gone off. The icy air bit the tip of my nose. I stared at the clock. Maggie was in Ireland and on her way to Meath. There was little point in trying to get up. The house was empty. There was nowhere to go. My head felt strangely compact. Sleep fell in on me again.

I dreamt I stayed with Aunt Moira. In the dream the sky darkened ominously, the wind freshened and whipped itself up and a rush of rain fell from the sky. I ran about the house calling her, searching for her, but all the rooms were empty. Then I ran out the back door, up the path and saw her ahead of me some distance, hatless and coatless, rain soaking her, wind rushing her. Where was she off to? I called out but the wind pocketed the words. I called out again and woke up. For a while I felt that dizzy, winded feeling you experience after a bad dream.

I decided to get up. When I went to get into a sitting position my body refused to move. I tried again and once again nothing happened. I struggled to stifle a fluttering panic. All sorts of dreadful explanations occurred to me. I had damaged my spine in the accident, I was paralysed. A nerve end had snapped. I tried again and, again, there was no reaction to the frantic messages my brain sent along the nerveways of my body.

Keep calm, I told myself. Keep calm. Think! Do this in an orderly fashion. I moved my head and lifted it off the pillow. Neck and head fully operational. I knew my right hand and arm were working. I struggled to get the left arm out from under the covers. Success. Then the toes. Wiggle, wiggle. Yes! Moved the knees up slightly then. Yes! Edged the right arm down the side of the bed as far as it would go and loosened the bedclothes. Dragged myself over onto my side, right to the edge of the bed. Rolled out. Thump! Cold floor. Then pushed up. Pushed up! Pushed with all my might.

Every fibre in my body protested as I levered myself up. Just very, very stiff I realised. I could feel perspiration from my upper lip trickle into my mouth. I clawed my way to the bed. The pain and effort didn't matter. Then, yes, I could stand and move and even manage a staggering walk.

I reached up and unhooked my dressing gown from the back of the door. Somehow I put it on. Everything took so long. Things were far, far away.

Difficulties later, I reached the kitchen, found the fridge and opened the door. I looked in at the Spanish omelette. Kind, thoughtful Maggie. Three cheers for Maggie. I let the door fall shut and balanced myself against the table.

My right leg was dragging, wouldn't be forced into line and refused to obey commands.

The doorbell rang, continued to ring – some obstinate person pressing on the buzzer. I started the journey to the front door. "Coming, coming," I muttered as it rang again. An age later I wrenched open the door and found myself face to face with Eoin. I staggered back, astounded and amazed.

We stared frozenly at each other for a long time. Eventually I motioned to him to come in. He looked utterly impassive, his face unreadable.

"What are you doing here?" I asked.

He closed the door behind him. "Maggie asked me to come. She rang last night in a bit of a state."

I leaned against the wall. "I don't know what she thought she was up to. I'd have managed."

"That's obvious," he said. "I can see you're in great shape." He helped me down to the kitchen. "Do a few press-ups. Give us a bit of a jig."

"I'm just a bit stiff," I said.

"Maggie felt you needed somebody. She was impressed by your bruises. I'm impressed by the Frankenstein walk."

Why did he have to turn up? How much better it would be to have Damien facing me. "Your whole family have been on the phone to me. You're lucky that I'm the only one who galloped over," he said. "Cup of tea?" he asked.

"I'd love a cup of tea," I said. I was parched.

"I always welcome a little drama in our lives," he said.

I let that pass. My body kept up its relentless campaign of pain. There were only degrees of discomfort.

"Tea's up," my husband said. "You look dire."

"Thanks very much. There are pain-killers in my bag in the bedroom at the top of the house. Would you get them for me?"

"Certainly, madam, my pleasure."

When he returned I swallowed the tablets. He sat on a chair very close beside me. I must have flinched or reacted in some way because he said, "This is a non-threatening situation," and moved the chair back.

I laughed. "You sound like somebody giving a day course, reassuring the victims before you psychoanalyse them to death."

"How are you?" he asked.

"Sore, very sore. I can't walk properly. I'm starving and I have a monumental headache."

He looked me up and down. "I'm surprised they let you out of hospital."

"Oh a nice nurse took pity on me and got me a taxi. She even got me a note for work."

"Still, it's odd that they discharged you."

"They weren't interested once nothing was broken."

He opened the fridge door and extracted the omelette. "*Voila.*" He grinned. "You needn't starve, said the prince." He served it to me on a plate and handed me a fork. "Delicious," I whispered. Although I thought I was ravenously hungry I had little appetite.

Afterwards, when I tried to stand up, he helped me to my feet. I clung to him. "Will I carry you?" he asked.

"No, no, I'm just very slow. Help me upstairs to the bathroom?"

"I'm at your command."

"You're always so glib," I complained.

"What way do you want me?"

"Oh, just sympathetic."

"I am sympathetic. I'd empathise if I could but, unfortunately, I've never had the pleasure of being knocked down by a car."

"I'll manage," I said at the bathroom door.

"Don't look so coy and don't lock the door in case you pass out."

"You might as well go off and pour yourself another cup of tea while you're waiting."

"I'll stick around and listen for crashing noises."

Everything was as painful and complicated as I'd feared but I managed to relieve my aching bladder, wash my hands and clean my teeth and felt infinitely better then.

As I emerged into the hall I felt stunningly weak. I was vaguely aware of Eoin catching me as I sagged into his arms. "It's bed for you," he said. "We'll do things the easy way." I felt him lift me, carry my creaking body up to my room and place me in my bed.

"I can't keep my eyes open," I apologised. "I have to sleep."

He tucked me in. As I fell into sleep I thought he said something.

Once I opened my eyes and saw him standing at the door. I smiled but he didn't respond. He seemed to be staring at me but not seeing me. I slipped back into sleep.

Hours later, it seemed, I woke in the dark and fumbled for the switch to my bedside lamp but sleep claimed me again.

When I woke up eventually in semi-darkness it was to catch him asleep on the chair, a blanket wrapped around him. I watched him. It was a long time since I'd seen him asleep. I thought of Damien and wondered where he was. Eoin opened his eyes and blinked, shuddered, shook himself, sat up straight, stretched and yawned. "Is the sleeping beauty hungry?" he asked.

"Starving."

"Wait here while I rustle up some breakfast."

He brought up a tray, backed me up against pillows and stayed to eat with me. We hardly spoke but it wasn't an oppressive silence. Once he glanced at me. "You look like a hen trying to lay an egg," he said.

"Cluck, cluck," I said.

"Oh, Maggie rang yesterday afternoon. I told her you were out for the count."

"What had she to say?"

"She was ringing from the house. They were heading out to the hospital for the removal. I gather things were pretty grim."

"How's Jean?"

"Almost demented. She was very attached to her brother. She's not coping at all."

"It's impossible to imagine what it must be like for her." After that we were quiet.

"It'll be difficult to get a flight back to Ireland at this time of year," he said. "They're heavily booked. We'll have to get something on standby."

"You don't have to worry about me."

"*Au contraire, mon amour*, it's one of the tasks Maggie set me. I'm to get you back to Mother Ireland."

"Well, I'm in no position to argue," I said.

"It's nice to have you biddable for once."

I remembered our previous encounter. "After the last time, I thought I'd never see you again," I said.

"Oh I heard you weren't yourself soon after that and I made allowances."

"That's big of you."

"Noble is the word you're looking for."

We were oddly at ease. Perhaps it was the strangeness of the occasion. We had to come to another room in another country to relax.

"What a Christmas this is going to be," he said that evening. He had bought a newspaper and, now and again, he read me out an article or an interesting letter.

"I'd like to avoid Christmas altogether," I said. "Christmas is all that family stuff. I didn't even think about buying presents."

The night closed in about us.

Chapter Eighteen

We sat in his car outside my parents' house. I felt like a fly on the edge of a spider's web. One false move and I'd be devoured. "Come in with me," I said.

We strolled up the long avenue. Walking was gradually becoming manageable, something that required less effort and concentration. I could just about walk without a limp. When I tired, I let the leg drag.

May opened the door. She stared at us. "You'd better come in," she said finally and walked down the hall into the kitchen. "We're in here."

I followed her down the shabby hallway and felt the sharp edge of dread twist in my chest.

"Surprise, surprise," May announced in that peculiarly flat way she speaks. I hurried into the kitchen.

Mother sat by the old range they had bought in the early days of their marriage. My father was eating his dinner at the kitchen table. He used to insist on taking his meals in the dining-room while his wife and family ate in the kitchen. They had never installed a central heating system. The chill of winter must have driven him back to the kitchen.

Mother gasped and stood up as May ushered us in. "I'll fetch more chairs," May said.

My mother approached us. "Sinéad . . . and Eoin," she said, "this is a surprise. Look, Dad, who's here!" She embraced us and held on to my hand.

Her eyes prompted me to speak. "Hello, Dad," I managed. "How're you?"

He chewed a mouthful of lamb chop, sipped from his glass of water and cogitated. "Well enough, all things considered," he said calmly. I broke away from my mother and planted a cool kiss on his forehead.

"Sit down, Sinéad," my mother said. "Rest yourself over here by the stove. You must be perished."

"I hear you nearly did perish," my father said. "How are you?"

"I'm fine really, still stiff and sore. I was lucky."

My father returned to the methodical demolition of his dinner. He looked thinner and paler than I remembered him. I noticed that he ate with a reluctant doggedness and ate very little . . . a small chop, one potato and some peas in gravy.

"He's getting his appetite back, thank God," my mother said. "He wasn't interested in eating for a long time."

"You'll have a cup of coffee," May said.

"They'll have their dinner," Mother said. She seemed genuinely pleased to see me. "When did you get back?"

"Yesterday. Eoin managed to get us a flight. I was sure we'd have to come by train and boat."

"It said on the radio that they'd a very stormy crossing last night," my father pronounced. "Give the visitors a glass of whiskey, Lizzy."

I stared at him in amazement. I'd never been offered a drink in that house before.

May brought the whiskeys in on a tray. She left a glass beside my father's place. "I thought you never drank, Dad?"

My mother smiled. "He takes the occasional glass now. It's supposed to help you avoid strokes and the doctor says it'll do him no harm at all."

"Everything in moderation," my father pronounced. He pushed his plate away from him. My mother jumped to her feet to remove it. That hadn't changed. "*Sláinte*," he said, lifting his glass.

"*Go mbeirimid beo ar an am seo arís,*" Eoin said. My mother beamed at him. She'd always liked Eoin.

We drank the whiskey in silence. I forced myself not to gulp it.

"Are you better now, Dad?" I asked.

"He has to go back to hospital for a check-up after Christmas, but he's greatly improved," May said. She finished her drink and began to scrub potatoes. She washed them under the tap and threw them into a saucepan.

"We won't stay," I protested. "It'll upset your routine."

"Nonsense," my mother said. "Of course you'll stay."

My father stood up. My mother bustled over to him and he leaned on her arm. This evidence of his frailty shocked me more than everything else. He hadn't ever relied on her before, had always gone his sullen way alone.

"The electric blanket is on," she said to him, "so the bed will be nice and warm."

My father faced me. "I take a little rest in the afternoon," he said. "You'll probably be gone when I come down again." I embraced him awkwardly.

"You'll see them over the Christmas," I heard my mother say as she helped him out to the hall. The door closed after them.

"He's changed," May said. "This illness really shook him. He hasn't been the same since."

"Yes," I said. "I can see that."

Eoin had been reasonably quiet since we had arrived. "He looks a lot older," he said.

May poured boiling water over the potatoes and put them on the stove. "It was very sudden," she said. "For a while we thought he was going to snuff it. He's a tough customer though. He pulled through."

"It's hard to believe. He was always so healthy. Those weekend walks up the mountains."

"Yes, always active, always used his bus pass. Poor Mother. Still, I bring her shopping once a week. That helps." My dour sister actually smiled.

"We're having bacon and cabbage. Dad won't touch salt meat now. He's taking good care of himself, trying to fend off heart attacks and strokes. It wouldn't surprise me if he became a vegetarian."

"I can't see that happening," I said.

She drained cabbage in the sink. "Nothing would surprise me now," she said. "He's become a bit of a hypochondriac. He's taken to reading books on health and diet. He's ranting and railing against red meat and dairy products."

"How're you?" I asked.

"It was tough when Dad was in hospital. Mam didn't like being on her own so I had to stay here at night for a while. Had to get up at the crack of dawn to dash home and make breakfast and lunches for the kids. These days I drop over in the mornings while the children are at school. He's much better and she isn't as flustered. This all happened when I was thinking of going back to work. I've had to put that on the long finger."

Our mother returned to the kitchen with a rolled money note in her hand. "Eoin, would you nip down to the supermarket and get a bottle of wine for the dinner? Get a cake or something sweet too."

"I'll pay for it," he said.

"Take the money," she said and pressed it into his hand.

"All right." He smiled. "Back soon."

"I'll come with you," I said.

"You stay put," my mother said. "You have to take it easy. I'm surrounded by invalids," she joked.

When he had gone she handed me another glass of whiskey. "To your good health!" she said. "Are you home for good?" she asked, as she pushed the cabbage down on top of the bacon.

"I'm home for Christmas."

She was silent. May sat in another chair and watched me. "I thought you'd given up all that London nonsense!" my mother snapped as she pressed the lid back on the saucepan.

"Nothing's settled," I said.

"It all seems very odd to me," she said.

"Eoin and I'll talk it out over the holidays. We're taking a cottage in Galway."

"That sounds like the most sensible thing you've done in years. I don't even know why you left him in the first place."

"He had some woman, didn't he?" May asked.

I glared at her but my mother took all my attention then.

She was pale. "Eoin had another woman. I don't believe it." She looked quite shocked.

"Didn't you know, Mother?" May asked. "Sinéad was the wronged wife."

"I'm sure there were faults on both sides," Mother said eventually.

"It's usually the man," May said. "It's the nature of the beast."

"It depends," Mother said.

"It really doesn't matter," I said. "We're the ones who'll have to sort it out."

"There's no denying that," Mother said. She threw a glance at May. "You should have kept your mouth shut!"

When Eoin returned with the wine the atmosphere was subdued. My mother put the bottle in the fridge.

The dinner tasted surprisingly good. I hadn't eaten a meal like it in a long while. The meat was moist, the cabbage tasty. The potatoes had a pleasing floury texture.

"Your Aunt Alice's trick with the muslin, it always works," my mother said when I complimented her on their flavour. "It dries them out."

"When are you and Eoin heading off to Galway?" May asked. I sat there tense, coiled like a spring.

"The day after Stephen's Day," I said.

"That's right. We're joining Maggie," Eoin said.

"That was dreadful, wasn't it? Her friend must be destroyed. I feel sorry for the poor parents," my mother said.

"What was that?" May asked.

"Oh, Maggie's friend . . . "

"Jean," supplied Eoin.

"Her brother was killed in a shotgun accident, messing

around with it with another young lad. It went off and he was killed. A terrible affair. I felt sick when I heard it."

May nodded. I could tell that the story affected her. Maybe she was thinking of her own children. She replenished our glasses.

"This is great. I hope you two make the right decision," my mother said to Eoin.

I met his ironic gaze. "I'm sure it'll all turn out for the best, Mam," I said.

She looked at me sternly. "I don't know what the world's coming to. When I got married you kept the bargain, good or bad. We didn't run out on our responsibilities. We stayed and made the best of things."

Across the table I met May's stare. Don't rock the boat, her look said.

A thought struck me. "Whatever happened to Auntie Sheila?" I asked. "We never hear of her."

"That trollop," my mother said. "She set up house with a married man. I haven't spoken to her in over twenty years."

No doubt I'd merit similar treatment if I absconded again. "I'm surprised you let me into the house, Mam," I said.

"You're not the first to go off like that and, I suppose, you won't be the last." She looked at Eoin. "We all have our crosses to bear."

Later, as we drove away, I said, "That was better than I expected."

"Yes, your father wasn't up to much and your mother was half afraid of you."

I scoffed. "I can't imagine her being afraid of anybody, least of all me."

"They're getting on," he said. "They're not invulnerable anymore. They've softened."

"Mellowed, you mean."

"Exactly." He put a hand on my knee. "Now I'm really looking forward to our Galway holiday."

I threw off his hand. "Sorry about that. I was under pressure."

"Actually I was going to offer to drive you and Maggie there. I fancy a few days away from the big smoke."

"Don't you have to work?"

"I have some holiday time due."

"I don't know what Maggie'll say."

"I've been told that I'll be very welcome."

"Nobody tells me anything," I said.

Chapter Nineteen

Eoin's hands were on the steering wheel. I was conscious of the practised movements of his feet on the pedals, the depression and release of controls and the hand foot coordination. Something like jealousy stung me as I watched his left hand push the gear lever into fifth. My own car, which lay rusting in the back alley behind our house, was in a bad way.

"I've never been to Leopardstown races, or any race meeting in fact," Maggie said. "It'd better be worth putting off the west of Ireland for."

"The west will always be there. This has novelty value," he said.

"I always think that horse-racing is a very masculine thing. I can't get excited about races and bets."

Eoin grinned. "They symbolise men's pursuit of women and success. You can't really understand Joyce's *Ulysses* unless you understand that."

"So women are always on the edge, is that what you're saying?"

"He's trying to rise you, Maggie," I said. "Don't let him. Don't give him a reaction."

"I can't," she said. "I don't know enough about racing to contradict him."

She sat in the back seat, stared out through the window, or looked at the roof of the car as though fascinated by the patterns that marked the plastic. I sat in the passenger seat with a folded newspaper on my knee. Once again it was a dull, chill day, like so many of those days, the sun lost to the earth, it seemed, forever.

"Did you send out many Christmas cards, Sinéad?" Maggie asked.

"Not a one," I answered.

"Very remiss of you," scolded Eoin. "Why not one to me?"

I clicked my tongue impatiently. In the driver's mirror I could see Maggie, her eyes closed as though she were deep in meditation. She looked exhausted. She had said nothing about her time in Jean's house.

"You didn't expect a card," I said to Eoin. "Cut out the teasing. It's one of your least endearing traits."

He flashed me one of his wicked grins. "And what does Madam find to be my most endearing traits?" he asked. "Do I have a ten out of ten quality?"

"Don't annoy me."

"But no Christmas card," he said, "no little gesture of tenderness or remembrance of times past?"

"I'm all out of gestures, Eoin," I said tiredly.

"I'm going to sleep, folks," Maggie announced. She stretched out on the back seat. "Wake me up when we get there," she said.

We saw a traffic jam ahead. He slowed the car and I looked across at him. "You didn't expect anything," I said.

"Of course I did. I got you a book." He leaned across me,

flipped open the glove compartment and extracted a small parcel. "There you are, wrapped up and all. I meant to give it to you yesterday."

"Damn you!" I said. "What did you do that for? I don't want it." I pushed it away.

"Take it," he said. "It's only a book."

"I don't like this situation any more than you do. It's worse when you go and play these games. Why not give presents to people who might want them? That mistress of yours probably has her tongue out for one."

He whistled. "Ouch! That's a bit venomous. My former mistress was good on the tongue work but reading was not one of her strong points."

"Former, current, future . . . what do I care? Leave me out of all this. Let's enjoy the races, have a few drinks and head off to Galway tomorrow."

"I'm all in favour of forgetting the past," he said. "I keep telling you that but you never hear me."

"I never will."

"Don't be like that," he said.

A fine drizzle was falling and he turned on the wipers. The car edged forward to close a gap in the line of traffic. "Can't you just let go?" I asked.

He sighed. "All right, we won't discuss it now," he said. The drizzle became a steady shower of rain. I rammed a cassette into the tape deck and the nasal tones of Elvis Costello cloaked our silence.

"I won't park too close to the race-course," he said. "We might leave before the last race." We joined the queue to the car-parks and were waved on. Umbrellas were up. People skipped in and out between cars, dodging impact, hurrying towards the stands. All the cars were mud-spattered. "Here's about right," he said and parked close to the edge of the track.

When we stopped Maggie sat up and stretched herself. She looked about her with jaded eyes. "Can we eat those sandwiches now?" she demanded. "I'm starving." It was only twelve o'clock but I was hungry too. The field was dark with people. This was only my second visit to Leopardstown races. The first was years before at a summer meeting with Eoin. In the reserve enclosure we treated ourselves to salmon, wine and strawberries. I remembered the taste of those strawberries. Eoin fed me his because I liked them so much.

"I suggest we eat in the bar," he said.

"Excellent idea. A pint would slip down beautifully. You never get a decent pint of Guinness in London." Maggie stretched again. "I'm stiff. I'll seize up if I don't move soon." She sounded cheerful. I risked a smile.

Eoin helped her out of the car. "Ever the gentleman, Eoin," she murmured. "I'm warning you I mightn't stick the pace. I'm whacked!"

"Well, there is the ancient and noble tradition of watching the races on the screen in the bar," he said.

I stumbled out. "You don't look too full of the joys of life," she observed.

"My leg's driving me mad. I can't sleep at night with it. It throbs all the time," I said.

"Maybe you should get it looked at again." She hoisted her umbrella and held it over me.

"You two must enter into the spirit of things," Eoin said. He closed the car boot and ran to catch up with us. "You'll have to place at least one bet each."

"I don't want to waste any money," I said.

He made a face at me. "Gamble some of this for me," he said, thrusting a tenner into my hand. He handed me a form sheet.

"I'm going to stick to the tote," Maggie announced. "That way I won't lose too much." She consulted her race card. "You'll have to help me out with this, Eoin," she said. "I haven't a notion about horses."

"We may as well do the jackpot," he said. "There's a big pool today."

"Ten or twenty thousand would suit me fine," Maggie smiled. "I could pay all my debts."

"Let's view the horses in the parade ring." He ushered us towards a large crowd.

We looked at the horses. "What's looking going to do for us?" Maggie asked. "I'm not the wiser for seeing them."

"What about the first race?" I asked.

"We could watch that from the bar," he said. "Come on."

"For which small mercy grateful thanks, O Lord," Maggie intoned.

"You all right?" Eoin asked as he steered me through the crowd. I nodded. We pushed into a little bar. Everybody seemed to be standing.

"Look what I've found," Maggie called out, indicating free chairs at a table. "Sit down quickly or we'll lose them."

Eoin went to buy the drinks. I looked about me and found myself staring into the incredulous eyes of my sister, Emer.

"Good God, Sinéad!" she exclaimed, "what are you doing here?"

"Maggie, this is Emer." I introduced them.

"Pleased to meet you." Maggie smiled.

"What're you doing here?" Emer demanded. She seemed to be in a state of shock.

"A day at the races," I said. In the distance I could see her awful husband with their three unruly children battling through the throng.

"Look what I've found," she said to him when he reached me.

"Look who you've found," I corrected.

He gasped and gawked at me. "I thought you were in hospital," he said.

"Not at all. I'm well on the road to recovery."

"Oh." He seemed to have lost the power of speech. That was a moment to savour, Jimmy bereft of words.

Emer spotted Eoin weaving his way back to us. "You're back with Eoin, Sinéad. Isn't that fantastic! But you never told us."

Eoin disappeared behind a group who pushed past him on their way out to the first race. "We're not back together," I said. I could sense Maggie's eyes on me.

Emer laughed. "Go away out of that. You can't expect me to believe you when I can see with my own two eyes what's going on. I suppose you wanted to surprise us all. Mam'll be thrilled."

"We're not back together," I insisted. "We just happen to be here today. That's all."

"Ah, Eoin." She smiled warmly at him. "Am I in your seat? Don't worry, I'm going." She stared at me, exasperation winning the day. "Your lady wife," she said, "is trying to make out that she isn't back with you. Isn't it just typical? Sinéad was always difficult."

He placed the drinks carefully on the table. It seemed that we were all stilled as we waited for him to speak, that he moved with extraordinary slowness and deliberation. Perhaps he spun out the moment, savoured the suspense and enjoyed being the focus of so much interest.

He straightened up, looked at Emer and smiled at her. "She's telling the truth. We're no more together than we were last September."

"Oh." Her jaw sagged. I saw Jimmy begin to edge away from us, dragging the reluctant children. I smelt their fascination with the possibility of conflict. I looked at the older boy, my godchild. His frosted, blond hair and his cool, blue eyes surprised me. I had forgotten what an attractive child he was. He smiled and raised a hand in greeting.

Emer gulped. "Excuse me, I thought . . . it was perfectly natural."

"Perfectly natural," I agreed. She stood up and backed away.

"Have you seen Mam?" she asked. Her voice had an edge to it.

"Sure. I called over a few days ago. Give her my best."

"I suppose there's no chance you'll get in touch with us," she snapped. "We were never good enough for you. We're going over to Mam and Dad for dinner tomorrow . . ."

"We're off to Galway in the morning," I interrupted and took up my pint.

When she had gone I passed Maggie her drink. "You were a bit hard on her," she said.

"Don't waste your sweetness on the desert air."

"You don't like your family much, do you?" she asked.

169

"Not much," I agreed. I opened the sandwich pack and distributed the sandwiches.

"She's not the worst, Sinéad," Eoin said.

"They leave you cold, don't they?" Maggie said. "Do you have any feelings for them?"

I shook my head. "Not really," I said.

"Sinéad won't forgive her family for the childhood she endured," Eoin muttered.

"That's not true," I rounded on him. "I'm doing my best to shake all that off."

"You can't let go," he said.

"Eoin thinks that some untapped devotion to my family lies buried deep in my soul," I explained. "He's quite fond of this theory but it's wrong."

"She reacts against them all the time. She loves to outrage them," he said.

"No. I was just unfortunate enough to be born into the wrong family."

"Weren't we all?" Maggie said. "Don't underestimate your feelings for them. You'll know what I mean when your parents die. Mine died a long time ago."

"You manage very well without them," I said.

She shook her head. " I do and I don't. I manage. My relationship with my father wasn't good. Even when he died, I was still trying to prove myself to him. I missed the boat with regard to love, turned opportunities down because I was greedy for other things." She laughed. "I wanted to be rated. I have all that now. I'm in demand but I don't have much else. Do you know what happened when Mammy died? I was in New York. It was my first production in the States. It was all a big wow and I went on a drinking binge after the first night. When I got back to the hotel there was a message for me to get in touch with home immediately. I went to bed to sleep off the drink. The next day I rang home. I'd missed the funeral by a day. They'd hung on for me but went ahead when I didn't get back to them. D'you know what I did then? I stayed on, reckoning that as I'd missed the funeral there was no point in going home. I can't believe all that now. Seems incredible. It haunts me. It's really weird when they die, Sinéad. You should make your peace with your parents."

"They're not bad people," Eoin said. "They just never had the knack for happiness."

"Just shut up about them," I snapped.

"See," he said. "You're just as rigid. Give them a chance."

"Ah, Eoin, can you see it? I go in to them and I say, 'I think we need to work on our relationship. I'll be a loving daughter and you stop telling me what to do with my life.' They'd think I was ready for the loony bin."

"They might surprise you," Maggie said.

"It'd be the first time then."

"Water wears away the stone," Maggie said.

"You're so wet," I said and we subsided into uneasy laughter.

"Finish up your pints. We'll watch the next race from the stands," Eoin said.

"Can't we stay here?" Maggie asked.

"You have to experience the thrill of the race, Maggie," I explained. She bit into a ham sandwich, remnant of the previous day's subdued Christmas dinner in our house. Eoin had dashed out on Christmas Eve and came back with smoked salmon, ham and a battered Christmas pudding from the local delicatessen. He and Maggie prepared the meal while I sipped wine and flicked through magazines in the front room.

"Come on," Eoin urged. "We have to get bets on." Outside a steamy drizzle trickled from the sky. We covered our heads and ran for the stand nearest the bar. My weakened leg dragged. Eoin dodged past us down the steps. "Back in a minute," he yelled.

"He's great," Maggie said.

"He's all right."

"Are you going to go back to him?" she asked, as if she didn't know the answer.

"Why ask?"

"You're always dodging the issue," she said. "You'll have to face it sometime." I watched the horses canter up to the starting point and looked at my race card. Fifteen runners.

"I'll face it if and when I'm ready."

"I think it's disgraceful. You string him along . . ."

"I do not!" I said. Heads turned in our direction.

She lowered her voice. "Of course you bloody do. I don't mind him coming to Galway with us – I've always liked Eoin – but you're sending out mixed signals. I'm sure he's reading all sorts of things into it. You should play straight with him."

I looked into her furious eyes and felt my own burn. "I don't feel obliged to do any such thing. He hasn't earned any entitlement to fair play."

"Oh, I see," she hissed. "It's the old revenge drama we're playing out here, an eye for an eye and a rotten tooth for a rotten tooth."

"I'm not playing out any role," I said. "He invited himself

along and you didn't veto it. If he chooses to read something into it, that's his problem."

"Why didn't you veto it if you didn't want him to come? God help any poor fool eejit enough to try to understand husband and wife. People are right when they say it's dangerous." She groaned. "You know, at your wedding, I'd have put money on you two having the marriage most likely to succeed. You had all the right ingredients. I could never have foreseen this. I don't know what games you're playing with each other. It's beyond me."

"People never knew what we were really like," I said.

"I just wish you'd get shut of each other altogether or make up. You're neither fish, flesh nor fowl now."

"These things are never neat," I said.

There was an ugly silence when she turned away. "Yes, break-ups are tough," she muttered. I felt she was remembering some bitter experience of her own.

"Have you been in touch with Jean?" I asked.

"Of course I have. She's in bits. What d'you expect?"

"How are her parents taking it?"

She sighed. "Badly, very badly. The father's old. Jean and Peter were all they had. I don't think they'll ever get over it."

"I keep on thinking about her," I said. "It must be horrific."

"Did you send her a card or letter?" she asked. I hated the way she asked this, hated her tone of voice.

"Not yet," I said. "I will, once the post offices open again."

A cold, sneering smile flickered over her lips. "You should know what's the done thing at this stage of your life," she said.

"Just in time," Eoin's voice said behind us. "I've placed our bets. Ours is number four, blue and yellow, yellow cap." He took out his binoculars.

"The white flag has been raised," the announcer's voice said over the PA.

"Want to look?" Eoin offered me the binoculars. I shook my head.

"They're off!" shouted the announcer.

"Who are we watching?" Maggie screamed.

Eoin pointed out a horse. "Third from the left," he shouted.

I watched the splurge of colours in the distance, heard the stampede of thudding hooves. The crowd was silent, straining to watch the horses, eyes on the race, steamy breath rising high in the air. The commentator's excited voice announced the winner as the horses scrambled past the winning post.

"Winner all right. Winner all right," he said after a while.

"What does he mean 'winner all right, winner all right'?" Maggie asked.

"They've weighed in. There's no dispute about the race."

"What happened ours?"

"Unplaced," he said.

"Damn! I wanted to win!"

I noticed a horse in front of the stand. His right hind leg dangled awkwardly.

"What's wrong?" I asked. Eoin looked through his binoculars.

"He's broken his leg," he said.

"Poor thing," Maggie said.

"Want to go back to the bar?" Eoin steered me down the

steps. I watched a veterinary ambulance drive up to the horse. They raised screens around about it.

"Wait," I said. "What's happening?" I asked. "What are they doing?"

"He has to be put down," he said. A shot rang out. After a long time the ambulance drove off and they took down the screens. "Poor bugger," Eoin said. "It was his first race."

"It isn't bloody fair," I shouted. I struggled to hold back tears.

"It can't be helped," Maggie said.

"I know it can't be helped. It's so awful. The poor bastard," I said. The drizzle stopped and, with rotten timing, the sun came out.

"You're really very odd," Maggie said. "You feel more for a horse than you do for people. It's a mystery to me."

Eoin came to my defence. "Sinéad's always had a soft spot for animals. I think we could all do with a drink after that," he said. We walked slowly in the direction of the bar.

Chapter Twenty

Close to a village, near a pebbled beach beside the dark sea, we found the cottage. "Sleeps eight," Maggie said, "so there's plenty of space."

The days were cold, wet and windy but the cottage was centrally heated. During the few daylight hours we went for long walks on the wet sand, and each night lit a blazing turf fire and drew up súgán chairs in front of it.

In the mornings I made for the wind-torn beach. For hours I watched waves roar and fling themselves dementedly against sand and rocks. It was exhilarating. I loved to be on my own, to feel the stinging wind on my face, stagger against its might, stand strong in the rain, fortressed against it by heavy raincoat and long Wellingtons.

The three of us shared the camaraderie of mealtimes and, sometimes, evenings in local pubs. During the day we were solitary.

I fell into a funny humour and imagined that we were all waiting for Jean to arrive. I hoped to walk in some day and find her sitting by the fire talking to Maggie. The more I thought about her, the more I convinced myself that she must come. I wanted to tell her how sorry I was about her brother's death. I started a letter to her, abandoned it and posted her a sympathy card.

I went to bed early and read for hours. Often I lay there and listened for sounds from the others. They sat in front of the fire until the early hours of the morning and, generally when I was on the point of falling asleep, I would hear them wish each other goodnight. This ease, this companionship between them excluded me. Maggie showed no further irritation with me. Eoin and she smiled pleasantly if I joined them, suspended their discussion or included me. If they were sitting by the fire, they drew their chairs apart and made room for me and Eoin fetched a chair from the kitchen table. I never once intercepted a knowing look or a shrug and never caught them talking about me. But I felt distanced from them.

This feeling began to vex me and I busied myself with domestic chores. I made beds, swept floors, washed up and dusted, emptied refuse sacks, shopped and did most of the cooking.

They were amused and bemused by this frenzy of activity. "You make me uneasy," Maggie said, "I feel you lurking about, ready to dust me down or put me in the dustbin. Relax. We're supposed to be on holidays."

"Eat, drink and take it easy," Eoin said. "We've only a few more days." He smiled at me and I choked down a strong feeling of irritation.

I couldn't stop. I saw how they suffered when I ironed their clothes or made their beds. "Stay out of my bedroom, I'll make my own bed," Maggie said.

As suddenly as this enthusiasm began, it abated. I bypassed the washing up and the cooking and this change found favour with them.

The shadow of Jean, the waiting for Jean, the thought of her brother's death clouded everything. The days became featureless and dreary like the weather outside.

"We're all very dismal," Eoin said one evening. I flicked through my book. Maggie looked up.

"I suppose we might be a bit more cheerful," she commented. She began to read again. I heard the creak of a chair as Eoin sat down.

I listened to the swish of pages being turned, the clock ticking on the wall, the gentle inhalations and exhalations of breath, an occasional sigh and the sound of a book being left down. The clock ticked. I became aware of my own breathing, the intake and expulsion of air. A log crackled and sparked in the fire and I watched the flames hiss at it and eat it.

"What on earth are you up to?" Maggie asked. I looked up to find them watching me.

"What do you mean?"

She threw her book on the floor, sat up straight and took a deep breath. "This," she said. "In." She took in some air. She held her breath. She exhaled. "Out." I had to smile. "I swear to God that's what you were doing," she said.

"You weren't practising Yoga by any chance?" Eoin asked. Their solicitous inquiries triggered an explosion of laughter in me. When I started, I found I couldn't stop. Eoin came over to stand by my chair.

"Sorry," I said when I could speak. "I know there's nothing to laugh at. I know it's not funny. Oh God." I felt a tremendous cathartic relief.

"You needed that." He grinned down at me.

"It should have been funny," I gasped.

"It nearly was," Maggie said. "You looked so solemn!"

"I wasn't aware of being so obvious. I became hyperconscious of us all sitting here quietly."

"I could sink a pint," Eoin said suddenly. "What about it?"

"I'm staying put," Maggie said.

"I'd like to go for a walk," I said.

"Put on your rain gear. We'll battle the elements."

Outside it was bitterly cold. Sharp needles of rain stung my face. We passed the houses on the boreen down to the strand. Eoin shouted something but I couldn't hear what he said. The sea surged wildly. It stormed over rocks and spray shot out from the crashing waves. Far out it was a breathtaking swirl of grey, green and black. It hit the beach with such force that it left behind a foaming white sludge on the sand along the line of water.

"I wish I could paint this," Eoin shouted. I nodded.

"It's wonderful!" I screamed. The sea drowned out all other sounds.

We made our way towards a cluster of tall rocks. I clambered on to a rock and perched there, buffeted by the combative wind, savouring the sea spray and licking the salt from my lips. I realised that he was behind me, close to me. He placed his hands on my shoulders as if balancing me. Then we picked our way back to the beach.

"Do you still hate Christmas?" he asked when we could hear each other again.

"Yes, I hate all the pressure to be cheerful."

He kicked a stone. "At least we escaped the craziness of the city," he said. "No mad rounds of visiting."

We paused at the turn in the boreen to look back down at the beach. Beyond that point it turned sharply and cut the sea from view. "Are things any better for you these days?" he asked.

"Not much. Nothing gives me pleasure. At least," I said, "we're not screaming at each other. That's an improvement."

"Yes, we're quite civil. It must be love."

I shook my head. "People don't change. I broke away from my parents but it didn't do any good. They taught me how to be unhappy. That's what I'm good at. You know the knack of being happy. I don't."

"You think it's all down to families."

"You learn everything from them and drag it through life with you."

"We're all flawed. I could live with flaws."

"I'm your well-trained domestic tyrant. I know all the tricks of fear. You don't want to live with that. You even told me you were afraid of me once. Do you remember? I was very hurt at the time."

"You can be pretty frightening. All that rage!"

"There you are."

"People overcome things. Change is part of life."

"I've thought it all out. I know me. I should have realised all this years ago. We should never have married. My tutor was right. I can't stay the course."

He swung me around to face him. "You're not on about that still! You don't really believe that what he said was true? He was way out of line."

"It's true."

"Oh, Sinéad," he said. "You've got to stop thinking like that. You're light years ahead of your parents. Don't you see that? In a million years they'd never see that they were behaving in a destructive fashion. They think it's the way things are. Recognising the problem is the first step."

"What's the good of knowing what we do if we can't stop it?"

"I believe in the next step," he said and suddenly pulled me to him. In the distance, over his shoulder, I saw the light in our cottage kitchen go on and saw a figure draw the curtains. I hadn't realised how dark it was. I pulled away.

"You're a good man, Eoin," I said. "You're better off without me."

He pulled me back. "Let's go to Galway tomorrow," he urged. I shook my head. "Come on," he said. "When were we last in the city? It's a great place."

"No strings," I warned.

"Word of honour. Just a day out," he promised.

Chapter Twenty-One

The pub was full of old men standing at the bar or sitting on high stools in front of the counter. Near me three of them crouched over a low table which held their drinks. From time to time one or other glanced across at me. I was the only woman in the pub.

The swishing, guttural Gaelic excluded me. They swilled words about their false-toothed mouths, contained them and swallowed them. My pint of lager seemed out of place in the sea of black stout. Crafty old eyes surveyed me. One old man poured a neat whiskey into his Guinness and swallowed the drink in a neat gulp. His collapsed mouth grimaced sourly.

As if attracted by a magnet, eyes swirled around and raked me. These were old men, village men, country men, I reminded myself. I wished that a stranger, any stranger, a woman, any woman would come in the door.

I sensed that assumptions were being made and judgements passed. Nicotine-stained hands cradled glasses while speculative eyes scanned me.

I was dressed in jeans, a multitude of jumpers, duffel coat and tall boots, a blotch of colour in all the darkness.

Some local men burst in and joined their elders. Slight

sneers twisted their lips. A youth started to stroll over towards me, thumbs in his jeans' front pockets, a swaggering nonchalance in his walk, but changed his mind and rejoined the men at the bar. I was relieved. There was something threatening in his stance.

Some local girls came in but they disappeared into a snug close to the bar.

An old man gave me an insolent, toothless grin on his way to the toilet. He threw a remark back to the others at the bar which raised raucous laughter. I outstared them all, fuelled by a burning anger and frustration. Still no sign of Maggie and Eoin.

Just then the door opened and a middle-aged, female head poked in, looked around, disappeared and then reappeared accompanied by the rest of its body and, lower down and on a lead, a Rottweiler. They strode confidently towards me.

"Mind if I join you?" she asked, throwing the words out. I nodded. She winked. It was a very reassuring wink. Her accent was difficult to place. It was either Anglo-Irish or English. She flung her hat on the seat beside me and shuddered.

"Absolutely rotten day. What're you having?"

"I'm fine."

"Nonsense. Keep me company for a while." She shook out her blond-grey locks.

"Páid, a Guinness for me and a pint of . . . Carlsberg . . . for my friend here. Bring it over."

The men at the bar muttered together. One of them spat on the floor. With a majestic indifference she ignored them and sat down beside me.

"Are you on your own?" she asked.

I nodded miserably. "Waiting for friends to turn up."

"Why didn't you go to the lounge up the road? This is a different sort of place, you know."

"I've been here before."

"Never on your own, I'd bet. Not a good idea to be unaccompanied here."

"You're on your own."

She patted her dog. "Rex here qualifies as company."

"I was just going to leave before you came. It was a bit scary."

"Even after twenty years I wouldn't venture in on my lonesome," she said.

"You live here?"

"Yah, got a little house a few miles up the road. We spend a lot of the year here."

"You know the place well then."

"Know what I need to know."

The Rottweiler nuzzled my hand. I started. Rottweilers make me nervous. She smiled. "He's absolutely safe. Won't do anything unless I order him to."

"He seems very fierce."

"He could tear you apart. He'd be more than a match for any of this lot." She jerked her head contemptuously at the crowd behind us.

"For a while there I was nearly afraid of them," I confided.

"Your instincts were dead-on. They're a primitive bunch."

"I thought they'd be more welcoming," I said. "They have the language, the music and the culture."

"That old chestnut!" She snorted. "Don't you believe it. They're as dark and mysterious here as you'll find in any city. Their lives are tough and they're tough too. They're cruel, without pity."

"If you think so little of them then why do you live here?"

"I've no illusions." She sat back. "Let's say I lost them." This was an extraordinary conversation. She leaned forward. "You don't believe me?"

"Well, it does seem harsh."

"Come here," she said quietly. She lowered her voice. "Sit in closer!"

I wondered if I was the prisoner of a bore, an eccentric, somebody avoided by others. But there was something compelling about her.

"Two years ago a group of English women bought a house on the outskirts of the village. They bought some land with the house and set up a commune. One of them had a daughter.

"The locals didn't like them. The women didn't fit in. They didn't attend church. They grew their own vegetables and kept some animals. They had very little to do with the local population. Occasionally they came in to buy newspapers or post letters. They kept to themselves.

"One night some of our brave boys here went up to the house, broke into it and raped all the women and the young girl. The fellows who did it broke furniture, destroyed the vegetable patch and killed the goats and hens. The guards sided with the locals and said that strangers did it, that the women had asked men in. They abandoned the place and went back to England."

She sank back in her seat as if exhausted from the telling. The brutality of the story jolted me. She was breathing heavily. "That's the sort of people these are," she said.

I stared at the men.

"I came in when I saw nobody with you," she said. "You're an outsider." I looked at her, half expecting to find traces of self-righteousness in her expression. The face I saw was full of desolation.

"I was away when it happened," she said. "The local schoolteacher told me about it. It shocked him." She laughed bitterly. "I suppose that's something, that it horrified a man from the place. Otherwise it never gets spoken about. It's never mentioned."

Still I couldn't speak. There was very little talk at the bar.

"How many women were there?" I croaked hoarsely.

"Four, and the girl."

"How old was she?"

"Fourteen. She went to school here."

"And they raped her too?"

"Yes."

I wanted to believe that this was some fantasy invented by her but I was convinced by her story. It had the ring of truth.

"It's hideous, horrible." In a way I hated her for shattering my illusions, resisted the idea of such pitiless cruelty.

A loud, coarse laugh from one of the men split the quiet of the pub. I saw her close her eyes as if in pain.

"Is it known who did it?"

Her lips barely moved. Like a terrible ventriloquist she said, "The tall one at the end of the bar. That young fellow with the cap. Those two sitting together. The two older men smoking pipes behind them. There's another one. He's not here. I dragged it out of the schoolmaster one night when he was drunk. I don't think he even remembers he told me."

She licked her stiffened lips, lowered her hand from her face. A muscle quivered in her cheek. "I can't point at them," she said. "They'd know what I was up to."

My face was burning. Her face was tense. I felt sick.

"I'm surprised you stay here," I said.

"Since that I haven't been able to rest easy. We're putting the house up for sale," she said. "We've been here twenty years but I've grown to hate the place."

There wasn't anything to say, anything that could be said.

"I appreciate the warning."

She drank her Guinness in one go. A terrible thirst overcame me and I followed her example. She stood up. "I must be off," she said. Wordlessly I stood up and followed her.

Out on the street I breathed in the cold air gratefully. We shook hands and she headed towards her Landrover with her fierce dog. She turned back and gave a little wave. I raised my arm but dropped it again.

The street was almost deserted. Two chattering women passed by. Their cheery normality was reassuring. I set off towards our cottage. I wanted to run but I forced myself to stroll along the street.

I looked back at the pub. Two men stood in the doorway. They began to follow in my direction. The day was darkening rapidly. I could see my breath smoking in the fading light. Stars winked down at me from the pale sky. Dark hedgerows shadowed the narrow little road.

The men were walking quickly. They were catching up on me. I couldn't decide whether to keep my pace or make a run for the cottage. The men came closer. I flinched. They overtook me.

"*Tá goimh ann,*" one grunted as they passed.

"*Tá,*" I said with relief. I felt weak with foolishness.

"There you are!" I heard Eoin's voice say. "You look like you've been turned to stone!"

"Rigor mortis," I said, and came back to life.

Chapter Twenty-Two

"Maggie's back at the cottage," Eoin said.

"What kept you two? I waited forever," I complained.

"It's a long story. We called into the hotel. She wanted to phone Jean. We had to wait ages for a phone."

"I suppose she didn't get a connection."

"Oh no, she got through all right. She'll probably tell you about it later."

"Bad news?"

"Don't know. She's hardly said a word since. She asked me to walk her back and then I came to find you."

We walked back to the cottage. When we reached it, I told him about the woman and her story. "A mysterious encounter," he said. "Still, it doesn't altogether surprise me."

"Why not?"

"Remember the time we got lost on that road that went on forever?" he said. "I wanted to park the car where the road ended and cut across the fields to the sea but you wouldn't let me leave it there. You had a thing about the people in one of the houses."

"Where they all came to the door and stared down at us. Funny lot. Made me uneasy," I said.

"You were right," he said. "I got chatting to a fellow in the pub the other day. Turns out he's from here, comes back on holidays. I was saying that we hadn't left the neurosis of the city behind. He got me to describe the place exactly. Turns out they're a well known criminal family. If we'd left the car, they'd have stripped it. The best bit is, he said that if we'd gone up to the house and asked them to keep an eye on it they'd have defended it to the death. Can you beat that? Your story reminded me."

I shivered. "I'm glad we're leaving."

"It's a fascinating place," he said. "I'd love to know how their minds work."

"We're more civilised."

He grinned. "Would you think so?"

"I think they're disgusting."

He threw a few sods of turf on the fire. "Imagine it," he said, "life pared down to essentials. No time for all that agonising we go on with. They're the survivalists."

"They're brutal and violent you mean. That story turned my stomach. I don't think I'll ever come back here."

"That's where we differ. I find them interesting. We cushion ourselves from reality. Whenever we come across it we're stunned. It repels us."

"You can't attack people just because they're strangers."

"Of course you won't if you're inhibited by the restraints of civilization. If we grew up here we'd be different. Sometimes I think we're over-refined. The old intellect has a lot to answer for."

"I hate to think what we'd be like without it."

He stared across at me. "We'd never get to that first step we were talking about the other day. We wouldn't be trying to reduce everything to sense."

"Oh." I sighed. "Back there again, are we?"

"Fair enough," he said. "Now I'm not going to let bottles of wine go to waste. I'm going to make the king of lasagnes tonight."

"If I lived here," I said, "the food and weather would get to me."

"It's a lonely place. The guts have been sucked out of it by emigration."

"I'd go mad."

"You probably would."

It was odd to be talking to Eoin in this fashion. I wondered if we were rehearsing for a future where we would be friends. I was beginning to like the idea that feelings could be closed down. I could put my life away, the way things get stored in a cupboard.

Maggie joined us that night. She looked pale and subdued. "I'm going to get drunk," she announced and poured herself a full glass of wine. "I don't want to have to think about anything." I didn't dare to question her. There was something fearsome about her.

After the meal she stared at her empty plate. "Whenever I need oblivion the fucking alcohol doesn't come through. If I wanted to stay sober, I'd be piddly-eyed by now," she said.

When Eoin went to take away her plate she grabbed his arm. "D'you know what, Eoin?" she said.

"No, I don't know, Maggie," he said. She held on to him.

"Jean's not coming back. She's not coming back to

191

London. She's going to get herself a job in Dublin to be nearer her parents. Isn't that a bugger?"

"How can she be sure she'll get a job?" I asked.

Maggie whirled around. "Search me," she said. "Says she's sussing out the job situation here. I think she's a bloody fool, a fucking eejit."

"Do you think she means it?" Eoin asked.

Maggie stared at him as if he had asked her a riddle. "How would I know?" She shrugged and poured out more wine. She filled the glass exactly to the brim. The wine spilt slightly as she lifted it to her mouth. "Bugger it all," she said. "Fuck it to hell!"

"Oh, Maggie," I said. Her head bobbed as if worked by strings. The Maggie I knew had always been in control of her drinking.

"She means it all right," Maggie said. "What it really means," – she put a hand on her heart – "I have no idea. I'll have to think about it. I have to work it out." She was about to cry. I hugged her but she shrugged me off. "I'm fine. I don't need comforting." Then she clutched my arm, her long nails digging into my flesh, marking and bruising it. She clung to me for a good while. "Sorry," she said abruptly and let go.

"We were always best friends, for years and years, ever since we first met up in London. When it really mattered, nobody else got in the way. She helped me and I helped her. I never thought she'd go away."

"Nothing lasts forever, Maggie," Eoin said. "You can't freeze time."

"Spare me the philosophy, Eoin. Please spare me that."

She stood up with difficulty. "You'll have to excuse me," she muttered. "All of a sudden I feel unwell." Swaying as she went, she walked towards her room.

"Check her out," Eoin said.

I knocked on her door. After a long while her voice said, "Come in, friend or foe." She was sprawled on the bed. When eventually she looked up she groaned. "Sinéad," she said. "Only Sinéad."

"It mightn't be as bad as it seems, Maggie. People often say wild things after bereavements. Jean could change her mind."

"She won't. I know her. She's given them a solemn promise. Fool. I bet she did it in a moment of weakness but they'll hold her to it. She's their sacrificial lamb."

"Some good'll come out of this, Maggie, you'll see."

"Whatever you have to say, I don't want to hear it," she said. Her eyes dared me to continue.

"Maybe it's all for the best."

"Cliché," she sneered. "Got any others?"

"Time will kill this."

"Give me a break, Sinéad. Go and leave me alone."

In the hall I leaned against her closed door. From inside the room I heard muttering and curses, the creak of bedsprings, the sound of a light switch, more creakings and finally silence. I crouched down to peer through the keyhole. Utter darkness met my eye. When I straightened up Eoin was standing behind me. I whirled about. He held out a glass of wine. I took a quick gulp. He beckoned me to follow him into the kitchen.

"She wasn't in a receptive mood," he said.

"She certainly didn't want to see me."

"You tried. That's all you can do. She'll be in better form tomorrow."

"I think she hates me," I said. "The way she looks at me." I edged over towards the fire.

"You hardly expected her to be reasonable. She was offloading some of that anger inside. You got in the firing line."

The wine tasted sharp on my tongue as though it had gone off. "I'm off to bed," I said.

He took my hand and wouldn't let me withdraw it. "She doesn't know what she's saying. She's drunk."

I wanted to cry. I wanted to drop my head on his shoulder. "She knows exactly what she's saying," I said. "The message is very clear."

He let go my hand. "Maybe not. Don't take everything at face value."

"Goodnight," I said. At the door of the kitchen I turned around. "Thanks," I said. I thought he moved towards me so I let myself out into the hall.

From Maggie's room I heard a gentle snoring. I hesitated. Should I peep in and check on her? The night was cold. I hoped she had pulled the bedclothes over her.

Chapter Twenty-Three

That night I groaned and tossed about in bed. I sat up, switched on the bedside light, got out, smoothed the wrinkled sheets, plumped up the pillows and got back in. Then I picked up Eoin's book, fingered a page but closed it again, turned off the light and lay there.

A dog barked and in the distance I heard men's voices. I pulled back the curtains and leaned out. I could see nothing. It was a moonless, wet night.

Maggie called out in her sleep and I thought I heard Eoin groan. The wind rattled the front door. The house creaked. I sighed in the dark, my heart sick with misery.

Then I dozed fitfully. The door of my room opened. Awake, but not properly awake, I sat up in alarm. My heart thudded. We'd locked the front door before coming to bed. "Maggie?" I whispered.

"It's me, Eoin." Surprise dried my mouth. "I want to come in," he said. I felt his hand touch my arm. He sat on the edge of the bed. I lay back. I wanted him to go away and I wanted him to stay.

He pushed back the bedclothes and came in beside me. He moved me so that his arm lay under my neck as it used to. His body felt cold. "I couldn't sleep," he said. He began to kiss and caress me. A panic that I mightn't be able to respond gripped me as his caresses became demanding. He kissed my mouth and neck. I felt his hot breath on my skin.

I pulled away. "Must sleep, I'm exhausted," I said. He ignored this and pulled me back to him with a sudden movement that was exciting. My body started to respond to the urgent rhythm of his needs. Still, something held me back. "Can't," I muttered.

"It'll be all right," he said. Like an unserviced machine my body took time to discover its own wishes. Then it seemed that the momentum of desire would become unstoppable. Who was this person? He was the man I had left.

"We can't," I panted after a while and tried to pull away.

"Why not? We've done it often enough before." He sounded bewildered.

It wasn't so important. I had always given it too much importance. "All right," I said.

He put on a condom and laughed. His laughter got caught up as he came into me. He shuddered and then I heard that harsh, frantic panting and felt my body jerked into spasms.

Later, as we lay together, he turned to me. "Where are you off to tomorrow?" he asked.

"London."

"Come back to Dublin."

"It wouldn't work."

"Give it a try."

"Can't."

"Christ, what's so difficult about it? Something has to be sorted out," he said.

"Not now."

"Jesus, you're an awful bloody woman to deal with," he muttered. "I don't know why I let you fob me off all the time." His fingers traced the outline of my breasts.

"Goodnight," I murmured. I was barely awake.

"Teaser," I heard him say as I drifted into sleep.

The following morning, when I woke and found him in the bed, I edged away from him. He was there. So what? I seemed to have remarkably few emotions about it. What had happened made no difference to anything.

I crawled over him on my way out to the bathroom. When I returned he was awake. He watched me as I got dressed. I pulled back the curtains. Drops of condensation ran down the steamy window pane.

"Sleep well?" he asked. I nodded. He moved restlessly in the bed.

"I'm going out for a while," I said and unhooked my coat from the door hanger. We looked at each other like tired, old warriors who had lost the stomach for fight. Finally he dropped his gaze.

On this last morning the rain had cleared and the sun shone fitfully through the coolness of the morning. It was always like that, I thought, tantalisingly calm with the promise of sun just when one was about to leave a place. From the door I looked at the drenched green grass, the glistening stone walls and the muddy boreen that led to the dark, sandy beach.

I had wanted to catch the beach in the early light, to

watch the sea in its brightness. Gulls hooted high in the air, their raucous screams shrill with greed. Cormorants perched on rocks or flew across the ocean, bellies close to the water. At the edge of the horizon dark clouds lurked, waiting to be blown in by westerly sea breezes. I smelt the strong salt in the air.

I felt a fondness for the place now that I was to leave. The wind had dried the rocks and I sat on one and flicked pebbles into the water. The tide lapped gently against the sand and the retreating water made a slurping sound as it dislodged small stones. Up on the main road I could see a tractor. The morning had a crisp, skittish perkiness about it, as if it felt better after a long illness.

Somebody was striding across the beach towards me. I recognised Maggie's bright green raincoat.

She stopped before she reached me, ignored my greeting and stared out to sea. I hoped there was no more bad news. I was tired of bad luck, bad news and terrible stories. "Morning," I tried again. She turned to look at me and something in her expression brought on that old familiar dip in my chest. I braced myself for whatever was coming.

She flung a stone into the water. It hit it a good distance out and skimmed the surface, and I gave a whistle of appreciation. She presented her profile to me and began to speak. "Right," she said, "I'm not going to shilly-shally or beat about the proverbial bush. Now that Jean has gone everything changes. It leaves you out in the cold for starters." I think I must have gasped. She gestured me to be quiet. "Don't stop me. I've got to say what's on my mind. If it hadn't been for Jean I'd have turfed you out long before. She always had greater reserves of tolerance than I had. She didn't mind listening to all that stuff about your parents, your marriage, your job and everything. Now that she's out of the picture, I'm not going to take up where she left off. I've had it with you. If you're going to end up on the streets or living rough, so be it. If you're going to make it, I don't care. I'm not going to be around to see it happen." She stopped and strode away to fling more stones into the water. When she returned she dug her hands into her pockets and glared at me, awaiting a response.

"I understand," I said. I was pleased that my voice didn't wobble. "You're clearing out the flotsam in your life, jettisoning the extra weight." I stopped then because I had to. I could say no more.

"You think I'm hard, don't you?" she asked. "I can see it in your face. You think that I've no compassion, no understanding of what you're going through. Maybe you hope that I'll reconsider. I won't, I'm telling you. No way." I noticed that the dark and distant clouds had dispersed.

"I've moved on, Sinéad," she continued. "That's the difference between us, isn't it? I know where I'm going and you haven't a notion of what you're doing. People can't support you all the time. You'll have to sort yourself out. Good old reality needs to get a foot in the door. You know that, don't you?"

"Of course," I managed to say. I thought she might hit me if I didn't say something. "I know what you're saying. I understand."

"Clever girl," she said but her voice had no venom in it. She looked tired and suddenly much older. She smiled suddenly.

"Oh I remember the good times," she said. "I remember

you at your best. That was when we were at college, another world." I couldn't look at her face, afraid of what I might see there, afraid of what she was building up to. She moved in close. "Get back to the person you were, Sinéad." I met her gaze reluctantly. "I have my own problems. I can't cope with you now. I'm sorry it came to this. Maybe when we're both sorted out you'll come and stay with me, wherever I'll be. Maybe sometime we'll laugh at today." She put her fingers to her temples in a distracted gesture. "I know, I know," she said, "I know you think I don't mean that."

Molten anger surged through me. Its pressure pulsed through my eardrums. I felt my head might burst under its force. For a while I couldn't speak. "I'll go and pack," I said eventually.

At the bend in the boreen I slid down the stone wall and sat on the wet grass. I could feel its chill dampness penetrate my jeans to my skin. I felt a tightness in my jaw. Bitch, I thought. You won't get me to cry. I unclenched my teeth and rubbed my tender jaw. "Oh Maggie," I said.

I don't remember much of the journey back to Dublin. Eoin tried one or two conversational gambits at the beginning but these met with no response. We shot through deserted villages and towns and there were few cars on the road.

We whizzed past outdated roadworks and detour signs. "Right turn here," I muttered at Kinnegad but no one heard me. Eoin drove like a madman or a man maddened.

We stopped at a pub in Templeogue because Maggie needed to go to the toilet. Eoin ordered drinks before I could stop him. We drank them in an atmosphere of sullen apathy. I glanced over at him and felt sorry for him. He looked defeated, like a sad child. We had barely spoken to him all day.

"I'm going to visit Aunt Moira for a while," I said.

He started. "I thought you were going to London."

"Change of plan. London's off."

"I'll send over your things," Maggie said.

"Mind if I have another drink?" he asked.

"I'll get it," Maggie said and went up to the bar.

Over, over, over, echoed in my brain. It's over.

"What a cheerful little company we are," he said.

"Indeed."

"Sinéad," he said. "Oh forget it," he said and turned away.

Chapter Twenty-Four

I poured tea from the pot on the old Aga range. The kitchen, heart of the house, contained countless childhood memories. I had danced, sung, recited verses, talked, argued, cried and eaten in this room. I fingered the solid, rather worn oak table. The big, old wall clock, half an hour fast, chimed. In a corner, on the floor beside the worn sideboard, lay a box. It contained a rejected offering, the new clock my mother had given Aunt Alice two Christmases before. Aunt Alice proved stubbornly fond of the old clock's eccentricities and ignored the gift.

"We really should put up your mother's clock," Aunt Moira said earlier that evening but, when we got out a chair and I stood up to take the old one down, I was stopped by a kick punch of nostalgia in my stomach. "You're right," she said. "We'll let the inheritors put up the new one." Honour satisfied, I dusted down the rich, walnut wood and the cracked glass face before I hopped down on the floor again.

I heard a light scratching sound as I washed up the teatime things and opened the door to let in Darcy, my aunt's black cat. He sprang into the kitchen and roped about my legs, pushed up against me, flexing and unflexing his claws and purred loud as a lawn-mower.

"In a moment, Darcy. Wait a while," I said as he mewed hungrily. His calls became more plaintive and demanding as I mixed up scraps of food with his cat food. "There you go," I said and laid his dish down. He untangled himself from my legs and darted over to the food. In Aunt Alice's time, Darcy had never been allowed in the house but Aunt Moira doted on him and spoilt him. He kept her company at night, she said. He would be her last cat. I returned to the main part of the kitchen and savoured the stillness. I had forgotten the utter quiet of the village.

I made my way down the hall to the parlour. From the window I could see if people were coming out from Saturday evening Mass. In the morning, to please Aunt Moira, I would sit through Father Guilfoyle's polished and condescending sermon, listen to the drone of the organ, the thin reedy voices of the children's choir and watch the processions of people up and down the aisle at communion. I would also see how much more of the church walls' damp paintwork had flaked away.

Across the street was Mrs Harrison's shop. She sat in grand isolation on her lofty perch behind the cash register reading a newspaper. She lifted her head and stared blindly in my direction.

When I saw her fold up her newspaper I glanced up at the church gates and saw shadowy forms move out on to the path. Mrs Harrison would catch a few late customers. They would come in looking for cigarettes, sweets, a tin of something or a pound of sugar. The light in the butcher's shop was also on.

A little later a figure passed the window and I heard the groan of the swollen front door, heard it drag across the floor tiles as Aunt Moira pushed it open. I met her as she made her way to the kitchen to hang up her coat on the back door. "You've cleared up, I see. Good girl. It was cold in the church tonight. Wrap up well in the morning." She drew a chair up to the Aga and settled down beside it. "The heating was hardly on."

"Were there many at Mass?"

"Not so many, mostly young people. They'll be off in the pubs tonight. What Mass are you going to in the morning?"

"Second, I suppose." She looked tired and I tried to look a little weary. "I put up the hot water bottles," I said.

"Pour us a little drop of the crater. I could do with something to warm me up. I was thinking we could get the bus into Cork on Tuesday. It's the day Father Duffy goes in so we might be lucky and get a lift back. I need a few things."

Later she said, "You'll have to call on people next week or there'll be complaints. That reminds me. I met Yvonne and she was asking after you. She wants you to call up during the week."

I sighed. "How is she?"

"Reasonable. She's expecting again. You know she had a miscarriage with the last one?"

"No." I knew what to say next. "When's this one due?"

"August. She had a lot of bleeding at first but things have settled down. Come on, pour us another glass. We'll be a long time dead. You were very mean with the first. I'll take mine up to bed with me and you may do as you please." This second drink was a surprise, further evidence of an easing of the strictly enforced rules of Aunt Alice's time.

Winter loosened its grip. There was a false spring. Everywhere the first thrust of growth could be seen. Snowdrops and crocuses nosed their way up from the earth and daffodil foliage had begun to sprout. I waited for a wily frost to nip in and shrivel up everything.

It was peaceful in the garden during the short afternoons. Aunt Moira went to her room for a read of the newspaper, a listen to the radio and a snooze, and I went out to the back of the house. Now and again a farmer tramped up the back laneway bringing cattle to another field and threw a greeting my way. Nobody stopped to interrogate me in the probing way of country people and I was left in the solitude of the blossoming garden.

One afternoon, as I repotted some of Aunt Moira's house plants in the garden shed, I heard a knock on the door. "Come in," I called and, to my surprise, Yvonne looked in.

"Are you busy?" she asked. I indicated the pots and fresh compost. "Your Aunt Moira said I'd find you out here. She says you're a terror for work these days."

The sight of her standing there awkwardly irritated me. She looked harassed and tired. I looked at this woman, this stranger. We weren't friends anymore. I wondered what still drove her to seek me out. "I was going to call up later this week," I said.

"You know you can call up anytime. You don't need an invitation. Why don't you come up for dinner next Thursday? Are you free?"

"Free as a bird unless Aunt Moira has something planned."

"You're looking well. How's Eoin?"

"He was fine last time I saw him. There, I've finished," I said, wiping off surplus clay from a pot. "You can help me bring these back to the kitchen and I'll make us a cup of tea. How are the children?"

"Grand. I find the young Tom a bit of a handful at times. He takes after his father's side of the family. I'm expecting again. Did your aunt tell you?"

I closed the door of the shed. "She mentioned it. Congratulations." I stretched my mouth into a smile. "You must be delighted."

"I suppose so," she said. Then she tried to smile. She had married the man she wanted and had his children. It was obvious that life had disappointed her but I didn't want to invite confidences. I disliked myself for that.

In the kitchen annex I stamped my feet vigorously on the mat. Aunt Moira would inspect the shed, the pots, my shoes and the floor when she came down later. "I was in the butcher's shop," Yvonne said, "so I thought I'd call."

"How's Tom?" I asked.

"Same as ever," she snapped. I wondered at the honesty of the reply.

"I suppose you're all kept busy on the farm."

"It'll be lambing season in a while but I won't be able to help."

"Why not?"

"Pregnant so I have to keep away from the animals."

"Are you hoping for a boy or a girl?"

"I'd be happy with either but Tom wants another boy. He says he's surrounded by women." I plugged in the kettle and she laid out cups, saucers and plates.

The taking of tea and cake was such a strained affair that

I wondered why I had offered her any, why she had accepted and why I would go up to their bungalow for dinner in a few day's time.

"Thursday." I smiled as we said goodbye at the door.

"Around five o'clock." She smiled tautly and left. As I washed up the tea things I felt quite cross with myself.

When I brought Aunt Moira's tea tray up, her fingers plucked at the sheets and she seemed out of sorts. "You never make the first move with Yvonne," she snapped when I put down her tray.

"I don't know why she bothers with me," I said. "We have nothing in common."

She smiled waspishly. "I talk to people that I've nothing in common with all the time. If I didn't, I'd never speak to a soul. Nothing in common with, indeed! You might as well go back to Dublin if you're going to ignore everybody."

She had broadcast my visit to a wide audience. Strangers stopped me in the street and said, "It's great for your aunt to have a bit of company" or, "She was so looking forward to your visit". An earlier than anticipated departure would give rise to comment. She might feel she had to make excuses which wouldn't be believed. This visit would have to be seen through. The time for running away was over.

Later as we sat in the kitchen and she knitted herself a new cardigan, I watched her. The festering silence between us was like a troublesome itch.

"How is it you never married, Aunt Moira?" I asked.

She looked up over her spectacles. In the glare of the light I could see that age was finally taking its course with her, creasing her fine skin and dropping folds from her chin. She was four years younger than Aunt Alice.

"If you must know I was never keen to marry when I was young. I always thought married women led awful lives. The men were dreadful. Of course now I'm not so sure I did the right thing. If I married I'd have children and that's the one thing I feel I missed out on."

"Was there ever anyone special for you?" I asked.

"A man?" Her knitting needles clicked away ferociously.

"Yes, a man."

"It's not as if it's any of your business, you know," she snapped. "But, if you have to know, I had two proposals in my life. One man was very keen to marry. I wasn't bad looking you know." I knew. I had seen old photographs of her in her twenties. "I can't say I wasn't tempted that once, but I don't regret turning him down. He married somebody else. That's the way it goes."

"Weren't you keen on the other man?"

"Oh, him." She snorted. "That was a flash in the pan. I brought him home and my mother wouldn't dream of letting me marry him and that was the end of that. She thought he was a ne'er-do-well. He was handsome though. He did quite well later on in life. As far as I know he's still alive. What's made you so curious all of a sudden?"

"I just wondered, that's all. Would you say you were happy?"

"What a daft question! I suppose I was. I never stopped to think about it. There's a lot of nonsense talked about happiness these days. We had nothing when we were young but we were happy. Now people have too much and it seems they're never satisfied. You make your decisions and you live by the consequences and that's that. Now, madam, we've had enough about that. I'm not going to satisfy you any further."

Darcy stretched out on my lap and yawned. I looked down at his clean, pink tongue and rubbed his belly. He arched back, closed his eyes and purred. "Get up and pour us out a drink," she said. "That's more your style than trying to ferret out other people's secrets when you're so tight-lipped about your own. Happy," she muttered. "That's a good one."

Chapter Twenty-Five

At breakfast one morning Aunt Moira fiddled with her teaspoon and coughed once or twice as if on the point of speaking. I was in a restless mood. "Today's forecast is good," I said.

"You should go for a walk after dinner," she said. "You're always moping about the house." I heard a letter plop in through the letter box.

"I might do that," I said and ran out to the hall. The letter I picked up had an English stamp. She snatched it impatiently from me and scrutinised the name and address.

"I don't recognise the handwriting," she said, ripped it open and began to read. Moments later I saw tears seep from her eyes. She mopped them furiously with a tissue. Her colour was up.

"What's wrong?" I asked.

"My friend, Gracie, is dead," she replied. "This letter's from her daughter. Gracie had a heart attack on Christmas Eve. Imagine, when I took down her Christmas card it was her last. I wondered why her New Year's letter hadn't arrived."

"Did I know her?"

"You never even met her. I knew her when I worked in Cork. We had such fun when we were girls, such fun. She married an Englishman and was widowed in the Second World War. Then she moved to Devon. Oh, we didn't see each other for about twenty years but we kept up a correspondence. She came here on a visit years ago." She took off her steamed glasses, wiped them with the edge of her apron and thrust the letter at me. "Here, you read it. I can't make out the rest."

I skimmed through the letter. "It was very sudden. Her daughter found her dead in her bed when she called around to collect her. She was due to have dinner with them on Christmas day."

"Still, it's a lovely way to go," Aunt Moira mused. "That's the way I want it to happen, suddenly, quickly. I'm glad she had an easy death. I'm always terrified of a lingering end. Your Aunt Alice suffered dreadfully before she went. Poor Gracie," she said. "Poor me," she added, "I've outlived all my friends."

I glanced at the letter. "There's something here, something about her mother never forgetting how you wouldn't let her give up in her darkest hour. Gracie always said your support kept her going. What's that all about?"

"Never you mind. Give me that back!" Aunt Moira snapped. "That's enough." She got to her feet. "Now, if you don't mind, I'm going to have a little lie-down. That news has made me feel a bit weak. Perhaps you'd get the dinner today." Clutching her glasses in one hand and the letter in the other, she left the kitchen and made her way down the hall. I heard her go up the stairs.

"Curiouser and curiouser," I said to Darcy who lay

stretched out on the floor, overcome by the heat from the Aga. "Even respectable old aunts have secrets from years ago but they're not telling." Darcy stirred and stretched out a languid paw.

I put out the bins. Monday was bin day. The travelling bank called every Wednesday and the travelling library called on Fridays. I joined the travelling library to satisfy Aunt Moira's craving for books. She was an avid reader of historical romances.

I would have to brave the butcher's shop where there was never any meat on show. Davy, the butcher, didn't believe in setting up a display. He was an abrupt man of few words and, if I found it difficult to deal with him, he found it easy to brush me aside. On the way down the street I rehearsed what I would say to him. "Show me a bit of bacon, Davy. Haven't you got anything a bit leaner than that? What have you got in the way of chops?" I steeled myself for a difficult encounter.

When I got back to the house I was clutching a fat piece of bacon which was leaner than the original piece Davy had offered me. "Your Aunt isn't too fond of lean," he said and that settled it as far as he was concerned.

I had paid for the meat. My stash of money was holding out well. I would make a withdrawal the next time we visited Cork. Aunt Moira refused to let me buy much. Aunt Alice's legacy was never mentioned.

That afternoon on my walk down by the river, a large grey car slowed down and stopped beside me. The driver wound down the window.

"It's a cold one for a walk, Sinéad," he said. I recognised

Yvonne's husband. To my surprise he smiled affably. "Can I give you a lift?" he asked. It was strange to watch him put away his grimness and see a lively man emerge. In their house, at mealtimes, he set up a challenging silence while Yvonne tried valiantly to keep a thin thread of conversation going.

"I can give you a lift anywhere you want to go."

"That's a bit reckless. What if I wanted to go to Donegal? I'm just out for a walk. I have to be back for tea."

"You might fancy a bit of company. We could have a drink in Casey's pub out near the monastery. You might as well get out while you're here."

I shook my head. He turned off the engine and winked up at me.

"I hear you've left your husband and that you've been gallivanting overseas."

"Goodness me, the wild rumours that circulate here," I said.

"There's been fierce speculation. You're the talk of the district."

"There's little enough to talk about, but I suppose there's a premium on news in a small place like this."

"You're not giving much away, are you?"

"Keep 'em guessing, I always say. Everyone needs a little mystery about them."

He leaned out the window. "Why don't you come out some night? We could have great times. You must be lonely down here. You wouldn't mind a little male company now, would you, a married woman and all?" A shiver of dislike for him rippled down my spine.

"You wouldn't be making improper suggestions to me, would you, Tom? I'm sure I misunderstood you."

He smiled coldly. "Get into the car and see how many suggestions I make. I'm very versatile."

"Goodbye, Tom. I'm sure you must be very busy," I managed to say. He started the engine of the car again.

"You're only dying for it, but you won't admit it. You're the same as anyone. You wouldn't say no to a good grope and a rough fuck in the back of a car, Miss Hoighty-Toighty."

"Go home to your wife, Tom."

"Much good that'll do me."

I was relieved when he drove off. I leaned against the wall of the bridge to catch my breath. The mix of lewdness and contempt in his attitude had shaken me. I couldn't imagine what Yvonne's encounters with this creature must be like.

Then a disturbing thought struck me. Perhaps Eoin cruised around Dublin like that. Perhaps he was also an exponent of the casual fuck and the furtive touch-up. I stared into the muddy depths of the river. There was no way of knowing what people got up to.

The following evening Tom turned a bland, impenetrable face to me. He was civil, inclined to banter. Yvonne looked relieved. She wouldn't feel the need to make up excuses for him. I wouldn't have to listen to what a hard time farmers had, how money was short and the banks were being unreasonable.

"How's the farming life these days?" I asked.

"Difficult, difficult," he said, "but then some of us have to earn a living."

"Goodness, earning a living," I smiled. "Yes, I remember that."

"What do you do to earn a crust now?" he asked. I saw Yvonne take a deep breath as she ladled out soup.

"Earn a few quid here and there, travel a bit. This is time out for me."

"Doesn't your husband keep you?" he needled.

"Goodness no, he never had to keep me. I kept him one year while he did exams so he owes me."

Abruptly he stood up. Yvonne threw an apprehensive look at him. "We've no wine on the table," he said. "The Dublin woman will be most unimpressed. Surely we have some wine in the house."

"I think there's a bottle in the parlour."

"Then get it, woman! It isn't often we have a guest."

He looked at me and I met his look. See how I make her jump, that look said.

Yvonne brought back a bottle of sweet German wine. I winced.

"Give me the opener, Yvonne. I used to be a wine waitress in my student days."

"That's a job for the man of the house I'd say," he said.

"I stand corrected," I said.

"You don't seem to have any man to do these things for you."

Yvonne shot me an agonised glance. My heart raced. I guessed she would pay for my boldness and kept quiet. He uncorked the bottle and filled my glass.

"Indeed," I said. "I do seem to have mislaid my husband. Rather careless of me. Cheers. *Sláinte*." I raised my glass and drank the sugary brew.

"What'll you do when you leave here?" Yvonne ventured.

"Return to Dublin and sort things out with Eoin."

"He should give you a good kick up the arse and knock some sense into you," Tom growled. Yvonne ladled casserole on to plates. "What's this?" he demanded, jabbing at it with his fork. "Stew?"

"There's plenty of meat in it," she said nervously.

He looked up. It was hard to read his expression. He could back off or he could destroy her little dinner. He looked across at me and winked. "Meat. Oh well, that's all right then. We'll let it pass. I don't go in for all this fancy stuff. I prefer plain food myself."

The children hadn't said a word. They cleared their plates without protest. They were taking in all of this, learning from it and recording it. Once their father had been a good-natured, good-humoured, gregarious man. Now he looked set to become the type of domestic tyrant his father had been.

It goes on and nobody learns anything, I thought, yea, until the next generation.

"I'm off to the village," he said after the meal. He smirked. "I'll leave you two to gossip."

"I expect Eoin would like to have you back again," Yvonne said as we sipped coffee later.

"I expect he would," I said. I drank my coffee under the unblinking stares of her children.

"You should call again before you go back," she said at the door. I smiled. The wind had sharpened. My ears ached with the cold by the time I reached the main street of the village. Outside Fennessey's pub I saw Tom's parked car. I looked up at Aunt Moira's room but there was no light in the window. I let myself into the darkened house, locked the door and tiptoed upstairs.

"Is that you, Sinéad?" she called. "Are you back?"

"Yes," I answered.

"Goodnight."

"Goodnight."

I threw myself on my bed. The village wasn't the serene place I had imagined.

Chapter Twenty-Six

Aunt Moira became sulky and withdrawn. Mealtimes were gloomy, fidgety affairs. Silence blanketed everything. I struggled to eat the food on my plate but it seemed I might choke on every bite. Aunt Moira pushed her food around as if being forced to eat an obnoxious dish.

It was a long, long time since she had used this tactic of silence on me. She was never one to slap a child but used to withdraw herself and radiate a distaste for whatever misdemeanour had been committed. It was almost as traumatic to experience this withdrawal now as it had been when I was a child.

In the evenings she took to her room, complaining that she felt tired. What had offended her so deeply? Perhaps I'd done something to annoy her, perhaps she wanted me to go, or perhaps she was sickening for something. That was the worst of it, trying to guess what was wrong.

The days before I left she was barely civil. I would have to face her down.

Nevertheless, I faltered when I stood outside her door one night. I heard the hum of a discussion on the radio and waited for music to end the programme.

She looked up when I went in. Her fingers froze on the page of the book she was reading. "I didn't hear you knock," she said.

"Aunt Moira, could I have a word, please?" She raised an eyebrow, noted the page of her book, closed it, turned off the radio and switched off her bedside lamp. She often lay in the dark and listened to the radio. Then she sat up in bed and took off her reading glasses. I rushed into speech, conscious that I might say nothing if I hesitated. "What's wrong?" I asked.

"What do you mean?"

"I get the feeling that you're unhappy about something."

"What gave you that idea?"

"I get the feeling that I've outstayed my welcome." The curtains rustled and I felt a cool breeze flutter through the open window. Aunt Moira's face was set. During the silence that followed I thought I'd burst with impatience.

"Sit on the bed," she said eventually. "There's no need to torment yourself," she said. "This last while hasn't been easy, what with your Aunt Alice's death, and now Gracie too. It's a dreadful feeling to be on your own. I'm really alone now. It's all getting me down." Impulsively, I covered her hand with mine.

"On top of that your mother's been writing me some awful letters, real stinkers some of them, telling me that I shouldn't have let you stay here, that it's wrong to come between husband and wife. We've nearly fallen out over it. She has very definite ideas about things and thinks she can order her big sister about. Mind you, if she imagines that she can tell me who I may have in my house, she has another think coming."

"Thanks for sticking up for me," I said.

"Don't get any wrong ideas, young lady," she said. "I only did it out of badness. Your mother isn't far wrong. You should be with your husband. In fact he always struck me as a decent sort."

"Oh, Aunt Moira," I said, "not you too."

"Don't Aunt Moira me, young woman and, yes, me too. I can't say I understand what you're up to and I can't say I approve, but you are family. It'd be a poor show if you couldn't stay here for a while."

"I'm going back to Dublin after this."

She cocked a sceptical eye at me. "Back to Eoin?"

"It's too early to say."

"Well I don't know what sort of a mess you two are in but it must be bad to throw up a good job and go gadding off to London. It would never have happened in my day."

"I dare say it wouldn't," I said, "but times are different."

"They must be," she sniffed, "when people give up on things so easily. I can't understand it. You shouldn't be looking for the sun, moon and stars. You should mind your marriage and try and mend it. I feel responsible in a way. If I hadn't given you an advance on your legacy you mightn't have been able to go that time."

I felt the gap of age and belief between us. "It'll work out fine, Aunt Moira. You'll see," I said.

"Time will tell," she said. "I hope you're right. It would be such a relief to me. You've no idea how much. Go downstairs and bring us up a drink. You're not here for long." She called me back. "And remember, my dear, don't ever get old. It's just too depressing and sad. Look at me," she said, "I'm not as spry as I was and the old memory's going.

Sometimes I can't keep track of things," she complained. "It worries me. It only takes one little thing . . . " she snapped her fingers, "and I could be gone, just like that, a case for the funny farm. Wouldn't it be awful if I went senile?"

"No danger of that," I replied, "you're as sharp as a fox. You don't miss much."

"Ah, Sinéad, I'm tired of this life. When you're old and alone it's dreadful. People shouldn't live so long."

"Go away out of that," I said. "You're, what is it, seventy-two years young? You'll be around for quite a while yet."

She waved me away. "Don't say that. I don't want to hear it. Off with you and get that whiskey." In the half light of shadows in the room her eyes glinted brightly. She gave a forced smile and closed her eyes. For a second she looked deathly and I really was afraid she would die. Then she opened her eyes again and I ran downstairs.

I opened the front door and looked out before I locked it. Down the street the butcher drew down the blinds in his shop window and locked the door. After a while the lights went out and the shop went dark. Mrs Harrison's shop was in darkness.

In the kitchen I took a slug of whiskey and refilled my glass before going back. Darcy stirred on a chair as I passed by. He stretched out his front paws and tucked them under his chin. He was the last of a long line of Ballycourt cats. I turned off the light and left him in the dark.

"Once," Aunt Moira said, "there were always things to do in this place. Somebody would go to the pump for water, people would talk in the street, neighbours called in to each other, men staggered home from the pubs or somebody cycled by. There was always time for a chat. Nowadays they're stuck inside in front of their televisions and they drive everywhere. There's no creamery, the market's gone, there's no hay gathering in the summer because all the farmers have that wretched silage, none of the young people want to stay on the farms. At times I wonder if I'm living in a ghost town. If I hadn't Mrs Deasy I don't know what I'd do for company. I don't know half the people in the village. It's not like the old days. Some of those young ones who work in Cork are only around at weekends and then there are the holiday homes. They're closed up all winter. It's a funny old life all right."

"Your mother's coming on a visit here next week," she said. I started. "She expects you might still be here."

"I'll miss her then, won't I?" I smiled. "Are you still upset over your friend's death?"

"That'll upset me for quite a while," she said. "Her life worked out well in the end but she had a sad history."

"Being widowed?"

"Well that I suppose," she said, "and something else." She sipped her drink thoughtfully. "I'll tell you," she said. "You're not a child any longer."

"You needn't if you don't want."

"It's not that I don't want," she said, "but that I don't want you to tell anyone. Still, you wouldn't know who to tell."

"Quiet as the grave," I promised.

"A lot of quiet graves about." She smiled. "Gracie was a great one for the men when she was young. They were all mad after her because she was so good-looking. Well, like a lot of attractive girls, she got into trouble. She wasn't the first and she certainly wasn't the last. She let some fellow seduce her and she got in the family way. Oh I know people are very blasé about that sort of thing nowadays but, in those days, a woman's life was ruined. I remember the state she was in."

"What did she do?"

"Well, she tried to lose it. She moved furniture, lifted heavy things, drank gin. She did all the things girls did then to get rid of babies. Her family disowned her, never had anything to do with her again. You were like a leper if something like that happened to you. In the end she went into a convent, a sort of workhouse, and had the baby there. You were treated like dirt in those places, a fallen woman, you see. To cut a long story short, she had the baby and it was given up for adoption. She didn't even see it. There was no question of keeping your baby then. They whisked it away. Afterwards she took off to London, met Basil and married him. He never knew anything about it. She told Bernadette, her daughter, a few years ago. Gracie never got over it."

"Isn't that strange?" I mused. "She never knew what became of the baby and it never knew anything about its mother."

"It was a boy," she said. "She came here once to try to trace him but the convent had closed down and she couldn't find any records. It had been a kind of orphanage as well. She could never be at ease about the adoption. She didn't even remember signing papers. It preyed on her mind dreadfully in later years. You know they've changed all those laws now and there's proper documentation but then it was something that was kept quiet. I always felt so sorry for her. Having an illegitimate child was worse than murder in those days. Gracie made a life for herself in England but not many had that chance. It's been on my mind the last few days. I wonder is that son dead or alive or what he's done with his life?"

"It could be that everything worked out and he was adopted by a good family."

"That's what she used to try and convince herself, but it tormented her that she never knew. I wish Alice were alive so I could talk to her. I really miss her."

I got us another drink. "To Gracie and Alice," I said and raised my glass.

She clinked her glass against mine. "Dear Alice," she said. "Poor, dear Alice. To Gracie too. God rest her soul and give her peace."

"Amen," I said.

Chapter Twenty-Seven

When the taxi dropped me off at the house, I saw it with a clarity that was almost unnerving. I felt a gut twist in my stomach. We had bought a dark, neglected house. "In need of modernisation" the auctioneer's blurb said and Eoin, temporarily rich after his father's death, had wanted to transform it. Eoin had always been the agent of our hopes, trying to impel us towards a kind of happiness.

"Promise me that you'll go back home," Aunt Moira had said. "You're to sort things out with Eoin. If I can tell your mother that I've sent you back to him then I'll be able to look her in the eye again." She extracted a reluctant promise from me. "You have to keep it now," she said, "or it'll be unlucky for you."

The taxi man pocketed his tip and drove off. I carried my case to the door. Back again. Not long ago that fragile coalition of Eoin, Maggie and I spent two days here. I opened the door and plonked my cases in the hall. Same as ever.

There was no sign of Eoin. My return to Dublin hadn't

sent telepathic vibes through his system, alerting him to my presence. He hadn't rushed to welcome me home.

Stagnant air hung heavy in the house. Everything was covered by a thin layer of dust. I gathered up post from the floor and flicked through envelopes, saw telephone, gas and electricity bills, letters from the bank and building society, advertising bumph and a postcard.

"Love and best wishes to Eoin from C."

I looked at the picture. C. was in New York. Who was C? Male, female, co-worker or friend? Did I care?

I felt a bleak relief. Being alone suited me much better than being with others. The fridge contained cheese, bread and milk. I sniffed the milk. It had gone off. Then I looked out at the garden and opened the back door. The grass showed little sign of growth but the hedge was in need of a trim. An overflowing dustbin was full of empty wine and beer bottles. I wondered if Eoin still lived here. My heart slowed at the idea of meeting him. The thought of that chilled the air and I shut the door against the world.

Days later, when the bins had been collected and emptied and the binmen had departed, I stared about me. Nobody had knocked on the door. No letters dropped in through the letterbox. Not once had the telephone rung or even tinkled. The world showed little interest in me. I searched the drinks cupboard but Eoin had cleared it out. I bought in beer, chilled it and drank it in the evenings.

One afternoon I lifted the telephone receiver and dialled Imelda's number. "Well, well, welcome back," she said. "You're a difficult woman to keep track of. What the hell have you been up to?"

"I'm back almost a week."

"It's great to hear from you. I'm just getting over a nasty dose of flu. Are you coming over?"

Imelda and Kevin lived in the suburbs west of the city, close to the Dublin mountains. "This is great," she said when she opened the door, "a bit of diversion." She coughed roughly. "I have a doctor's cert to the end of the week," she said as she ushered me into the living-room.

Her baby, a crawling creature, followed her about. I had forgotten about him and he was a surprise to me. She caught him to her and hugged him. "This is Martin. You've never met. Hold him," she said. "Isn't he gorgeous?" She thrust him into my arms and he dribbled on to my shoulder. I tried to unprise him from me. "Not a single tooth yet," she said. The child clung to me, pulled my hair and made cooing, gurgling noises. "See, he likes you," she smirked. Even I knew this mother's trick to charm the unwary and warm the unenthusiastic.

"He's a fine child," I said and she removed him, satisfied by this declaration. I saw that she couldn't imagine anybody unmoved by him. I could never understand women's obsession with babies. They were messy, smelly, noisy, wakeful and helpless. They demanded everything and gave back nothing. Where did Imelda find her reserves of love and tolerance for her child? I was sure I had no such feelings.

When she offered me coffee I tried to think of what I could say to her. "How's work?" I asked to forestall questions.

Her face tightened. "A pity you asked that," she said. "It's awful, absolutely dreadful."

"Tell me about it."

"It's good to be able to talk to somebody who knows something about it," she said. "Kevin says that all my troubles will be over in June. He reckons that wherever I am next September it's bound to be better than where I am now. He has no sympathy with me." She scooped the baby away from a large potted plant and sat him on her knee. He wriggled and protested and she set him back down on the floor.

"It must be very hard," I said.

"It's dire. You'd think that we'd all stick together but we've grown apart. The staffroom is really depressing these days. We're all jealous of the people who were redeployed last year. I miss everybody." She put a hand on my arm. "I miss you. Marianne, Constance and Fintan are gone. There are none of my old pals to talk to. Some people are terribly bitter. It's great to be sick and get away from it all." She laughed but it was a hollow laugh.

"What about Sister Ruth?" I asked. "How's she managing?"

"She isn't. She's not there. There's another nun, a Sister Mary, taking her place until after the Easter holidays. She's a right bitch, heart of stone."

"What happened Ruth?"

"We reckon that she cracked up under the strain. Very few of us were on civil terms with her."

"Why so?"

"What you'd expect. The kids blamed us for what happened and we passed the blame along the line. It was supposed to reach the source of the anger but it stopped at her. She couldn't take it."

"There wasn't much she could do," I said. "It was out of her hands."

"That's not the way some of us saw it. She should have stood her ground."

"They'd have pulled her out and put somebody else in her place."

"She let a lot of people down. After running the place for so long you'd imagine that she'd have made a protest of some sort."

I tried to see Sister Ruth's face in my mind's eye, but the picture I resurrected was blurred, out of focus. "Well," I said, "isn't she bound by a vow of obedience?"

"Bollox, Sinéad," she snarled. "She didn't do the right thing. She copped out."

"Well, she's paying for that now. Do you really hate her? You always got on so well with her."

"I just can't forgive her."

"Ah, you're asking too much. She couldn't step out of line after all those years of doing what she was told."

"Doing what you're told isn't half good enough, Sinéad." The baby crawled over to me, hauled himself to his feet and dribbled on my jeans. Imelda rescued me.

"Well, they got their way, didn't they?"

She shrugged, "They can hardly wait for us to be out of the place. It's crawling with fellows in suits surveying the grounds and measuring everything in sight."

"I'm glad I'm not there."

"You're lucky," she said. "It's awful. We're like prisoners waiting for an execution."

I shuddered. "I wouldn't have been able for that. Are you annoyed with me for bailing out?"

The baby chewed the rug. She sat beside me. "Not at all. You had your own troubles." She smiled at her baby. "Thank God he came along. He was so demanding that he took my mind off things. I'll be all right if I end up somewhere half-decent."

"How are the girls?"

She considered. "There are so few of them now. The better ones just about manage to keep their heads above water. Some can't handle it at all. They're completely soured."

She took her baby up for a rest. When she returned she poured us both a drink. She coughed her nasty cough. "I probably shouldn't drink. I'm still on antibiotics, but I'm not going to pass up a good excuse for a bit of a booze-up. Jesus, let's lighten up. Bring us up to date on your adventures. What have you been doing with yourself?"

"Very little."

"Come on," she urged. "I lost track of you that time you went to London. Your flatmates fobbed me off every time I rang, so I gave up. I want to hear about this nomadic life of yours."

I sighed. "It's not a success story."

"Stay for dinner. Tell me all about it while I chop up vegetables."

"It's not worth telling," I said. "Nothing much happened."

"I still want to hear about it."

"You're going to be disappointed."

"Into the kitchen," she ordered. "You talk and I'll cook."

Chapter Twenty-Eight

Imelda held her baby in her arms. "Mama," he said.
"Mama. Goo boy." She jiggled him on her hips.

"Say goodbye to Sinéad," she said.

He screamed joyfully. She inclined him towards me. I felt
a wet, sloppy kiss on my cheek.

"Look after yourself," she said anxiously, "and you're to
keep in touch, mind."

"Sure." Kevin hooted the car horn. "Got to go," I said. I
waved back at her. Kevin smiled in the manner of a man
who finds himself giving his wife's friend a lift into the city
centre. He was a giant of a man, a rugby player. Already his
powerful body was troubled by arthritis. The previous night
he had sung his heart out after a few drinks. Now we sat
uneasily beside each another, occasionally glancing at each
other and smiling awkward smiles. He hummed along with
the radio music, his fingers tapping the steering wheel at
traffic light stops.

"Traffic is desperate," he said.

I nodded. "I'd hate to work in town."

"I like town," he grinned. "Reminds me of my misspent
youth."

"Did you have one of those? Rugby players have a bit of a reputation."

"I don't play now. Reformed character and all of that."

"Don't tell me that you're into fidelity and domesticity." I smiled.

"Nothing like it," he said. "It beats everything else."

"Don't you miss the fleshpots?"

He looked straight at me. "It palls," he said. "Believe me you get tired of it."

When he dropped me off on the quays I imagined we each felt relief as we smiled goodbye. He kissed me on the cheek. "Keep in touch with Imelda," he said. "She likes you." He hooted as he drove away.

"You're a dark horse," Imelda had said the previous evening. "I couldn't imagine you even considering taking up with another man. So you never heard from Damien again?"

I shook my head. "Typical," she said.

"I thought that you'd be pleased I didn't stray."

"Not really. I always thought you needed to loosen up. If you'd a bit of a romp with somebody you might end up appreciating what you have in Eoin."

"God, virtue has no reward," I complained.

"Fear of Hell will get you to Heaven," she said, "but it's not the same thing as love of God."

"No more lectures," I said then.

By the time a bus arrived it was raining. When I got back to the house it was obvious that Eoin hadn't been near the place. Suddenly the idea of being there on my own seemed unbearable and I rushed out again. For a while I walked around without any clear idea of where to go. I ordered soup in the local pub and drank cups of coffee for a while. Finally I found myself on a bus to my parents' house.

"Oh, it's you," my mother said with the marked lack of enthusiasm that characterised her greetings. I stood in the shadow of her disregard. "You might as well come in. We're in the kitchen."

"Aren't you supposed to be in Ballycourt?" I asked.

"I had to cut the visit short. Himself got a chest infection and I thought I'd better come home. It's Sinéad," she said as we entered the kitchen. My father sat in the corner reading *The Irish Independent*, half-glasses perched on his nose.

"Hello Dad," I said. He raised his eyes from the newspaper and nodded.

"The kettle is on," my mother said. I realised that she had stopped putting colour in her hair. She looked years older than when I last saw her. For some reason this shocked me.

She noticed me looking at her. "Oh, I haven't had time to get it done recently. I've been so busy. Anyway, I suppose I'm not fooling anyone at my age." She passed a faltering hand over her hair. I was surprised to discover this vanity in her.

"How's Aunt Moira?" I asked.

"Not too good I'm afraid. She has a dose of the flu. She had to have the doctor while I was there. She's all right but she wasn't back to herself when I left." She gnawed her lower lip. "I don't like her being on her own in that house." My father put down his newspaper and cleared his throat.

"Hello Dad," I said again.

"It's unusual to see you in this neck of the woods," he said. "We're honoured, I'm sure."

Mother got straight to the point. "How's Eoin? Moira said you were going back to him."

"Fine. He's grand."

"You're back with him then?"

"I'm back in the house," I equivocated.

"Did he get that transfer to Brussels he put in for?"

There was a certain stale smell in the kitchen that I couldn't identify. I searched for an answer. "He hasn't heard yet," I said. My reply passed muster. I accepted the mug of coffee she offered and sipped its scalding hotness.

"I'll have a cup of tea," my father said. He was stuck to his chair like a fixture such as the cooker, fridge or stove. She filled a mug and handed it to him without comment.

"You may as well stay to eat since you're here," she said. I didn't imagine that she particularly wanted me there but guessed that she wanted to be able to say I had visited and stayed to tea. Outsiders would be told that a proper family occasion had taken place.

"May usually calls over today. The children are at their music so she'll be on her own." May was always held up as an example of what I should be like. I swallowed the strong, bitter coffee. She knew that I preferred weak tea and coffee but always made them strong. She used to say that I drank shamrock tea - three leaves of tea - her only assessment of me that might have passed for a family joke. "Dilute the coffee if you want," she said as if she read my thoughts. "You're here so seldom I forgot you like it weak."

"I think I'll go up now," my father announced when he had finished his drink. He held out his empty mug to her and she took it, placed it on the table and helped him to his feet. When I stood up to assist her she waved me away.

"I can manage," she said throwing me a baleful look. "I do it everyday on my own with nobody to help me." I sat down again. They shuffled slowly out of the kitchen leaving me with the coffee, the smell and the silence. The room was gloomy, slightly dank and stale, as though it needed to be aired.

When she returned she put on some eggs to boil. Egg sandwiches for tea I guessed. "How is he?" I asked.

"You have eyes in your head, haven't you? Can't you see how he is? You needn't pretend to be concerned. You've never been much interested in us." This I answered with my usual silence. I glanced up at the clock.

"Will I butter some bread?"

"I'd prefer to do that myself." There was acid in her voice. I felt that constriction in my chest as if a stone had lodged there and felt a weakness in my limbs. She cast a dark glance in my direction. I looked at the hard cast of her face. I had to struggle to drag oxygen into my lungs. I couldn't stay in the house a moment longer. "Do you need anything from the shops?" I asked.

"Why would I need anything from the shops?" she retorted. "I was down there this morning. What's wrong with you? Can't you bear to be in the place more than five minutes?"

"You say you don't need help."

"Help!" she snorted. "Fine help I'd get if I was to rely on you. I'm lucky that some of my children have a sense of what's due to their parents."

"And what is due to you?" I asked. I felt my voice break away from me, thin and reedy.

She buttered the bread fiercely and carelessly. "You'd know that if you knew anything, but I suppose you don't.

235

You're the oddest one out." There was some justice in what she said but I still felt the clawing need for air.

"I have to go to the post office before it closes. I need stamps," I said and ran into the hall. "I'll be back soon," I called out.

She followed me. "If you're going to the post office you can get me a stamp," she said and fumbled in her apron pocket for change, the way she did when I was a child.

"I'll buy it."

She threw some coins on the hall table. "Here's the money."

"I said I'll get it for you."

"Take it," she said. "We never got much out of you, so you needn't think you're doing us any big favour by buying a stamp."

"Certainly, if that's the way you want it." I picked up the money and her lips curved in a strange smile. At that moment I was certain I hated her. "Anything else I can get you?" She just looked at me.

I raced down the steep lane that sloped to the shopping centre, passed by the pub, a converted cinema, and resisted the temptation to run in.

In the post office queue a woman turned around to look at me. "Is it Sinéad?" she asked. I stared at this thin, old woman. "Don't you remember me?" she asked and I shook my head. "I'm Mrs Morris from next door." With a shock I recognised her. She had aged dramatically in the few years since I had seen her last. Although we shook hands and smiled at each other I could barely recognise the woman she had been from her features. "We never hear anything about you now," she said. That fitted. My mother only mentioned her successes. "What are you doing with yourself?"

"I'm home on a visit from London," I said. I wished that this woman would go away but I couldn't brush her off. I remembered too many kindnesses from her during my childhood. Her house had been a refuge where she fed me biscuits and fruit and let me feed her cats. She had sent me postcards from places she visited on her holidays and always gave me a little present on my birthday. I struggled to find some magical phrase of gratitude. "I'm really very glad to see you," I said.

An impatient official said "Next please" very loudly and she started. It was her turn.

"Drop in any time," she said as she passed me on her way out. "Give my best to your Mam."

While I was being served I fretted for fear she might be outside the post office waiting to walk me home. I wasn't in the humour to talk to anybody, least of all her. How had I forgotten this woman's thoughtful friendliness towards a lonely child? "Eaten bread is soon forgotten," my mother would have said. The girl behind the counter gave me a searching look when I remembered to take the stamp.

Outside I was relieved to find that she hadn't waited. I found myself crying. I went upstairs to the restaurant and ordered coffee and a bun. "You get your own coffee from the machine," a thin, surly girl informed me. The girl at the cash desk sighed when I offered her the exact amount as if I had offended her. The whole world seemed at odds with itself.

A woman and a child of about four sat in beside me. The mother laid out the things from the tray before them. She put an enormous jam doughnut in front of the child. "You'll never finish that, whatever you think," the mother said.

"I will. I'm a big girl." The woman glanced at me and smiled. I looked away.

"I'll cut it up," the mother said. The child nodded solemnly and I was surprised by her reasonableness. I wanted to hear the mother's voice rise, sharp with irritation. I wanted to witness a surreptitious slap from the mother. "You're a good girl," the woman said and patted the child's head. A pang of jealousy shot through me. None of us had ever experienced such tender gestures from our mother. I finished my coffee quickly. As I left the table the woman was wiping the child's jammy fingers. I prepared a non-committal smile but the woman didn't raise her head. She was intent on her task.

May offered to drive me home in her new, silver car. My mother insisted on dragging me out to admire it. "Donal gave it to her for Christmas. Isn't it great?"

May looked at the car as if it failed to please her in some way. "What happened to your car?" she asked.

"It's in the back laneway, at home."

"You'd better go in and say goodbye to your father," my mother said. I might have resisted this order but May stopped me with a look. Her eyes sent me messages all the time, guiding me through the labyrinth of our mother's expectations. May seemed lessened or diminished by life, as if contact with the world wasn't all that satisfactory.

In sleep my father looked like an old stranger. As I watched him I was reminded of the fifteen-year age-gap between him and my mother.

"I'll tell him he was asleep when you looked in on him," Mother said as I got into May's car. "I suppose we'll see you again sometime," she said to me through the open window.

"I'll pop over tomorrow," May said. "Give Dad my love."

"You're a glutton for punishment," I commented as we drove away. "Still, you seem to get on with them. They never have a good word for me."

"Ah, you know what they're like. They're easier to get on with since Dad's illness."

"You're very good to them."

"I'm not all that far away and I have time on my hands."

"You decided against going back to work?"

She grimaced. "Donal's job more or less decided it for me. He has to do a lot of entertaining and he wants me on tap for dinners, lunches and all that."

"The high life plus the bonus of a car. Not bad going," I said and hoped I didn't sound as insincere as I felt.

"That's the reward I get for being the good wife." She looked at me. "All things considered I'm exactly what everybody wants me to be."

I couldn't miss the edge to her voice. "I thought you were happy," I said. "I thought I was the only misery boots."

She laughed shortly. "You have rivals," she said. "Look, don't let them slot you into a neat little box or put you in a corner. You know what I mean."

I was confused by this show of support. "I can't make you out at all," I said. "You're the last person I would have expected this from."

"You were expecting the elder sister routine. Take two teaspoons of good advice and wash it down with some humbug. Well, you never really know other people, do you? Who'd ever think us sisters?"

"We're not exactly close."

"We could go for a drink," she said.

"I thought you didn't drink."

"Wrong again."

"Ah sure, why not?" I said, surprising myself.

She drove the car on. "We'll go to that grotty little place near you."

"How are the children?"

"Good in parts, like the curate's egg."

"I don't suppose," I said when the barman brought over our drinks, "you bring them up the way we were brought up?"

"You must be fucking joking. Exactly the reverse. Mind you, I can see the benefits of terrifying your kids. Mine can terrify me, they're so demanding, so articulate. I'm sometimes tempted to lash out." She sipped her drink. "But I always remember how I felt when Mammy lost the run of herself. I hold back."

"Maybe they won't be as fucked up as we were."

She laughed. "Ah, Sinéad, you're not still harbouring grudges, are you?"

"Of course I am."

"The statute of limitations on parental crimes expires when you're thirty, you know."

I smiled. "I got an extension."

Later she stopped the car at the top of my road and I hopped out. "That wasn't too bad, was it?" she said.

"No, we might try it again."

"Give me a ring," she said and drove off. I gave a brief wave.

Then, as our house came into view, my eyes were drawn to Eoin's car parked outside and suddenly I was full of nerves.

Chapter Twenty-Nine

The security lock was off. My key turned and the door opened. The house seemed extraordinarily quiet. I pushed open the living-room door but the room was empty. The kitchen door was slightly ajar and I advanced down the steps towards it.

By the window stood Eoin. He lifted a glass of red wine to his lips. I noticed a tall vase of flowers on the kitchen table, a profusion of daffodils and carnations. Propped against it was a large envelope addressed to me. "What the fuck is this?" I asked.

"Shouldn't 'Hello' or 'Nice to see you, Eoin' come first as a general rule of politeness?" he asked.

"Hello. What's all this?"

He pointed towards the envelope and watched me. That hypercritical gaze of his made me uneasy.

I picked up the card and discarded the envelope. "To my dear wife," I read, "on the occasion of our ninth wedding anniversary."

"You always complain that I never make gestures," he said.

I faced him. "You're drunk," I said. "I can smell it off you."

"Of course. I started long before you arrived." He indicated an empty wine bottle on the worktop. "Would you care to join me?" His words slid into one another.

I ignored the offer. "What would you have done if I hadn't come back?" I asked.

"Got stinky, rotten drunk." He grinned. "Don't you like the flowers?" he asked. "You always said you loved flowers." He smiled morosely. He was usually the reasonable one, the calm and rational face of our marriage. I resented this drunken idiot who grinned at me. I felt cold, almost icy.

"What's the meaning of all this?" I asked.

"It's our wedding anniversary tomorrow. Don't you remember?"

"It's nine years down the drain, isn't it? I don't see any cause for celebration." I wondered if this was some sort of vile joke, an elaborate mockery he had concocted to confuse and embarrass me.

"Don't be like that, wifeen," he murmured. My head pounded. I could hardly see. I clenched my fists and struggled to control myself, and all the time I was aware of his unwavering stare, aware of him waiting for my reaction.

He moved towards me and caught my arm. "Sinéad," he said in that horrible, slurred voice.

"Let me go," I said. I tried to pull away but he held me firmly. "I told you you're drunk. Leave me alone." His grip slackened and I pushed him away. "What's all this nonsense with the flowers?" I asked.

"A romantic gesture," he said. I caught up the vase of flowers and flung them at the sink. Even as it flew through the air I thought, Oh God, too extreme. The vase shattered against the wall tiles and the wet flowers spun through space. My fingers had a life of their own. They snatched the card, tore it up and dropped it in the bin. After that there was silence except for a dripping sound in the sink. When I looked up he was watching me. In that moment I really felt afraid of what I had done.

Then he looked down at the wet floor and the scattered flowers. He nodded very slowly to himself and looked up at me. "You've got an awful lot to answer for," he said quietly and left the room. I heard him stride up the stairs. Somehow this calm distaste was worse than any fit of anger.

Almost blindly I made my way into the living-room and sat on a chair. I wondered if I should follow him.

Not long after I heard movement from upstairs, doors being opened and shut and Eoin walking about. In a flash I realised what he was up to.

I ran upstairs. He was packing shirts and the last of his suits. He looked up when I came in and continued with the packing. He went to a drawer, extracted some ties and flung them on the bed.

"Please don't go," I said.

"Listen to yourself," he said. "Do you ever listen to yourself? You fling everything in my face and then you have the nerve to ask me not to go. You despise me. I've had it. There has to be a resolution. It looks like this is going to be it."

"I'm sorry about the flowers," I cried.

"Sorry, are you? I wonder about that. This has been going on a long time, hasn't it? Almost from the beginning of our marriage. Are you sorry about all the scenes and rejections? Are you sorry about the nights when you couldn't bear to let me touch you? I'll bet you'll say you are, that you really care for me – you can never quite bring yourself to say the word love – and that you want to start again. I'm sick to death of false starts and empty promises. Everything has its own logic you know. The logic of this situation is that we're all washed up." He closed the suitcase, drew the zips together. "Do you know why you married me?" he asked. He didn't seem to want an answer. "You married me because I was completely different from your family and you wanted to get away from them. You thought you wanted love and affection and understanding but you don't. You're as twisted and warped as that family of yours. You've no idea what love is." He put the suitcases on the floor. "You're addicted to conflict. You can't live without it. You need the buzz. I'm not like that."

"Eoin, please!"

He looked at me coldly. "What are we going to get now, the old 'I can't cope' routine, the 'can't we talk about it?' line? Don't you think you've put me through the mill often enough, Sinéad? Isn't it time we called it a day? I've got only one life and I'm not going to spend it fighting pathological battles with you. Face it. You're sick. You need help."

"Don't Eoin. Don't say those things," I begged. "Please stay. I'll change. I will try." Our eyes locked. In his I saw the pity that one might feel for a stranger. I heard a sort of choking sound and realised that it was me. "I'm going to get sick," I said and ran to the bathroom.

"Keep your head down," I heard him say behind me and felt him push my head into the toilet bowl.

"He's going to kill me," I thought as I retched and vomited. "So much the better." Eventually the nausea subsided and I sat up on the floor. He wiped my face with toilet paper.

"I should kill myself," I said. "Everybody would be better off." He helped me to my feet.

"You're very pale," he said. "Do you think you could manage a drink?

"Oh Jesus," I moaned. "I wish I were dead. Everything is completely fucked up."

"Downstairs. I think we'll go down to the kitchen." His calm voice guided me to the kitchen. He sat me down on a chair. "Swallow this," he said and I saw that he was offering me a neat whiskey. I coughed at the shock of its bitterness, then felt slightly better.

He faced me across the table. He looked infinitely tired. "Poor Eoin," I smiled. "You'll be much better off without me." I thought he tensed when I said that. His eyes refused to meet mine. "You should go now," I said, "before I do something like attack you."

"You've done that before."

"Strange, isn't it? I don't understand why I lash out at you."

"Because you hate me."

"No. No. I never hate you. If I were capable of it, I'd love you. I don't feel real. Other people feel real to themselves. Why can't I be just bloody ordinary?"

"Don't know." He sounded weary and uninterested.

"Do you really think I need help, Eoin?" I asked. I was desperate to hold his attention. When he judged the time to be right he would get up and go.

He sighed. I thought he mightn't bother to answer me. He looked dreadful, drained of all emotion. "You know I think that," he said. "I've said it before. Look, I haven't the energy to hop back on this merry-go-round. It's the same old story, again and again and again. Right now I don't see much that can be salvaged. I want to move on."

That was it. I tumbled into the pit. "Then move. Go. Go on," I said faintly. It seemed that he would never budge. When he finally moved he went upstairs to fetch his suitcase and I heard the slam of the front door. I threw myself on the floor, felt it wet beneath me. Something brushed against my face. I looked up. A broken daffodil had entangled itself in my hair.

One morning, exhausted by tears, I decided to visit the doctor. I would tell him that my husband had left me, that I couldn't sleep, that I needed pills, that I had to sleep. Maybe, with sleep, the days wouldn't be so unendurable, the nights so horrible. Perhaps, if I couldn't go on, I could hoard the tablets, store them for the day when I'd have the courage to use them.

The waiting room was full of people who coughed, spluttered, moaned and complained. I almost left at the sight of so much illness. A mother held a flushed baby with a horrible wheeze to her. I saw the fear in her eyes as she pressed the crying thing to her. I recognised that fear.

The doctor was resolutely cheerful as he called out people's names. The receptionist handed him files. My file looked pristine, almost untouched. I had visited him a few times for heavy colds and chest infections. The waiting room looked out on to the back garden of the house. I saw crocuses poking their heads up through the sodden earth. How tiresome, I thought. When my name was called I thought I might run out of the surgery.

I followed him into his consulting room and tried to hold my head up. I wanted to seem perky, a little under strain perhaps, finding life difficult. Hopeful. I had to seem hopeful.

I finished my story and looked up. He didn't seem to be paying any attention to me. He glanced out through the venetian blinds at the road where cars whizzed by. I could see their lights and hear the swish of their tyres through the sounds of the rain. "It's a filthy day," he said. He closed the blinds. "And what is it that you want from me?" he asked.

"I think I need something to help me sleep. I just can't get off at night. I think it's the strain of everything." I willed my voice to sound reasonable and controlled.

He looked down at my chart. "What do you do?" he asked. I hardly knew the man. He was a stranger. "Oh yes, you're a teacher."

"I'm on a career break," I volunteered.

"That place is closing down, isn't it?"

I agreed with him. He was taking so long over everything. I'd better humour him, I thought. What a fool!

"Tell me about that," he said. I sighed and rattled off something. "Tell me about your husband again." Really, the man was brain dead, incapable of absorbing straightforward details. I tried to keep my irritation under control. I had a sudden fear that he would dismiss me and tell me that I was fine, that I'd be able to sleep once the initial trauma of the break-up had subsided.

"It's just a little hump that I have to get over," I said. I was running out of energy. I felt tired to the point of sickness. The clock on the mantelpiece ticked. I had no idea what time it was or how long I sat there.

After a long while he spoke. "You sound terribly depressed to me," he said. "Everything you say leads me to believe that you have a serious problem." After the shock of hearing this I found that I couldn't stop crying.

He handed me a tissue and I dried my face with it. The surgery light caught the glass of one of the framed certificates on his wall. I read my swollen and blotchy reflection there.

"You must be honest with me," he said. "You have to decide whether you want the problem or the solution. Let's start again."

Chapter Thirty

"It's well for some," Marianne called from the door of the pub. "Tearing off to London and wandering about the countryside. Some of us have to work for a living!"

"If I catch you in this establishment again I'll have you thrown out," Imelda called after her.

"People like you lower the tone of places," Marianne shot back. "It's a wonder they let you in at all."

"They recognise quality when they see it. Riff-raff like you need to be kept in their place."

"Bye!" Marianne called out. "Great to see you, Sinéad."

Imelda sat back. "Sorry about that," she said. "I never expected to meet her here."

"It was fine. I didn't mind. It's nice to know how people are getting on."

"Marianne's doing well. She likes her new school. Did you hear what happened George? The place he was sent to is going to close down too! He's taking a career break, says he's getting out of teaching."

"Close down?"

"Ah, it's only starting. It's happening all over the country. Falling population."

"Poor George."

"Pity really. He's really good in the classroom, has the kids in the palm of his hand. Says he doesn't want to spend the rest of his life working in places that are for the chop. Well, where were we," she said, "before we were interrupted?"

"I can't tell you much. I've been to only three sessions."

"You're doing the right thing. I think we could all go to a psychiatrist at times. I don't understand why there's such a hoo ha about these things. What's your woman like anyway?"

"A person," I answered. I resisted the sharing of heart's secrets, the bonding of souls. Her eyes pricked me into effort. "The first session was just information gathering. We went through everything you'd expect - parents, brothers, sisters, childhood, schooling, relationships, friendships, work and my sense of self. She sits behind a desk and I sit in front of it. I feel so stupid telling you this," I said.

"Why should you? My sister's been through it. As long as I've known you I always thought you were unhappy. I could be doing the same thing myself some day."

"There are no guarantees," I said. "It may not work."

"I'm sure it will. I think that you're really brave to have gone in the first place. I don't know if I'd have had the nerve."

"Well, I don't know if I'll keep it up. I'm supposed to sort myself out." I laughed. "That kind of annoyed me. I thought she'd do all that. First she says that she has to decide what has made me dysfunctional. I might have a tendency to be that way or it might be a combination of events that sent me over the edge."

"Is it easier to talk to a woman?" Imelda asked.

"I don't think it matters. You just need somebody who's good at their job."

"So will you be trotting off to your analyst every week like the Americans?"

"That's the good thing about it. I haven't signed up for life. When I'm functional she'll give me my marching orders. None of this going over the past again and again and again, which is a great relief. That's over and done with and can't be changed. I'm supposed to look to the future."

"You know what they say, Sinéad?" she said.

"No. What do they say?"

She grinned. "The future works!"

"Spare me," I groaned. "I have to read this book. It's all about thinking processes. I go to a psychiatrist because I can't read books anymore and what does she do? Gives me a book to read!"

"Do you feel that you're getting somewhere?" she asked.

"I do and I don't." I drank a little wine from my glass. She sipped some of her soup. "I resist her a lot. I gave out to her last week. I'm afraid I'll lose control in front of her."

Imelda threw her eyes heavenwards. "I wouldn't worry about that. I'm sure that she's well used to people having all sorts of reactions. If you have to have a good old cry, I'd say go ahead. It's your money."

"Well, actually it's Eoin's money. He said he'd pay when I threatened to give up after the first session."

"Jesus, how's Eoin taking all this? Are you two dealing with each other?"

"Sort of. He calls over. He's staying with his mother. He's interested in what's going on, but he hasn't committed himself one way or the other. Yer woman wants him to come along to the next session and he's agreed to that."

"That's progress, isn't it? It's an advance on a total break-up."

"Take it easy, Imelda. No banner headlines yet. I've had so many false starts that I'm afraid to think of this as the magic solution."

"My doctor says half the world is cracked," she said. "I don't know how most people stay sane. I think it's a miracle."

"Well, there you are. I didn't stay completely sane."

"Shush. It isn't as if there's a black mark against you. You lost the balance. You'll even out. You'll see."

"The eternal optimist, eh Imelda? You never give up."

"If I ever gave up I'd be dead."

I nodded. "That's the way I was. Dead. I couldn't seem to feel things."

"See. Already you're staging your resurrection. You'll get there."

"That's what the psychiatrist says. One day I'll be better but it'll take a good while."

Imelda looked at her watch. "Jesus, talking of time, look at the time. I'll have to make a run for it. I have a class in ten minutes. You don't want to come back to see the place, do you?"

I stiffened and shivered. "No thanks. I don't think I could face it. I might come down after Easter."

"Whatever you feel able for." She stood up. "You'll have to come to the final, final farewell party. We're inviting everybody we can think of. We're going to hire a room and get caterers in." She smiled. Her eyes were moist. In that moment I knew why I considered her a friend. "Awful, isn't it, but you must come." She clasped my hand.

"I will," I said. "That's a promise." We hugged.

"That's the spirit," she smiled. "We'll go down fighting."

"See you soon."

"Ring me after your next session," she urged. "Keep in touch. Remember to keep the faith."

When she had gone I ordered another wine and a dessert. The girl brought me apple tart and I sat back in my seat and thought about Eoin. We had met the day before, gone to a film and then for a pizza. We had been extraordinarily polite to each other, aware of the fragile nature of our truce. He was the person who knew most about me so, in an odd way, he was the person who could best understand what was happening to me. He asked questions and we mulled over the therapy. It was enough to be going on with.

I opened my bag and looked at the prescription I had carried about with me for days. Antidepressants. The word sent a shiver through me. A mild dose she had said. She had to see me undepressed, normal. I feared those chemicals. How would they change me? How much control would they leave me?

"Take the damn things," Eoin had said impatiently, tired of my agonised indecision. "You won't be on them forever. Come on, take the medicine."

Between a rock and a hard place. Was that what they said? Other people were begging to be given drugs. Why was I so frightened of them? I folded the indecipherable prescription and put it away. Only slightly off the wall. Most of the time I pass for normal, I thought. I pondered Imelda's last throwaway remark. Keep the faith with myself I supposed she meant. I would emerge from the valley of darkness. Yes I would! I closed my eyes. When I opened them again I was looking into familiar eyes.

"How're ye doin'? Still drinkin' red wine." Stunned into silence, I looked up at Damien. "A woman of few words I see," he said.

"I'm amazed," I said.

"So it would appear."

"What are you doing here?"

"I could ask ye the same question, couldn't I? I thought ye were in London."

"No. What are you doing here? I've never seen you here before."

"I was with some people, They've gone now. I spotted ye when I was goin' to the jacks."

"I'm dumbfounded." It was as if years had passed since I last saw him.

"Ye never turned up." It was almost as if he were speaking of another person, another life.

"There was an accident. I got knocked down."

He smiled grimly. "Ye don't have to give some dramatic excuse. All ye had to do was phone to say that ye'd changed yer mind, or that ye'd decided not to come. Ye could have done that much."

"I was in casualty. When I got out it was too late. You were gone and there was no way of contacting you."

"Jean knew my address." I explained about Jean. "Murphy's law," he said. "Ye could have written to me care of the publishers," he said.

"I never thought of that," I had to admit. "It never

occurred to me. What would you call that? A failure of imagination?"

"A failure of some sort," he said. "I suppose that it wasn't meant to be."

"I suppose not." I couldn't understand what his attitude to me was. He seemed composed but withdrawn. "I'm sorry," I said, "I wasn't badly injured but I did have to go to hospital. I can't show any of the bruises. They've all faded."

"That's fine," he said. "I believe ye." I wasn't sure he did. He looked down at the floor. I had forgotten how compelling his presence was. "Ye were with another girl today."

"Another woman," I said. This politeness was extremely wearing. "We used to work together."

"Are ye back in Dublin?"

"It looks like it. I'll probably live here now."

"Are ye living with your friend?"

"My friend? Oh, you mean Imelda." I wondered what he was getting at. "No, no. We just met for lunch."

"Ye're back with your husband then?"

I hesitated. "That's debatable. I might be. We're giving ourselves another chance."

"I guessed right. Would ye have told me that?" He threw me an odd look.

"I don't understand you. Would I have told you what?" I asked.

"Well, would ye have mentioned that situation if I had asked ye out?"

"I probably would. Yes, I would have."

"So ye'll probably get back together again. What made yez decide to have another go?"

"Everything deserves one last chance. We're making an effort. We're . . ."

"Let me guess. Yez are goin' to a marriage counsellor."

He was unnervingly close to the mark. "Something like that," I said.

"So the outcome of the counselling decides whether yez stay together?"

I took a drink from my glass. My mouth was dry. "That's about the size of it," I confirmed. "Do you want a drink?" I asked. I wasn't sure if it was the thing to say.

"No thanks," he said. "I have to go." Instead he sat there and watched me.

"How are you?" I asked. I felt uneasy under this scrutiny.

"Oh, I'm thrivin'," he said. "The world is treatin' me well."

"I'm glad."

"We never got anywhere, did we?" he said.

"You had a lucky escape." I smiled. "I have a history of failure in these things."

"It's the possibility of success that's excitin'," he said. He stood up. I felt numbed, unable to think of anything sensible or meaningful to say. He took my receipt and scribbled something on it. "That's my phone number. If things don't work out and ye're interested, give me a ring." He handed it to me.

"Thanks," I said. I took it. He paused a moment before muttering goodbye. We shook hands limply. I felt sure that he must consider me some sort of fraud. I put aside the apple tart. My appetite had gone.

When he had paid and left I stared into the emptiness of the afternoon and cursed my luck in meeting him. He had unsettled me. I looked at his telephone number for a while, then slipped it into the inner chambers of my purse where I hoarded everything that I couldn't quite let go.

Chapter Thirty-One

"A year to the day. It's unbelievable," Mother said to me. "You'd think they planned it. I can't get over it." She looked down the garden at Aunt Moira's house. We were out in the back while neighbours prepared and dressed the body. I saw the gaunt figure of the doctor making his way towards us.

"Sorry I wasn't able to be here when you arrived, Liz," he said, "but I got called away."

"That's grand, Mick," she said. They shook hands for a long time. He took out a cigarette and lit it. He inhaled deeply and, when he exhaled, the smoke blew into my eyes.

"Sorry," he said. "It's a great day, don't you think?" He held the burning end of the cigarette in close to the palm of his hand.

"She chose a good day all right."

The doctor extracted a piece of paper from his pocket. "Here's the death certificate, Liz. I put down heart failure. She went out like a light, no suffering or anything."

"That's the best way. Mrs Deasy told me she got Mass and confession this morning so she died in a state of grace."

The doctor threw his half smoked cigarette on the ground after a long interval of silence. "That's the way of it," he said. "Aren't you going to introduce this young lady to me?" He smiled and turned to look at me.

"This is my youngest, Mick. Sinéad, this is Dr Lawlor." We shook hands. "We went to school together," she said. "God how the years fly by. It doesn't seem all that long ago now."

"We're the old ones now, Liz, and these young ones," he winked at me, "think that we know nothing. It's all in front of them." He looked at his watch. "I'll have to be off now. I've a surgery in the afternoon. I'll drop in tonight."

"The way it is, Mick, is that I can't take it all in. It's like I'm in a dream." Again they shook hands and he patted her shoulder and whispered something in her ear.

When he had gone she looked around her. "They'll probably let us see her soon," she said. "I feel lucky to be in one piece. Eoin drove like a maniac. I was sure there'd be a second funeral."

Mother was a nervous passenger, never happy at speed. I looked down the shortcut to the graveyard. "It's hard to think that she was alive this morning and now she's gone forever," I said. "At least she got her wish and died quickly." I felt cold even though there was warmth in the September sun.

"Good for her and bad for us," said Mother. "It's a shame she didn't live to see the child."

"She knew it was on its way. I'm glad I told her."

"You'll start to show soon," she said. "People'll notice then and you'll have to talk about it."

I smiled. "That's fine by me. I'll put up with it when I

have to. No point in drawing attention to it yet." It seemed almost sinful to be talking easily.

"Here's Mrs Deasy. They must be ready." A cloud obscured the sun. I shivered. Even my hands were cold.

"You don't have to look if you don't want to," Mother said.

I shook my head. "I'll look at her. Why wouldn't I? I looked at Aunt Alice."

"You can come down now if you're ready," Mrs Deasy, lighter of Aunt Moira's fires, said. I shook her hand.

"Thanks very much, Mrs Deasy," I said. "You're very good. We appreciate everything you've done."

She shook her head of luxuriant white hair. "Not at all," she said. "What else would we do?" She caught Mother to her and embraced her.

Unexpectedly I found I was crying. I turned to see my mother dab her eye with a tissue. For a moment the world seemed hushed and silent. Mrs Deasy took Mother's arm and guided her down the path to the back door. The sun came out and once again I heard the birds singing.

Aunt Moira looked exactly as I had seen her on my last visit. Dressed in her Sunday best she lay stretched out on the bed, a rosary beads strung through her folded fingers. They had placed a book under her chin until the jaw set. Her eyes were closed.

"She's a lovely corpse," Mrs Deasy whispered in my ear. "She looks wonderful, doesn't she?"

Mother knelt down beside the bed and took out her beads. I knelt down beside her. She chanted a decade of the rosary and I muttered half-forgotten responses. She stood up abruptly and helped me to my feet. "We can come up later. I'm done in."

We straggled down the stairs, Mrs Deasy following us. "Your aunt was a fine woman," she said to me as we entered the kitchen. "I'll pour you two a drink. You look as though you need one."

"Eoin'll be back later," mother explained. "He's gone to the city to buy in supplies for tomorrow. We'll have plenty of food and drink."

"He's very obliging," Mrs Deasy said. She handed me a neat whiskey and another to my mother who caught my eye and smiled.

"Have one yourself, Mrs Deasy," she said. "You earned it."

The aftertaste of the whiskey exploded in my mouth and at the back of my throat, and I felt faint stirrings of heartburn in my chest.

"The rest of the family'll be down later today," Mother told Mrs Deasy.

"All the beds are aired and everything's ready," Mrs Deasy said. "We can settle up who'll be sleeping where tonight. You come over to us and have a bite to eat in about an hour or so. We'll be expecting you."

When she had gone my mother sat silently by the stove. There was such a stillness about her that she might have been posing for a study in dejection. Her face was a mess of conflicting shadows in the dark kitchen, her mouth and eyes downturned. She sighed to herself once or twice.

"There's no will, you know," she said suddenly. She issued the information like a gloomy news bulletin.

"Maybe there's one you don't know about."

"No, no," she said impatiently. "I know there isn't a will. Moira was always very reluctant to draw one up. We were supposed to go to see the solicitor that time my visit was cut short. She had finally agreed to it. She was going to leave the house to me."

I was holding my breath as she spoke. I released it gently. "What difference will not having a will make?" I asked.

"Don't you know?" she asked. I shook my head.

"Ignorance is bliss, isn't it?" she said. She seemed to be fighting to keep herself under control. "Without a will the house'll be divided between Sheila and me. That'll involve selling it and sharing the proceeds between us."

"Sell the house!" I exclaimed. "Why would you do that?"

She stared hard at the floor and took a deep breath. "It stands to reason. Sheila has no interest in the place and she won't let me have it. In order to get her share the house will have to be sold."

"I don't believe it!" I cried. "Why should she get anything? She hasn't set foot in the house for years. She has no interest in it. What entitles her to any say?"

She smiled a grim smile and twisted her glass around in her hands. "It's the law. She's Moira's sister and that entitles her to a share. The rights and wrongs of the situation don't come into it."

"That's outrageous," I said. "You've a much stronger claim."

She shook her head. She looked old, tired and defeated. "Rights don't count. Moira died intestate and that means a field day for the solicitors. It'll take years to sort out and there'll be precious little at the end of it all. Whatever's left will be split between your aunt and me."

"How could Aunt Moira have done this? Did she know what would happen?" A dull flame of anger glowed in my stomach.

"She was allergic to making a will. I think she was sort of

superstitious about it. The charitable thing would be to assume she didn't know what she was doing." She knocked back the remains of the whiskey and stood up. "I'm doing my best to be charitable," she said, "although I'm finding it very hard. She's broken my heart." She left the room abruptly and walked out into the hall. I was left with the full whiskey glass in my hand, a burning heart and a sense of furious helplessness. My mother would lose the property, and her last link with the place would be gone.

When Eoin returned from Cork it was time to go across to Mrs Deasy's for our meal. I buried this news deep in my heart and kept faith with my mother's silence on the matter. I felt him glancing at me during the meal and couldn't rise to reassuring him with a smile. The damp, decaying stone house had been in my mother's family for almost a century. Generations of people had lived in it. Now the O'Gibbon Mahons would have nothing more to do with the place.

I had to admire my mother. She chatted to Mrs Deasy about old times, reminisced about her childhood and told funny stories about her girlhood.

"Remember the time those young fellas blocked up all the chimneys in the village and smoked everybody out of their houses?" Mother was saying.

"We were run out of the village," Mr Deasy said. "We couldn't show our faces about the place for weeks."

"Proper order," Mother said. "You almost gave my mother a heart attack."

It was hard to recognise this spunky person as the defeated, dejected woman I had spoken to earlier in the kitchen and even harder to recognise my once despised mother in her.

A few people called to the house that evening to pay their respects. That night when Emer helped my father out of the car I realised how feeble he had become. I looked at this remote, puzzling man who had spawned me but I was no closer to understanding him than I had ever been. My mother sat him down in a high-backed chair by the table and he sat there quietly, like a docile child, and waited for her to bring him a cup of tea.

Brian and Joe and their wives were expected the next day.

Later May settled my father in the sofa bed downstairs. We had a long argument with my mother over who would take the spare bed and who would sleep on the sofa bed.

"You need a firm bed, Sinéad, and you need to be close to the bathroom," Mother said. She drifted about the house that night as though she couldn't make herself go to bed.

"She's like a lost soul," Eoin commented, "I feel sorry for her."

"It's hard on her, very hard."

"Did she tell you that there's no will?" he asked.

"Yes," I answered. In the ensuing silence he caught my hand and pressed it gently. We sat close without moving, like a frozen tableau. After a while I had to move to another chair. In my pregnant state no position remained comfortable for very long.

"Off again, my nomad?" he asked.

"I'm too restless," I said.

"Oh, I know all about that. I hear you at night when you go padding up and down to the toilet or trot down to the kitchen. You've turned into a night wanderer."

"I'd love a cup of tea," I said. "I'd really love a drink but I know it'd just give me heartburn."

"I'll get you your cup of tea. Do you want some toast? I'm hungry."

He went out to fill up the kettle and my mother strayed in again.

"I've locked the back door," she announced. "I'm in for the night. I'll leave the key here in case you want to go out." She placed the key on a shelf.

"We're staying in," I said.

"Will you join us in a cup of tea?" Eoin asked.

"No thanks, Eoin. If I have any more tea today I'll burst."

"You go to bed, Mam," I urged. "You look done in."

"I'm really exhausted," she said, "but I don't think I'd sleep if I went to bed now. I'll go up and sit with Moira for a while. I'll keep her company." Unexpectedly she smiled. "We can recall old times. There's a lot to remember." She left us with a subdued "Goodnight".

I got up to follow her but Eoin held me back. "Let her be," he said. "She needs to be on her own for a while." I sank back into an armchair and he brought me tea and toast.

"She'll come round to the idea of losing this place," he said after a while. "It'll take some time but she'll adjust. You have to admire her. She's tough."

"Well, losing here is an idea that takes some getting used to," I said. "It's as if a blood supply was cut off. I wish we could buy it."

"Yes, now all she'll have here is graves to visit."

"I wonder where we'll be buried?" I speculated.

"Not here," he said. He thought for a while. "Who'll be here tomorrow?"

"My family, a few cousins from around here and all the village. It's going to be a busy day. May and I will make mountains of sandwiches and cut acres of cake."

"Great," he said. "I'll take care of the drinks. That'll keep me occupied and help me forget all the gloom."

"Yeah, being busy gets you through. I think I'll turn in for the night. I might get a few hours' sleep."

I plodded up the stairs to Aunt Moira's room and went in to say goodnight to my mother. She sat in the chair by the window, asleep. In the dim light I could make out Aunt Moira's prostrate form on the bed. The radio was silent and all her books had been stacked neatly on the window-sill. On her bedside locker lay a black-covered old prayer-book. I had often seen her lift it and read it. Somebody had placed a crucifix on the prayer-book. I thought I could hear the gentle stir of her breathing. A soft breeze fluttered the open curtains and I realised that I heard the sigh of the wind. Silently I placed a kiss on each forehead and bade goodnight to the sisters, one living and one dead.

Later, as I lay stretched out in our bed, I stared up at the stars that I could see through the uncurtained window. The village seemed quiet, almost deserted. Tomorrow evening a crowd would follow Aunt Moira's removal to the church. Some of them would be attracted to the house that night, drawn by feelings or memories, or the desire for drink they wouldn't have to pay for. They would burrow their way into the house, whisper condolences and mutter words of comfort to my mother, who was already a half stranger in the place. I didn't think she would discourage them this last time. She might even be glad to have others in the house, pleased to have things to do for them, moved to remember Aunt Moira through their stories, happy to tell a few stories herself.

Much later I heard my mother's dragging steps on the stairs as she made her way down to the chilly sofa bed to join my father. I could hear low exchanges between them as she got into bed and then the house was silent. I was conscious of the lonely presence in the other bedroom. My mind wandered up the main street to the church surrounded by trees, out past it, down the narrow road that twisted back behind the houses of the village to the cemetery. I found the opened grave, felt Aunt Alice's spirit waiting for Aunt Moira's arrival. The day after tomorrow they would be together again forever.

Eoin came into the bedroom and undressed in the dark. He crept in beside me and drew me towards him. "Remember this time last year," he whispered. Sleepily I laid my head on his chest. I snuggled up to him. "Everything was hopeless," he said. "Now there's something to look forward to. It wouldn't have seemed possible then, would it?"

"No." I answered, only half awake and unwilling to shake off sleepiness for wakefulness. He stroked my hair and ran his other hand along my belly.

"How's junior?" he asked. "Do you feel anything?"

"I felt something yesterday, a funny little fluttering inside, like the flapping of a trapped butterfly. I forgot to tell you when you came home and I never thought of it when we got the news today." I was fully awake now. "It was so slight, so fleeting, such a delicate, quivering movement that I'm not sure it was that quickening they talk about in books." As I spoke I felt it again. His hand must have felt it too. When it stopped we embraced.

"Our child," he said. In the darkness I smiled. He was so confident that we would be good parents, that our marriage would strengthen and we would endure. Even I, trusting my untested confidence, was convinced by this.

The pregnancy wasn't planned but neither of us was dismayed by it.

"Did I tell you Imelda's pregnant too?" I said.

"What a life - babies, nappies, night feeds! I'd better get fit for this. I can see serious demands being made on the spirit."

"Well, it'll keep our minds off the school. I got a shock when we drove by today."

"Yeah. I hadn't realised the bulldozers would move in so quickly. I thought the site wouldn't be cleared until next year."

"They couldn't wait."

"What's going to be built there?"

"Houses."

"The convent's still standing."

"That's a nice building. They'll convert it into flats."

"I bet it's full of ghosts." He pressed my hand against his cheek and kissed my fingers.

"All its ghosts are alive," I said. He snorted.

I turned to speak to him but he had tricked me and escaped into sleep. I was conscious of his warm breathing beside me. Disgruntled and restless I turned away from him, feeling wide awake.

Suddenly I heard a plaintive mewing from the back yard. There had been no sign of Darcy all day. I crept into Aunt Moira's room. Her body was lit by a shaft of moonlight. She looked as if she were smiling in her sleep. I tiptoed over to the window, looked down and saw a dark form silhouetted against the kitchen's white window-sill. His paw tapped at the window. "Wait, Darcy," I whispered. "I'll come down and let you in."

End